HOPELESSLY BROMANTIC

LAUREN BLAKELY

For Kayti. For Tuesdays. And Sundays. And Fridays. And every other time I demanded a brainstorming session and you showed up with your very big brain. And your can-do spirit. And a knife ready to slash all the bad ideas.

ALSO BY LAUREN BLAKELY

Big Rock Series

Big Rock

Mister O

Well Hung

Full Package

Joy Ride

Hard Wood

Hopelessly Bromantic Duet (MM)

Hopelessly Bromantic

Here Comes My Man

Happy Endings Series

My Single-Versary

A Wild Card Kiss

Shut Up and Kiss Me

Kismet

Rules of Love Series

The Rules of Friends with Benefits (A Prequel Novella)

The Virgin Rule Book

The Virgin Game Plan

The Virgin Replay

The Virgin Scorecard

Men of Summer Series

Scoring With Him

Winning With Him

All In With Him

The Guys Who Got Away Series

Dear Sexy Ex-Boyfriend

The What If Guy

Thanks for Last Night

The Dream Guy Next Door

The Gift Series

The Engagement Gift

The Virgin Gift

The Decadent Gift

The Extravagant Series

One Night Only

One Exquisite Touch

My One-Week Husband

MM Standalone Novels

A Guy Walks Into My Bar

One Time Only

The Bromance Zone

The Best Men (Co-written with Sarina Bowen)

The Heartbreakers Series

Once Upon a Real Good Time

Once Upon a Sure Thing

Once Upon a Wild Fling

Boyfriend Material

Asking For a Friend

Sex and Other Shiny Objects

One Night Stand-In

Lucky In Love Series

Best Laid Plans

The Feel Good Factor

Nobody Does It Better

Unzipped

Always Satisfied Series

Satisfaction Guaranteed

Instant Gratification

Overnight Service

Never Have I Ever

PS It's Always Been You

Special Delivery

The Sexy Suit Series

Lucky Suit

Birthday Suit

From Paris With Love

Wanderlust

Part-Time Lover

One Love Series

The Sexy One

The Only One

The Hot One

The Knocked Up Plan

Come As You Are

Sports Romance

Most Valuable Playboy

Most Likely to Score

Standalones

Stud Finder

The V Card

The Real Deal

Unbreak My Heart

The Break-Up Album

The Caught Up in Love Series

The Pretending Plot (previously called *Pretending He's Mine*)

The Dating Proposal

The Second Chance Plan (previously called *Caught Up In Us*)

The Private Rehearsal (previously called *Playing With Her Heart*)

Seductive Nights Series

Night After Night

After This Night

One More Night

A Wildly Seductive Night

ABOUT

An irresistibly sexy, emotionally-charged, forbidden MM romance between a broody American and a charming Brit!

My first day in London feels ripped from the pages of a rom com when I meet a charming, witty guy in a quaint bookshop. We vibe like crazy, and our chemistry is almost too good to be true because...*It is.*

Turns out he's my new roommate. For the next year, I'll be living with the English hottie in a tiny flat that's barely big enough for a mattress. That means no walking around wearing only a towel and definitely no accidental kissing. I do my best to resist the swooniest guy I've ever known.

But after a very-much-on-purpose kiss I find a loophole to the roomie rules – *we'll give in for one night as long as we promise we won't get our hearts involved.*

Too bad in the morning, I find out that hiding my true feelings is the least of my worries, compared to what fate has in store for us.

Contents Include: Incendiary flirting, opposites attracting, forced proximity, flat-sharing antics, a broken shower that needs fixing, and the first novel in a scorching and emotional two-book epic romance that'll take you from London to New York to Los Angeles!

HOPELESSLY BROMANTIC

BOOK 1 IN THE HOPELESSLY BROMANTIC DUET

By Lauren Blakely

Want to be the first to learn of sales, new releases, preorders and special freebies? Sign up for my VIP mailing list here! You'll also get free books from bestselling authors in a selection curated just for you!

PRO TIP: Add lauren@laurenblakely.com to your contacts before signing up to make sure the emails go to your inbox!

Did you know this book is also available in audio and paperback on all major retailers? Go to my website for links!

PROLOGUE

SOME GUYS ARE JUST LIKE THAT

TJ

Present Day

Seven years ago, when my boss hit me with the news that he was sending me to London for the next twelve months, I could picture my nights unfolding like a dirty fairy tale.

After working my ass off all day, I'd hit the music bars, check out cool new bands, and meet hot guys. They'd charm me with their accents, and I'd charm them with my wit, and we'd bang till Big Ben struck morning O-O-O-and-one-more-O'clock.

My sex life would be nothing like it was in college, which was a lot like a drought—a famine from which, two years post-graduation, I'd only recently started to emerge.

But Ye Olde London? It would be a beefeater feast.

And sure, yeah, a great work opportunity. Obviously. And I wanted that because I had goals. Big ones.

Little ones too.

First, I wanted to stop at the bookstore on Cecil Court I went to on a family trip when I was an awkward teenager. While my parents hunted for a guidebook, I browsed the paperbacks, and for the first time in my life, I visualized my name on a cover. I left there with an armload of books . . . and a dream.

The bookshop was one of the first places I went when I arrived in London seven years ago. I wanted an auspicious beginning to my year abroad. Full circle and all that.

But that time, when I reached Cecil Court, it wasn't a paperback that sparked my dreams.

It was a man.

This bloke had more charm and appeal than any hero I could write into a novel.

But he wasn't simply between the covers of a story, where I could mastermind the ending. He was vibrant, real, and the most thrilling time I'd ever had. Soon, my London life was full of him.

And—spoiler alert—this guy in the bookstore was going to upend my world, not once, but twice.

Some guys were like that. They stayed with you, even when you wanted them out of your head.

And they left, even when you wanted them to stay.

PART ONE

Seven Years Ago

And so it begins . . .

1

WHAT KIND OF LAP DANCES DOES HE LIKE?

Jude

This is the greatest vacuum cleaner ever. There has never been a better one in all the land. It's literally going to change your life.

I repeat those notes from my agent before I head into the audition room—a drab, windowless shoebox of a place above a strip club on the outskirts of Leicester Square.

I've got no problem with the business of exotic dancing. But all things being equal, I'd rather audition for a new commercial above, say, a Tesco or an insurance office.

But a gig is a gig is a gig.

I put on my best smile as I give the casting director my name. "Jude Graham with Premier Talent. Harry Atkinson reps me, and it's a pleasure to be here."

The casting director looks up from her tablet, question marks in her eyes. "Harry? I thought he was—" She makes a slashing gesture against her throat.

"I hope not. I saw him a week ago. Very much alive. And also, not headless."

"Ah, must have been someone else," she says.

Yes, I've noticed the epidemic of talent-agent beheadings in London lately.

"Sorry for whoever that might be," I add.

She smiles faintly, the thick coat of plum lipstick cracking. "All right, show us you're in the market for a Cleaneroo."

Somehow, she manages to keep a straight face when she says the brand name—something I'll be required to do in *three, two, one . . .*

I become a cheerful, British businessman returning home to his flat after a hard day at the office. "Sweetheart, I swear the floors have never been prettier. Did you get that new Cleaneroo?"

Could this script be any more 1950s?

"Thank you," the casting director says, revealing zilch about how I did.

"Thank you for having me," I say with a gentlemanly nod as old-fashioned as this script.

Shit.

That was more of a bow. I meant to be jaunty, not obsequious. No matter. She didn't even notice. She's dragging her chipped red fingernail on the tablet screen, already done with me.

I grab my messenger bag and make my way down the rickety stairs in the back of the building, heading out through the strip club. A brunette dancer weaves past me, pink thigh-high boots jacking her up several inches, white seashells covering maybe half her breasts. An unlit cigarette dangles from her lips as she gives me a once-over. "Fancy a lap dance? Half off for you . . . I like blonds," she says.

"Thanks, but I'm on a lap-dance fast," I say, making my way to the exit.

Once I hit the street, I call my agent. "Why do these Cleaneroo people think you're dead, Harry?"

He chortles. "Ah, that's so typical of Vicki. When I don't send her anyone for a while, she assumes I've kicked the bucket."

That's not the most reassuring answer. But last year, Harry did book me a sweet spot that's still paying the bills, so I let rumors of his demise slide. "Maybe let her know you're still alive?"

"Oh, I already told her, Jude. She just called."

I perk up. That has to be good. "Did I get a callback already? I can turn around right now. Or is it even better? Did I get the job?" Antiquated gender stereotypes aside, I wouldn't mind the money.

"She said you look too much like Apollo. The Greek god."

What the hell does that mean? "Is that a good thing?"

"Of course it is," he says, too chipper to trust. "But they think you're too good-looking to peddle a vacuum. Like, no one believes you'd think about anything besides abs or kale smoothies, let alone cleaning. So it's a compliment, in a way . . ."

I sigh. "And, also, kind of not."

"It's a double-edged sword—your godly good looks."

I'm not sure what to say to that. "Should I forgo

showers for a few days ahead of time for the next audition?"

He laughs. "Chin up. We'll find some more commercials for you soon. But in the meantime, the body spray people just sent a residual."

"Well, there's that double-edged sword too." I played a complete douche in that advert, spraying Hammer Body Spray on my armpits before I sauntered into a nightclub. "Thanks, Harry."

I hang up and check the time. I'm not due at An Open Book for a half hour, but I might as well head over. Too bad the Cleaneroo commercial flopped—I rearranged my schedule at the store today to do that audition. *C'est la vie.*

I pop in my earbuds and tune into Carrie Fisher's memoir—someday, I'd like to have a secret affair with someone like Harrison Ford—as I make my way to Cecil Court. I turn down the next street, and there's no way I can miss the strapping man on the corner, staring up at the TK Maxx sign. He looks perturbed and, also, really fucking hot, with a strong jaw and thick dark hair.

A brooding sort of stuntman, he's all casual in jeans and a black T-shirt, no pretenses.

Time to take out my earbuds right now.

He sighs in frustration, flings a hand at the store.

"It's literally the British equivalent of T.J. Maxx," he mutters.

He's loud enough for me to hear and American enough for my happy radar to beep. I happen to be a connoisseur of American accents.

I stop a few feet from him. "It is, indeed," I agree. I've

heard that about this shop, and I'm so bloody helpful to lumberjack-like men.

He turns, giving me a full, close-up view. *Those eyes.* Fuck me with a ten-inch dildo—they are a dreamy chocolate-brown with gold flecks.

I am not walking away.

I will continue this conversation for as long as I possibly can, or until I learn what kind of lap dances he likes. "It's our discount shop. It has a little bit of everything," I say.

He doesn't answer right away. Maybe he's straight. Sadder things have happened to me today.

"What do you know?" he asks in a voice that sounds like he just got out of bed after having sex.

I like that image—a *lot*.

His dark eyes flicker, perhaps with dirty deeds. Maybe he's got the same images running through his head that I do. "I might be in the market for a little bit of everything," he adds. "Where should I start at TK Maxx?"

How about letting me show you around?

But best to make certain he's into the same things I am before getting too flirty. "Depends on what you're looking for. They have surprisingly fashionable dog clothes, excellent popcorn, and also home furnishings," I say, starting with a bit of charm.

His lips tilt into a bit of a grin as if I've entertained him. "Good to know, in case I get a late-night craving."

I've got a craving right now, all right.

The American gestures to his shirt. "But I'm on the hunt for a new shirt."

I wave a hand at his firm chest. "You might want to

try Angie's Vintage Duds around the corner if that's your thing. They have cool retro tees and stuff," I say while I cycle through tactics to get his number.

To satisfy my craving.

"Thanks. Maybe I'll hit up Angie's. You never know who you might meet your first day in London."

He shoots me a smile.

Trouble is, it's only a friendly one, not quite a come-and-get-me one.

I'm getting ahead of myself. I should get on my way because I don't usually hit on men on the street. Maybe the thing to do is leave him a clue and put the ball in his court.

"True. You never know." I pause for a moment, then . . . What the hell. You're only young once. "By the way, I'm Jude. I work at a bookshop on Cecil Court."

With that, I turn and get on my way, and I don't look back.

Not until I reach the end of the street. Then, I can't resist one more glance his way.

He hasn't moved, except to turn his face toward me, watching me walk away.

A kernel of warmth spreads in my chest, and I know later, at the shop, I'll be staring at the door, hoping he walks in.

A few minutes later, as I reach Cecil Court, I realize what a daft idiot I am.

I didn't tell him *which* store I work in, and there are *only* twenty bookshops on this street. I check my watch. I can make it to Angie's to correct my mistake and still be on time for my shift. Spinning around, I walk quickly to Angie's. But as I peer in the window for a few long seconds, I only see the purple-haired woman who works there. I give her a wave, then head off.

Sigh. Another tiny heartbreak today, since I've a better chance of selling a Cleaneroo than seeing the American again.

2

JUST IN CASE

TJ's Travel Journal
London, Day One

My life was not a rom-com today.

It's been more like a manifestation of Murphy's Law. Everything that could go wrong on my trip to London did go wrong. The flight was cramped, turbulence hit an 8.0 on the Richter scale, then the airline lost my luggage. On top of that, the hotel said it wouldn't have my room ready for another few hours. I was tempted to crumple into a jet-lagged ball of stinky misery on the rundown lobby floor. I smelled like a ripe, day-old T-shirt, and I felt like a zombie. The front desk attendant took pity on me and sent me to a nearby store to buy some new clothes.

THANKS, FATE, FOR CHOOSING THAT EXACT

MOMENT TO SEND ME THE WORLD'S MOST BEAUTIFUL MAN.

When Jude gave me his name then walked away, my life was distilled into two choices:

Go to every single bookstore on Cecil Court and find him.

Or miss out on what felt like the first chapter in my new life here in England.

Wait. There was a third choice. Get my ass over to the thrift store he recommended, buy some new clothes, and then beg, borrow or steal for a shower if I had to.

I was not going to let this chance pass me by.

Cecil Court, here I come.

3

WE MEET AGAIN

TJ

When I wander down the little lane in Covent Garden, it's as if I've traveled to my personal paradise. Shops line the quaint alley full of books—my favorite things after sex and pizza.

I could get lost and never want to be found. Except I *do* want to find Jude. What are the chances he'll be in one of these shops *right now?*

Maybe it's best to focus on my original mission. Even before I left the States, I wanted to go to the bookshop I'd visited as a kid. No, not that one with the medical textbooks.

Definitely not the children's bookstore with the stuffed dragon in the window.

And for sure it's not the shop with globes in the window.

When I've scoured nearly the whole alley, I'm

convinced the store I camped out in a decade ago has closed.

Until a sign beckons me.

An Open Book.

It feels like déjà vu.

Peering inside, I breathe a sigh of relief. This is the store. Jude is probably history, and soon, he'll be a hazy memory of my first day in London—just some cute guy I met one afternoon.

A bell tinkles as I enter. I don't see a shopkeeper. Maybe they're in the back?

I browse the shelves, checking out row after row of colorful spines, stories in each one that lure me to read and also to write. I reach a row of works by Oscar Wilde, one of the greatest Irish writers ever. That dude was funny as fuck.

As I tip a copy of *The Importance of Being Earnest* into my hand, the thump of a hardback tome rattles a shelf behind me and I jerk my head.

Then I turn.

And wow.

This must be kismet.

Jude's paused in the act of sorting books, surprised to see me, it seems. And he looks—impossibly—even better than he did a few hours ago.

"You found the shop," he says, his lips twitching with the hint of a grin, his blue eyes full of mischief.

All at once, everything feels a little heady and a lot possible. Like this is the start of something. My fingers tingle, and I'm not even sure why. But maybe it's just from this dizzying sense of . . . fate.

And fear.

I don't want to fuck this up. Life doesn't give you a lot of chances. So I don't answer him right away. "Well, I had a few clues," I finally say.

Maybe I was wrong. Maybe I *did* step off the plane and into my very own rom-com.

"It's good to be an amateur detective," he tosses back.

So that's how we're doing it—going toe to toe and quip to quip. Bring it on. "Who said anything about amateur?"

His lips curve into a sly grin. "Ohhh . . . you're a professional detective?"

"How else would I have found An Open Book?"

His eyes travel up and down my body. "Sheer determination."

I laugh. "Yes, a little bit of that, but someone left a few hints. It was like a scavenger hunt. Maybe that's my new calling—scavenger hunting."

"Didn't know that was a thing. You do learn something new every day," he says. Then he makes that wildly sexy move again as he did outside TK Maxx—he coasts his teeth over that lower lip. I stifle a groan. My God, does he know what that does to a man?

Who am I kidding? Of course he does. A guy who looks, talks, stands like that—he's gorgeous and knows it.

Hell, he makes leaning against a shelf sexy.

"You know what I learned today?" I ask, plucking at my new Tetris shirt. It's nice and snug and makes my chest look good.

"Dying to know."

"That Angie's Vintage Duds does, in fact, have good clothes. Appreciate the tip."

"Would I lead you astray?"

That's an excellent question. I glance down at *The Importance of Being Earnest* in my hand as I hunt for retorts, then I look up, our gazes locking. "I have no idea, Jude. Would you?"

He laughs easily. Bet he does everything easily. Pose, walk, talk, read, live.

"Not when it comes to important matters like finding just the right shirt, and just the right store, and just the right book." He steps closer, taps the Wilde I'm holding. If an electrical charge could jump through pages, it just did. My skin is sizzling, almost like he touched me rather than paper.

"Like this book. Is that what you came to the store for?" Jude asks it so damn innocently, like he's goading me into admitting I came here for him.

Of course, I did. But two can play at this flirting game. I waggle the book. "I just needed to brush up on my Wilde."

"Naturally. You're just here for the books," he says, calling me on my patent lie.

"It's a bookstore. Why else would I come?" I counter.

"There couldn't be *any* other reason," he says. "But I'd be a terrible shop assistant if I didn't help you find just the right Wilde." He takes his time with his speech so that each word can send a wicked charge through me.

They all do.

"Except, I don't even know your name," he adds.

I glance around. The shop is empty, except for a couple of young women parked on comfy chairs in the corner, flipping through guidebooks, maybe. They're wrapped up in their world. I hope they stay there for hours.

"I'm TJ," I say.

A laugh bursts from Jude.

"My name is funny to you?" I ask.

"That's so very American," he says.

"What do you know? I am American," I say. "And I know you don't do the whole initial thing here. Does that mean you prefer to be Jude the Third?"

Another laugh. "If I'd told you I was Jude the Third, I doubt you would've come looking for—" He sounds like he's about to say *me,* but he amends it, quickly shifting to, "All the Wildes. Besides, I'm just Jude."

But he's not just Jude.

He's not *just* at all.

I keep that thought locked up tight. "And if I'd told you what TJ stands for, you'd know exactly why some Americans prefer initials," I say.

His blue eyes sparkle with intrigue. "You have to tell me now, TJ." My name sounds like a bedroom whisper on his lips.

"You'll never get that out of me," I say, matching his breathless tone.

He arches a brow. "Never? Never ever, you say?"

I could dine on his charm. I could eat breakfast, lunch, and dinner on his wit. I never want to leave this store. We can play word badminton till after dark. I'll stop only when the lights go down, and we can do all the other things—the things I'm already picturing with that lush, red mouth of his.

"Never," I repeat, then take a long, lingering moment. "Unless you have your ways."

He hums, a rumbly sound low in his throat. Then he taps his chin. "Perhaps I could guess. Thomas James?"

I shake my head. "Not even close."

"Theodore John." He makes a rolling gesture. "I could go all night."

"I hope so. And, perhaps, you should," I say.

Over drinks. Over sex. Over breakfast.

But the shop bell tinkles.

Jude groans as a customer strolls in. "I have to go wait on a customer."

And I have to make sure you and I go out tonight.

But before I can say *You'll find me here by the Oscar Wildes,* Jude adds, "Don't go anywhere, Thiago Jonas."

"You're not even warm," I say as he walks past me, brushing his shoulder against mine.

"But I bet you are," he whispers.

I try to stifle the hitch in my breath. But it's hard with this man, and his mouth, and his face, and my good fortune.

"Very," I say, low, just for him.

"Good," he says, then strides to the front of the store and chitchats with a customer. The whole time he ushers her around, my neck is warm, my head is hazy, and I feel like this is happening to some other guy. Like this is just a figment of my jet-lagged brain.

I flip open the book, turn it to one of my favorite scenes, and hear the lines in Jude's voice.

It's never sounded better.

A few minutes later, Jude returns, sliding up by my side to read over my shoulder, his breath near my ear. "*I hope you have not been leading a double life, pretending to be wicked and being good all the time. That would be hypocrisy.*"

He stops before I melt, because yeah, that's the best I've ever heard this play. "Do you like Oscar Wilde?"

"Very much so," I say, trying to stay cool. "You?"

"A lot," he says, and neither one of us is talking about the Irish poet.

But I feel Wilde would approve of everything I'm about to do.

"Go out with me tonight, Jude," I say, as a tangle of heat rushes down my chest, curls into a knot in my belly.

"I was hoping you'd ask. *But . . .*" He pauses, and my stomach plummets. This is when he'll disappoint me. "I have to work till nine. Can you meet at nine-thirty?

That's it? That's the *but*? I would meet him at three in the morning. At noon. Now.

I keep all that eagerness to myself. "Yeah. Want to meet at a pub? Get a beer? That sounds so very English."

"And it also sounds so very good," he says. "Where are you staying?"

"Not far from here. My hotel's near Piccadilly Circus."

"Meet me at The Magpie."

"I'll be there."

He points to the book. "Is this the edition you came for? The one with the two men in top hats?"

"It's perfect."

"Did you really want the book?"

I swallow roughly, meet his eyes, speak the whole truth. "I really want the book," I say, and it's not a lie. It also might have a double meaning.

As he heads to the counter, I follow him. I feel like

I'd follow him anywhere, and that's a dangerous thought. But now's not the time for analyzing.

Now is a time for doing.

Jude rings me up, slides the card reader across the counter, then takes out his phone. After I swipe my credit card, he says, "And I believe you were going to give me your number, TJ."

As I slide him the card reader, he gives me his phone. I keep my head down, so he can't see the size of my smile as I tap in my digits then swivel the device back to him. Seconds later, he sends me a text.

Jude: Mark my words. I'll figure out what TJ stands for. I have my ways.

TJ: Just try them on me.

Then, since it's always good to leave them wanting more, I take the Wilde and go. As I walk off, I can see the rest of my days and nights in London in a whole new way.

4

A GREAT DICK WITH A GREAT DICK

Jude

I've had dates that started worse.

There was the guy who turned out to be my second cousin, though we thankfully learned of our interconnected family tree branches before we smacked lips. Then, there was another guy who informed me the second I sat down at the table that he liked to take cold baths before sex.

Give a bloke some food before you reveal your fetishes. I mean, that's just polite.

But let's not forget the man who cried the instant I arrived at the café. I don't even know why. He just blubbered for thirty minutes till I called him an Uber and sent him home.

With that precedent, a night out with a hot, but exhausted American likely won't crack the top-three worst dates. But when I catch sight of TJ through the window of The Magpie, yawning wide enough to fit a double-decker bus, I suspect the evening won't end the way I imagined—with *mutual finishing.*

Well, there are other uses for mouths.

I go into the packed bar and head straight for his booth, where he's reading the book he bought. "Usually, it takes a few beers before I bore my dates, so I'm ahead on that count," I say.

"Sorry about that," TJ says with a tired laugh as he sets the Wilde aside. "But I assure you, boredom is not the issue."

"It's past your bedtime?" I suspect that's why he's zonked.

A sheepish look flits across his tired eyes. "That obvious?"

"Yes, but you said it was your first day in London." I slide onto the dark wood bench across from him. On the wall above us hangs a vintage poster of London from a century ago.

"Who's the detective now?" TJ counters.

"It's a useful skill," I say drily, tapping my temple. "Remembering, that is."

"Sure is. And hey, if it helps, I haven't slept in more than twenty-four hours. But thanks for the heads-up that you're dull." TJ points to the door. "I'll just make my great escape right now."

"I don't think you're going to slip away just yet."

His eyebrows dart up. "And why is that, Just Jude?"

"Oh, I have a nickname already?"

"You made it easy."

I'd like to make a lot of things easy for him. Like, say,

having me when he's not knackered. "And you've made it hard for me to figure out your real name."

"But you like it that way. *Hard*," he says.

I shrug coyly. "I do enjoy a hard man."

He chuckles, then he holds up a finger for a pause. "One sec." Grabbing his mobile, he quickly taps something out on the screen.

I peer over the table, intrigued. "Are you taking notes on our conversation?"

"It gave me an idea—what you just said." He finishes typing and sets his phone down, a little amused with his own notes.

That ratchets up my curiosity. "And, are you going to keep that idea all to yourself, like your real name? Or will you share?"

TJ gives a sly smile. "Depends on what I do with it," he answers in a tone that says *Let's leave it at that.*

Fair enough. I don't need to push him on his note-taking. People reveal things when they're ready. But I want him to reveal *something* to me. I have a hunch about it, but I'll have to get the answer out of him in a roundabout way. "Great table. Did you get here a while ago?"

"Yeah, I did," he says, scratching his jaw like he's playing at "laidback" too. "I mean, I didn't know how long it would take to walk here from my hotel, or whether the GPS directions are right, or whether The Magpie would be crowded since it's a Saturday night. So, I showed up a bit early."

The way he overexplains is endearing, and confirms my hunch that he was as eager to impress me with a good table as I was eager to find him earlier. Call me a glutton for compliments, but I do like knowing when someone's into me. I can blame my ex for that, I suppose.

"That's why I didn't think you'd slip away," I say. "Who'd want to give up such a great table?"

"Not me," he adds, as if he's trying not to smile.

A waitress swings by and asks us our poison. I pick a lager, while TJ opts for an ale. When she leaves, I'm tempted to confess I doubled back to Angie's to see him again. But if I admit I chased him to the thrift shop, he might put me in an Uber like I've blubbered to him.

I'd deserve it.

I play it cool instead, opting for a safer topic. "So, how are you finding London so far?"

He shrugs, all no big deal, but keeps those dark eyes on me. "It's not so bad. I guess we'll see if you can keep me up."

"That's a tall order. But I think I'm *up* to the task. I happen to be a scintillating conversationalist."

"Then, Just Jude, you really should keep scintillating." Something about the way he says that—all faux naughty—rips a laugh straight from my chest. He cracks up too. "All right. Tell me for real about your first day in my hometown. Besides meeting a fabulous Englishman who has the same tastes."

"Thank God for that," TJ says, relieved.

"Same here. It's always a welcome moment when you know you're not barking up the wrong tree," I say.

"I prefer the right trees. And England is . . . pretty good so far. Even though the airline lost my bags, my room wasn't ready, and I had nothing clean to wear until this afternoon. Also, apparently, I can't stop yawning." Another one racks him as the blonde server returns with our drinks.

"Here's your lager and your ale," she says, setting down the glasses. "Shall I start a tab for you?"

"Yes," TJ says, just as I say, "No."

She holds up her hands to show she's not getting involved. "I'll let you gentlemen sort that out."

I hand her my credit card. "Here you go, love. We're all set."

"Thank you," she says, then spins on her heel.

I turn back to TJ, who's crossing his arms. Oh, no, no, no. He's not getting it. "You think when you said yes, and I said no, that I meant I was taking off straight away?"

He scoffs in denial. "It's all good. I'm happy to call it a night," he says, so damn nonchalant.

"I'm not letting you get away that quickly."

Like that, his cool demeanor cracks. A smile breaks through.

I get up, move to his side of the booth, and slide in next to him. When we're thigh to thigh, his breath hitches, then it catches as I drape an arm around him.

"Are you trapping me?" he asks.

"Yes. Is it working?"

"Depends on what you want to do."

"Keep you here for this drink."

He's quiet for a few seconds. "It's working quite well."

"Good. I'd hate to be presumptuous if it wasn't working."

He clears his throat. "You should be very presumptuous."

"Then I'll presume about other things too." I curl my hand over that big, strong shoulder that feels so fucking good. I do like a man who's bigger than I am, broader than I am. Who can climb over me and pin me down.

"What sort of things?" he asks, a little breathy.

Ah, fuck it. He's probably only in town for a short while. Might as well enjoy this while it lasts. "Things like . . . tomorrow."

That wins me the start of a smile, then the slight turn of his face toward me. "What are you presuming about tomorrow?"

"That I'll see you again," I tell him. "When you're not falling asleep. When you're not yawning into your fucking beer."

With a laugh, he rolls his eyes then leans back in the booth. "I'm only a *little* tired," he says, so much gravel in his voice now.

"That's why I gave her my card. That's why I said we were set. So we can have this one drink to your first night in town. And something more tomorrow."

He nods a few times, clearly liking my plan. If he only knew all the dirty plans I have for him tomorrow. "I'll drink to something more," he says, and we lift glasses and clink.

"Cheers," I say, then drink and lick my lips. "So, what brings you to London? Give me the two-minute version since I'm going to put you in an Uber soon."

"I'm writing an exposé on bookshops," he says, deadpan.

"So, this is all a ruse to get me to reveal the hidden secrets of the shelves?"

"Seems to be working too. I already uncovered critical details, like how much you adore helping customers and which edition of *The Importance of Being Earnest* is your favorite."

I try to remember when I told him but draw a blank. "I didn't tell you the one you bought was my favorite."

"You didn't have to tell me. I figured it out from your clues," he says, and this man would make a good detective because he's spot on.

"Perhaps all this Sherlock Holmes work of yours brought you to London then?"

He takes another drink and casually sets down the glass. "Or maybe I'm a Wilde scholar here in London to research the man."

"But we're all Wilde scholars, aren't we?"

"Excellent point," he says, then his tone shifts like he's letting down his guard. "When I was in high school and first learned he was gay, I checked out all Oscar Wilde's works from the library. Devoured them. I've read this one several times." He taps the top hat cover. "Maybe I felt I should have an affinity. Do you know what I mean?"

"I do—on both counts. And probably that's why I was the most excited I've ever been when I was cast as Jack Worthing in uni." I pause to replay in my head what I just said. "I hope I didn't sound like a braggart then. I was truly thrilled."

"Not at all. I can completely understand that excitement." This is our first stripped-down moment, free of flirting or trying to impress the other. It's nice, and I like it, but I don't want it to last too long. I don't want too much closeness in my life, and I doubt TJ does either, judging by how quickly he returns to the banter.

"And is that your way of telling me you have a second career?" he asks. "That you're an actor?"

"Yes. Clever, isn't it? How I dropped that in?"

"Very much so. So, the bookstore thing, then?"

"I moonlight there. Bills and all," I say, offhand. I don't want to reveal the full extent of my acting dreams. Don't want to let on that I spend my days auditioning for hoover adverts and bit parts on web shows and every single fringe theater production that might be right for me. That I'm chasing a wildly unlikely dream of making it big in film and on stage. He'd probably laugh. "And I'm guessing you're a writer?"

A surprised laugh bursts from the man next to me. "It's as obvious as me being tired?"

"Pretty obvious, TJ." I don't go into how I caught on. It'd be evident I'm paying too much attention to every detail of him—like how he sometimes takes his time with his words like he's writing them out in his head first. Rather than say that, I tease, "Your whole look kind of screams writer."

Okay, I can't help it.

His jaw drops, and he gestures to himself. "Am I disheveled, unshowered, and dressed in sweats? No. Not to cast aspersions on other writers, mind you."

I lean closer and whisper, "I won't tell all the other writers in the world that you mock their wardrobes."

"Thank you so very much. Anyway, you're right. I am a writer—well, I'm a business reporter—and my news organization sent me here to cover the financial markets."

"Ah, stocks, bonds, money, money, money," I say.

"That's the gist of my days," TJ says, then takes a

breath like he's not quite sure if he wants to say the next thing. But then he goes for it. "I'll be here for a year."

I flinch in surprise. "That's a long time."

He laughs, but it's defensive. "You're rethinking that offer for tomorrow, aren't you?"

Am I? Does the score change with him living here rather than being on holiday?

I'm not in the market for a relationship after the way my last one ended. But first dates aren't the best time to lay down the rules of my solo road.

I keep my answer on the level—the physical level. "I'm thinking I'm still quite interested in seeing what's underneath this writer's garb."

He laughs. "So, I do dress like a writer."

"A little bit. But that isn't stopping me from wanting to touch what's under the Tetris T-shirt," I say playfully, plucking at the fabric near his belly.

I'm so very tempted to check out his abs. But I don't want to be handsy. I'll just have to imagine what they're like. Or maybe not, because TJ grabs my hand and places it on his stomach.

Oh, yes. They're as firm as I imagined.

TJ gives a slight smirk. "Figured this was easier than you surreptitiously trying to check out my abs."

"Was playing with your shirt what we'd call surreptitious?"

"Not in the motherfucking least," he says.

This is my chance to turn the tables on him, to grab his palm, and set it on my stomach.

But he lifts his hand and takes another drink.

Maybe he wants to leave me wanting him more. And I do want TJ, even this tired version—make that dog-tired because there he goes again with another yawn.

"All right, stud. It's well past your bedtime," I tell him.

"It's not even five in New York," he protests.

"And yet, you look like you could sleep for days," I say.

"I do like sleep, but I also like doing other things in bed," he says, his voice husky and hopeful.

"Tomorrow, Troy Jett," I say and ruffle his hair. I like touching him. *A lot.*

"Troy Jett? Please."

"It was worth a shot."

He arches a dubious brow. "Promise me something. Promise me you'll never date a douche named Troy Jett."

"That is a particularly dickish name," I say.

He hums, tapping his chin. "Why is dick an insult?"

"That's an excellent question, considering how much I love it," I say, giving a little roll of the tongue with those last few words.

"That's why it should be a compliment of the highest order," TJ adds. "Instead of saying *he's a dick* when someone is a jerk, we should save *he's a dick* for a really awesome dude."

"Like, if I met a rather handsome stud, I'd say *I met a great dick today*." I take a beat to adopt a thoughtful expression. "At least, I think he's a great dick," I say, feigning worry. "What if he's not?"

TJ sighs heavily. "That'd be such a shame if the guy you think is a dick turns out to be a not-dick. But I'll let you in on a secret. I have a feeling this dude you met is definitely a dick. Like a big, huge dick. The biggest dick."

I groan, half in the promise of pleasure, half in amusement. "But I won't say I hope he has a big dick. Because, sure, size is nice and all. But great dicks come in all sizes. It's not the length or the girth, but what a great dick can do with a great dick."

TJ laughs, long and a little slaphappy. "You have a way with words too. And I will drink to your ode to all shapes and sizes," he says, and we toast once more.

Soon, we take our last sips of beer, reaching the end of the date. But before I can say good night, TJ leans into me and brushes a kiss onto my cheek.

I freeze and moan at the same time.

I didn't expect a kiss, and I definitely don't want it to end. His lips are utterly delicious on my skin. I close my eyes and revel in the barely-there stroke of his soft lips down to my jaw, where he's more insistent, a little rougher, that stubble scraping my chin in the best way.

I shudder out a breath. He lays a hand on my other cheek, holds me in place. "If you're a good dick, I'll give you a good night kiss," he whispers, and I'm so damn glad I lost the Cleaneroo gig. If the casting director had asked for a callback on the spot, I'd have missed my chance to run into TJ outside a discount shop.

"I'll be the best," I say, and I'm tempted to turn into his lips. To get lost in one of those endless, dreamy kisses I suspect he can give.

But I'm acutely aware of the power of waiting.

I've never edged with kisses. I plan to tonight.

A few minutes later, we're outside The Magpie. With

the book in hand, he gestures in the direction of his hotel. "See you tomorrow sometime," he says.

"Text me when you're up, Sleeping Beauty," I say, nibbling the edge of my mouth absently for a second.

TJ stares wantonly at me, then steps closer. He's mere inches away. "You do this thing where you bite your lip, and it kind of drives me crazy." He drags his thumb along the corner of my mouth then chases it with his lips, giving me one more kiss right there. A spark sprints through me from that barest touch.

TJ steps away, walks backward, lifts his free hand to wave. "Goodnight, Just Jude."

"Welcome to London, Tobias Jangle."

With a smile, TJ turns and strolls into the London evening. The whole way home, I think of great dicks. Because that was the best goodnight kiss I've ever had, and it was also the most innocent.

5

ALL THAT PRESUMING

TJ

I was born and raised in Seattle and lived there till I left for college. It rains every day in the Pacific Northwest, and no one there uses an umbrella.

To London weather, I say, *bring it on,* and the gray sky does just that the next morning, piddling rain on me as I hunt for coffee.

Coffee will help me decide when to text Jude, and it is a veritable hunt because I'm a little ashamed to admit this—I'm a terrible coffee snob. Like, the worst of them. The kind I will undoubtedly mock in a future book someday. The guy who asks *Do you know the elevation where the beans were grown* while the barista wonders if it's acceptable to flip a customer the bird for being a pretentious fuck.

Google tells me the nearby Coffee O'Clock has the

best reviews in the hood, so I make a beeline for the shop's red awning then wait in line.

When I reach the barista, I place my order, then ask, "And I just wanted to make sure you cleaned the hopper?"

Don't want my beans' oils mixed with some other beans' oils.

The barista—a tattooed guy with a leather apron—sears me with a dead-eyed stare. "The second I woke up, mate." Brits are known for their dry humor, and his is desert level.

"Cool, cool. I won't have to cancel my order, then," I quip with a smile that he declines to return. "And did you purge the steam wand?"

His stony expression and lifted brow tell me what I can do with my steam wand. I hold up my hands. "Sorry. It's all good. Do what you're doing." I'm particular, but I'm not a complete coffee douche. "I'm new to town."

"You don't say." He relents and gets to making my coffee. "So, New York, is it?"

"Yes. But originally from Seattle."

"Ah. That would explain it."

"I know. Seattle is the root of all manner of coffee sins."

The barista hands me my drink. "Have faith, mate. This is the good stuff."

I take a sip as I leave the shop and decide he's not wrong. But he's not right either. This is only a passable cup of coffee. To be fair, though, a true coffee snob is never satisfied. There's always a better bag of beans out there.

With the cup in hand, I head to the river, stand at the railing, and stare—*Portrait of a moody American on a Sunday morning.*

Except, I'm not moody. I'm antsy.

FOR PEOPLE TO WAKE UP.

It's only nine here, so it's four a.m. in New York, which means I can't text any of my buds back home. And I'm not sure when to message Jude. He said *Text me when you're up,* but what if he's a late sleeper? I'd look way too overeager if I texted him before ten.

Wait, make that eleven.

Actually, noon is better.

With that decision made, I finish the cup and toss it in a recycling bin, then take a walk along the Thames, the river my companion.

But I still want a human voice, even if it's in text. I could reach out to my brother. Chance won't be up for hours, but there are friend rules and then there are sibling rules. Besides, he messaged me late last night, writing: ***Don't make me go all mom on you and ask if you arrived and why you didn't let me know you were safe?***

I replied before I crashed: ***Safe and sound, Mom.***

Now, awake and strolling through London, I itch to say more. Like: *This sounds crazy, Chance, but I met this guy already, and I'm seeing him today, and he works at An Open Book, that store we went to, the one the travel journal came from, which is kinda wild. And I'm kinda really into him.*

But once I've typed those words, they look too good to be true. Hell, last night *felt* too good to be true, and I don't want to put those sentiments out into the ether. I don't tell my friends or family about my hook-ups, and that's all Jude will be. A hook-up. Nothing real is happening between us, nothing meaningful.

This bout of pragmatism was brought to you by a cup of passable coffee.

I head to a nearby bench and break out my travel journal, taking it from my back pocket. Better to get these thoughts out of my head and onto paper. Maybe they'll be useful for a book someday.

So there's this guy, and we clicked from the start. We vibed like nobody's business. It's a little nutty how much I can't wait to see him again.

There. I said it, okay? I am not cool about this. I had to tell someone. So I'm telling you, Travel Journal.

Keep it to yourself.

There. Done. Rolling my shoulders, I let go of the giddy feeling. I shut the journal, sliding the pen back into its slot. Then I stuff the journal in my pocket and resume my pace along the water as the rain lets up and the gray skies turn blue.

Earbuds in, I work my way back through Covent Garden, listening to Too Big For Their Britches as I go. On the flight over, I made an executive decision to listen only to English bands while I am here—my own sort of travel immersion. Plus, Too Big For Their Britches is performing in a couple of weeks. Not that I've already researched all the cool music bars I want to hit up in my first ten days in London. Not that I have a list on my phone. Not that I'm obsessive about music.

Hmm. Does Jude like new Brit-pop? Would he want to go?

Stop. There will be no music dates. In fact, I'm not even going to reach out to him today. He can text me. That will prove to the ether that I can take it or leave it where he's concerned.

Besides, my day is busy. I need to move into my flat-share, shop for food, and if my bag doesn't arrive today, buy some clothes. Maybe I should stop in at the thrift store just in case.

See? My day is too packed to fit in a text.

I plug Angie's shop into my GPS, and it turns out I'm only three blocks away. When I reach the store, I take out my earbuds and head inside.

"You could be our new store ambassador!"

I turn to find Eggplant Helen—her nickname—grinning at me and glance down at my *The Dude Abides* shirt, which she picked yesterday. "You have the best duds, Eggplant Helen."

"It looks stellar. Are you already back for more?" she asks.

"I believe I am," I say.

She picks some more shirts, sliding me a wide-eyed, *I'm waiting* look. "So, how did it go? Did you see that guy? Does he have a name, so I don't have to keep calling him *that guy* every time you come by to share the little juicy details?"

I wish I knew details. In my mind, I've already detailed his body, his hands, his mouth. For a hookup. A casual fling.

"Yeah. I did. We got a drink last night," I tell Helen.

She howls with delight, "So I was right!" Then she slugs me on the arm. "Told you as much. He fancied you just the same."

I laugh, not sure what to say. It's hard to know if a guy digs you *just the same.* I return to her question. "And his name is Jude."

Her lips twitch. "Jude?"

My brow knits. "Yeah. Like 'Hey, Jude.'"

"Jude from the bookshop?"

"You know him?" I ask, unsure where this is going.

"Jude as in 'looks like a bloody fucking movie star'?"

Never has there been a more fitting description. I smile. "Yeah. That'd be him."

Helen slaps the counter, wildly entertained, it seems. "Well, I'll have you know, he happened to be walking by the shop yesterday after you left."

"Okay?"

"Like he was looking for someone . . ." She sighs impatiently, her tone telling me to connect the romantic dots.

But really? Should I? "Are you saying he was looking for me?"

"Yessss. It's obvious. He decided he'd been too vague in his come-hither and went to find you himself."

No. Because that's too good to be true. Although, I do like the way her brain works. "Those are a lot of logic leaps there, Eggplant Helen. But I appreciate the matchmaker in you."

"Mark my words. You'll be seeing him tonight. Did you make plans?"

"Yes. Sort of. We made plans to see each other, but I'm supposed to text him to set it up."

"Don't wait too long. A man like that won't be around forever."

No one's talking about forever. I only want Jude for tonight. And maybe tomorrow if it's good. And the next night if it's great.

That's all, though.

After buying another shirt, I leave the shop, my phone buzzing once I'm on the street. Jude's name flashes across the screen, and my pulse spikes.

Jude: It's tomorrow. And I've presumed a lot already this morning. I presumed last night too, when I got in bed.

I go up in flames as I reply.

TJ: I could help you with that. All that presuming.

Jude: Good. I hoped as much. Let's meet later. I have a bunch of boring things to do this afternoon but plenty of time for non-boring things tonight. How's seven?

TJ: That's the perfect time for presuming. And I promise it won't be boring.

Jude: I'll hold you to that, Tool Johnson.

TJ: How long were you waiting to whip that one out?

Jude: I just came up with it. I was hoping to find the right moment to slide it in. How'd I do?

TJ: Great. But then, you're kind of a dick.

Jude: You're kind of a dick too.

He sends me the name and address of a bar. A quick Google search tells me it's nearby, but I'd go all the way across the city for him. I don't tell him that, though. I just tell him I'll be there.

When I put the phone in my pocket, I punch the sky. "There. I was super chill. And now, I'm getting laid. That's how you do it."

The freckled brunette jogging past gives a thumbs up.

I salute her jauntily because today will be an excellent day for sex and more sex and then even more.

When I return to my hotel, I head straight for the front desk, where the attendant gives me the good news that my luggage has arrived early.

Everything is falling into place. "Perfect. I'm going to head over to my flatshare now," I say.

Then, with two bags in tow, I head to the nearest tube station, checking the email from my company along the way to confirm the details for my flat in Waterloo, just across the river.

There's a lockbox outside the building. A key will be in it.

Just take one since your roommate will be moving in today too.

Cool. I hope he's a good dude. All I asked was my roomie be a non-smoker and queer-friendly.

In short—the kind who won't mind if I kick him out tonight while I do Jude.

6

A BIG BITE OF ONE THING

Jude

I sling my bag into the back of Olivia's Fiat, then breathe a deep sigh of relief.

"Don't take offense, Liv," I tell my best friend, "but if I never have to beg you or anyone else for a ride into the city again, never will be soon enough. Not that I don't totally love you for having a car."

The fiery redhead stares daggers at me. "I hate you, Jude. You know that, right?"

"You've only mentioned that twenty times since I told you I was moving out of Reading," I say, closing the boot of her sister's car.

Olivia huffs again. "I am so jealous that you're getting out of here. You're going to be close to the theater, to all the studios, to the casting directors. Fuck you, fuck you, fuck you."

That's exactly why I'm leaving. I've lived in Reading

since I finished uni, but it's been brutal getting around. I sometimes have only a moment's notice for an audition or a callback, and being an hour away—by train, no less—from my job and the center of the art world has cost me a couple of job opportunities.

My agent was not pleased. Harry's sternest voice is the equivalent of anyone else's regular voice, but he used it on me. A clear sign that I needed to *be more accessible*.

His words.

And so, I searched the city up and down, listing my name with all the flatshare services, and then finally, a few weeks ago, this place became available. A steal of a deal and in a great location. This will be fantastic for my nine-forty-five audition tomorrow in the Savoy Hotel for a new web show about scientists and robots in love.

"Feel free to tell me to piss off tomorrow morning when I only have to walk fifteen minutes to try out to be a grumpy scientist falling for his robotic creation."

Olivia taps her chin, fire in her green eyes. "Do I really want to give you a ride into the city? Or shall I make you take the train with all your things?"

"Of course you want to help me, Liv. Because you love that I'm the only gentleman you know." I prove my point by opening the driver's side door for her. "See?"

"Thank you," she says, relenting briefly with her vitriol as she sinks behind the wheel. "You're the only one who does that. And I'm such a sucker for manners."

I get into the passenger side. "If you only knew what a gentleman I was last night with my date."

"I would ask, but I think you're about to tell me," she says as she pulls away from the curb.

"Don't pretend you don't want to know every salacious detail." I give her the best ones from last night, including how I sent TJ home. "Which means tonight he'll be rested and ready for me."

"I hate you for that too—your planned trip to Pound Town," she says, slowing at a light.

I pat her thigh. "I'm sure you'll visit there again soon. With Rufus. Or Ginny. Or whoever you decide is worthy of you." I stage whisper, "Even though no one is."

"Damn straight."

"Well, straight's not the word I'd use," I say.

That makes her smile. No easy feat. "It's much more fun having a little bit of everything," she says.

"I'll have to take your word for it. Tonight I'll have a big bite of *one* thing," I say, imagining how my evening might play out with the American. "One very yummy thing. And I'll still make it to my audition on time tomorrow even if I can't walk straight."

"Fuck you. That's the best kind of sex to have."

"The kind you can feel the next day." I couldn't agree more.

She huffs, flicking her gaze at me. "Can't I just move in with you too? Maybe camp on your pullout sofa so I can sleep in and still make it to auditions?"

But we both know she'd never really do that. She lives in her sister's house in Reading, and her sister travels for work most of the time. Liv would never give up the free rent or access to her sister's car. "Poor Liv with her rent-free lifestyle and her ability to audition for anything whenever she wants," I say.

"You did want me to drive you all the way to your

new place, right? Because I can drop you a few miles from it too," she counters.

"Fine, fine. You can crash at my place anytime. My bed is your bed."

As she slows at a light, she waggles a brow. "Or maybe I'll fancy your roommate and get free rent that way. Maybe your new roomie is some gorgeous babe."

"You never know. His name is Terry." The flatshare company sent me that info this morning. "Though, Terry could be a woman. I said I'd live with either gender as long as the person's not a homophobe. So, this is perfect for you. You can fall in love with Terry, and I can see you all the time."

"And since I'm so fabulous in the sack, Terry will pay my way, then the three of us can live in your magical, wildly inexpensive flat that I hate you for getting."

I laugh again. "Promise me something, Liv? Don't ever change."

"I don't plan to," she says.

After an hour of stop-and-go traffic—on a damn Sunday, no less—she pulls up in front of my new place and casts her gaze longingly at the white, six-story building with the yellow door. "It has a pretty door." She pouts. "I'm literally going to die of envy. All I want is a flat with a yellow door."

"And for Terry to bang your brains out and offer you a free place to live."

"That too. I have dreams," she says, raising her chin defiantly. "Just like you."

And it's a damn good thing I have a friend like her to share them with. "Yes, I know. And we will keep chasing them." I stretch across the console and hug her.

"Come over for dinner soon. I'll make you something amazing."

That cheers her up. "Can you make me something with cauliflower? I read it's basically the best food ever, and I'm considering going on an all-cauliflower diet."

"Ah, cauliflower, the latest vegetable to enjoy a renaissance."

"First, there were Brussels sprouts. Now cauliflower. Next, it'll be carrots," she says.

"I truly appreciate the ride," I say.

"I know. Don't go sentimental on me. Just get out," she says.

I do as I'm told, grabbing my bags. But she doesn't pull away even as I head to the lockbox to fetch my key. When I glance back, the saltiest person I've ever known gives me a big wave, then the middle finger.

Laughing, I give the finger right back to her, then blow a kiss.

Once she leaves, I head inside, ready to see my new place and meet my new roomie.

* * *

Jittery with excitement, I turn the key in the lock. I don't even care that this flat is on the stinking fifth floor of a rickety building. Don't care about the garlic I smelled on the fourth floor or the barking dog on the third.

When the door swings open, I call out, "Hello, Terry."

But my voice just echoes.

Cool.

I got here first. That means I can pick the better bedroom. Or, wait—is that kind of piggy? Perhaps I should wait. I'll be polite. Olivia's not the only one turned on by manners—they kind of make me swoon. Not that I want to make my roomie swoon.

But I'd like to be a good roomie, so, yeah, I think I'll wait.

I shut the door behind me, drop my bags, and drink in the sight of this furnished flat that I nabbed at a pittance. I am fucking proud of myself for my persistence.

Even if the couch is a drab gray.

And the kitchen table *might* be missing a leg.

Also, the sink looks like it's seen better days.

Even if I wind up with the shittier bedroom, who fucking cares? Not this bloke.

This flat is close, close, close. That's all I care about. Spinning around, I turn down the hallway—though that's a generous term since it's about three feet long. There are two doors off it, and I knock then open the first one.

There's a bed, a dresser, and little square footage for anything else. But it's big enough for bonking, and what more do I need? Nothing.

I knock on the second door. No answer, so I open that too. Two bags sit on the floor. Okay, so Terry picked a room already.

Fine, fine.

They're pretty much identical.

This makes me wonder . . . I step back into the hall, peering back and forth at the two Lilliputian bedrooms.

"Are you fucking kidding me?" I say to myself.

This place is not a true two-bedroom. They cut a one-bedroom in half. Well, this just shows that if something is too good to be true, there's a reason.

But this is still better than a mansion in Reading.

I return to the living room to grab my bags, and I spot a note on a coffee table. Leaning over, I glance at the first line. It says *Hey, Roomie,* so I pick it up and read the rest.

I tossed my stuff into one of the bedrooms, but if you'd rather have that one, it's cool. I'm good with anything.

Just ran out to grab a coffee. I'll be out tonight, so if I miss you later, I'll see you . . . whenever.

I know everyone says they're chill, but seriously, I am. I don't care if you take long showers, have friends over at all hours, or even play loud music.

As long as it's not Zeppelin.

Sounds pleasant enough.

Setting down the note, I survey the tiny pad once more, then settle on the dull gray couch. "Well, Terry. I'll be out tonight too, so it looks like we'll get along just fine," I say to no one.

The key rattles in the lock. Terry must be back with that coffee already. Maybe next time, I can put in a request for a proper cup of English Breakfast. But for now, I'll be the casual roommate, sitting on the settee with an easy smile.

"Hello there, roomie," I call out as the door opens.

And in walks the American I planned to shag.

7

THE CONSOLATION PRIZE

TJ

I'm a ponderer.

Every spare minute I'm asking myself questions.

Like right now.

Did I hallucinate or time travel to eight-thirty tonight when I hoped to bring Jude back to my place and have my wicked way with him?

Because . . . why the hell is he sitting on my couch?

"Hi, Jude?" It's a question. Or really, it's a slew of questions that all spill out at once. "What are you doing here? Why are you in my flat? Aren't we meeting later? How did you get a key?"

Behind all those questions is the mother of them all, sitting leaden in my gut. I wish it were the dreadful coffee and not the feeling that I know the answer already to this question.

Are you the queer-friendly non-smoker I'm living with for

the next year? Because I never got your name, and please, please, please tell me this is a giant mix-up or maybe a hilarious practical joke we'll laugh about later.

"I'm here because this is the flat I'm sharing with . . . someone named Terry?" Jude sounds as if the floor just fell out from under him too.

I groan and rub my face with my free hand, still standing on the threshold. "24News used my real name with the flatshare?"

"Seems they did." Jude hasn't moved either. He's still spread out on the couch, one arm casually draped over the cushion, looking too fucking good to be my roommate.

Stepping inside, I shut the door and face the inevitable. "So, you're definitely . . .?"

I can't even finish.

"Your new roommate?" Jude asks, going up at the end like maybe, possibly, this could be a case of mistaken identity.

"Do you think maybe there's a misunderstanding? Like maybe it was another flat in this building?" I offer.

"That could be it," Jude says, hopeful, then he grabs his phone from his pocket.

I set down my coffee and do the same, swiping to the email from 24News. I read off the address.

So does Jude.

This building.

And at the same time, we both say, "Flat 5E."

I open the door and check the number, just to be certain. This is undoubtedly 5E, and we both have keys that work. Ergo . . .

Jude slumps into the couch. I slump against the wall.

"The universe is fucking with me." I wince at my word choice; it seems insult to injury when my forecast has plummeted to zero percent chance of boning.

"I'm not fucking with you, Terry." He grimaces and I'm guessing his boning app has the same grim prediction. "I've been living an hour away, trying to get a place in the city for a long time. This came through from the flatshare service, and it's a total steal. I need this apartment." He sounds a touch desperate.

It dawns on me that maybe he's worried I'll bail and he'll have to pay the freight until the flatshare service finds someone else. I don't know how these situations work—24News handled the lease and is covering my rent.

Which is why I can't move out. I don't want to rock the boat at work, especially not when I'm just twenty-three and building momentum up the ladder. "My company rented this for me," I say to Jude. "I can't tell them I was going to . . ."

The sentence dies unfinished. *This setup won't work for me because I planned to fuck my roommate* makes me sound as douchey as I did in the coffee shop.

But the idea's about the same. *I wanted my roomie to purge my steam wand with his mouth.*

I offer a sanitized version. "I can't go back to 24News and say I need a new place because I want to date my roommate," I say, and I squirm a little inside from the discomfort of that honesty. I wanted to sleep with him, and I wanted to date him.

But doing either of those while we're living together would be a huge mistake. What if we bang once, and it's terrible? Or, what if it's great and we don't stop? Until we do stop—because eventually, we will.

That's just how things go.

They end.

Then, our daily lives would be comprised of awkward tiptoeing around each other while he sees someone else, and it would mean kicking myself for getting involved in the first place.

Thank fuck we didn't even really kiss.

"Right. We can't live together and go out," he says. I wonder if he just went through the same thought process. If he saw the exact ending I watched play out in my head.

"Right," I repeat.

Jude pats the couch. "So, it's just you and me, living here. Just reprogramming my brain," he adds, tapping his temple. "Roomie, roomie, roomie. Not hottie, hottie, hottie."

I give a small smile that disappears in a second. "Guess we aren't meeting for that drink."

"Or that presuming."

"There will be no presuming."

"Shame, that," he says, but he's not cheeky Jude now. He sounds resigned to our new reality.

The sex genie is going back in the bottle. I'm not sure how to rank this on the bad-news scale, but on the bummer scale, it's damn high.

We're both quiet for a minute, then Jude breaks the silence. "So, the T is really for Terry?"

I sink to the floor in despair, then wrap my arms around my knees. "Yes," I say dully. "But don't call me that, please. No one does. I hate it."

"You made that quite clear. But what does the J stand for?"

I meet his gaze head-on. Gorgeous blue eyes twinkle with mischief like they did when I met him.

"Doesn't matter," I say, waving a hand dismissively. "I've been TJ for a long time. TJ Ashford. I do everything I can to avoid my given name."

Especially after I was incessantly mocked for it when I was younger. Kids can be such jackasses.

Jude nods. "I'll stop pressing you."

That's another thing that won't happen—Jude using his ways to get my name out of me. I was looking forward to learning how long it'd take for his tongue to get me to break. With those lips? Probably a minute, tops.

"Thanks," I say.

"Though, I'd be a lot happier if I could introduce you as Terry, the guy I'm shagging, not TJ, my new roomie because fate decided to fuck me without lube."

I level a steely stare his way. "Jude, I would never fuck you without lube."

We both crack up, breaking into peals of *you've got to be kidding me* laughter.

Eventually, we catch our breaths. "I guess we'll have to be friends," I say, then I stand and extend a hand.

Jude rises and shakes. "To friendship. But I do have one question. What if I like Led Zeppelin?"

I shudder. "Then I am going to teach you about music."

That'll be the consolation prize.

8

THIS IS THE PERFECT DIVERSION TACTIC

TJ

Maybe I pissed off the Fates or incurred some spectacularly bad Karma because it's Sunday night, and Jude and I are not dueling with words over drinks and then with tongues over at my place. We're wandering through the home decor section of TK Maxx, looking for a shower curtain.

"What about this one?" Jude asks, pointing to a curtain printed with rubber ducks.

Is he for real? Oh, wait. This could be good. Maybe I'll learn Jude and I don't see eye to eye on anything, and all my red-hot desire for him will drain away in one shopping trip.

Yes! "We're not getting that," I say. "We're not three."

"It's ironic," he explains.

"No, irony is when I say *That shower curtain is so nice.*"

Jude whips out his phone, taps furiously, then reads, "Ahem. *Irony: incongruity between the actual result of a sequence of events and the normal or expected result.*" He grabs the curtain and holds it out as if I could somehow miss those bright yellow ducks. "This shower curtain is the opposite of what you'd think two young blokes would have in their flat."

"Hold on," I say, then grab my phone, and pretend to read, "*Irony: still the most often misused word in the English language.*"

Jude rolls his eyes. "Call it kitschy, then. Will you allow kitschy, Mister Word Police?"

"I will definitely allow kitschy."

"Great. Then let's get this shower curtain."

"No."

"Don't you like kitsch?"

I shoot Jude a searing stare. "About as much as I like the irony of living with you."

He chuckles, almost despite himself. "But we're still getting a new shower curtain. I am not showering in that travesty of a bathroom with that horror of a curtain. It had about twenty layers of mold on it," he says, shuddering.

"I'm aware. I'm the one who took it down and tossed it in the trash because you refused to even go in there and touch it."

Jude presses his palms together. "And I am still so very grateful for your chivalry, roomie."

I point to a white shower curtain. "How about that one?"

Jude stares at me, challenge in his eyes. "TJ, are you secretly boring?"

"No. I'm openly interesting."

Jude scoffs, muttering out of the corner of his mouth, "Who gets a white shower curtain?"

"Who cares about the color of a shower curtain?" I ask, and yes, it's working. We're bickering. This will douse the flames in seconds.

Jude points at his chest. "I do. And I'm putting my foot down. We're not getting a white shower curtain. It's boring with a capital B. I refuse to be boring," he says, and he squares his shoulders like he's going to battle on this front.

"I don't understand how the shower curtain says anything about whether you're interesting or not. Who cares about the color of the shower curtain?"

"Everyone," he says.

His answer awakens the beast in me, and I hiss, "You mean everyone, as in, people who are going to come over?"

"Everyone," he emphasizes.

I grit my teeth as the creature thrashes harder in my chest. "Everyone like…?"

"Everyone like *me*," he says, indignant.

Whew.

Stand down, dragon.

While that's not an admission that he *won't* bring a dude over, at least he's picky about bathroom decor for an aesthetic reason rather than a look-tidy-for-a-hookup reason.

And maybe this whole shower curtain persnickety-ness will cure me of my lust. Please, pretty please.

"A classy bathroom sets the mood for the day," he continues, sweeping an arm out, setting the scene. "You want to walk into the bathroom in the morning, enjoy some nice, fluffy towels, and have a shower curtain that welcomes you."

I chuckle at his *Downton Abbey*-esque description. "It sounds like what you need is a valet."

"Don't tease me like that. A bathroom valet is only the height of my fantasies."

"You and I have very different fantasies," I say.

Jude grabs my arm, his touch practically singeing me, and I'm right back on the attraction merry-go-round.

Don't let go of my arm, hottie.

"I assure you, TJ, our fantasies are not that different," he says, low, sensual, and way too dangerous. "And I have loads of fantasies. But I'm speaking specifically of household fantasies. Don't you have household fantasies?"

Sure, but my household fantasies are more along the lines of fucking him while he's bent over the counter. Blowing him at the kitchen table, jerking him off behind the shower curtain. "No. I don't," I lie.

He lets go of my arm. "Well, I do. And mine include a nice bathroom for getting ready in the morning."

This must be an actor thing. I'm going to have to go along with it, and hopefully, it'll dull the shine of Jude Graham.

He waxes on about cheery colors and patterns as he sifts through the selection of shower curtains, picking up a purple one, a plaid one, a green flower one, dismissing each with a careless flick of the finger. "We want something with a little perk."

"Perky shower curtains," I repeat, processing this term. "I didn't know that was a thing."

"How about something bright and yellow?" Jude suggests.

I wave a hand dismissively at the selection on the shelves. "Sounds fine. Just pick."

He laughs deeply, very *oh, silly boy*. "You didn't think I was going to let you pick, did you, TJ? If you picked, it'd be something you ordered from Zazzle and with a guy in a bathrobe on it."

"The dude?" I point to my shirt, the one with the illustration of Jeff Bridges's iconic character from one of the greatest cult classics ever.

"Yes. Or Tetris," Jude adds.

Fine, if he's going to poke at me like that, I can poke back. "You didn't have a problem with my Tetris shirt last night," I point out.

Jude slides just an inch closer, lowers his voice. "Actually, I did."

I put my hands on my hips. "What was the problem?"

His eyes sparkle as he tugs at the fabric of my shirt again. "My problem . . ." He takes a deliberate pause as he holds the material in those fingers. My blood heats as I imagine those fingers tearing that shirt off me, then traveling down my chest. "Was that it was on."

I laugh—I wasn't expecting that. Jude laughs too, then turns away from me, which is for the best. If he keeps looking at me like that, with flirt in his eyes, I just might grab his face and kiss the fuck out of him in the shower curtain aisle at TK Maxx.

I move to new topics. "I'm getting the sense you're saying I have no style?"

Jude swivels around and adopts a too-sweet expression. "Let's just say, the way I feel about your style"—he waves a hand dismissively at my T-shirt then at the shelves of curtains—"is on par with how you feel about my love of Led Zeppelin."

Yes! Another thing we don't have in common. Shower curtains, clothing style, and musical taste will work in combination to turn me off. "Fine, go ahead and play Zeppelin tonight. It's cool," I say with a shrug.

He snort-laughs. "Oh, please. You're a terrible liar."

"I'm not lying," I lie.

Jude stares at me with a smile that says he's caught me red-handed. "You only want me to play Zeppelin so you don't think about me naked."

Jesus.

He's electric. He's unstoppable.

"Feel free to add in Jethro Tull, then too," I say. I've got to try to keep up with him.

"Wait. I figured you out. You hate all the English rock bands that had their heyday in the seventies?"

"Yup. But not just English bands. American ones too. Case in point: The Allman Brothers Band." I cringe for effect. "Queen aside, the seventies were a musical wasteland worldwide."

"But what about ABBA?" He sounds like hating the Swedish pop group is blasphemy.

"Especially ABBA. So yeah, feel free to love on them all you want," I challenge.

With curious eyes, Jude seems to size me up.

"Because . . ." He wags a finger. "Because that would help our necessary friendship? If I love the bands you hate?"

"Yes, exactly." Though, so far, that doesn't appear to be true whatsoever.

He stares at me like a cat, taking his sweet time. "No. I don't think I will play them."

"Why not?" I ask like I don't care, but I really want to hate him. I swear I do.

"Because I think you'd rather I play some alt-rock. Some cool new bands. Something I find in the clubs. I bet that's your scene, right?"

I am cellophane with him. I need to find a trench coat to cover my see-through self. "No," I say with an offhand shrug.

"You're a terrible liar, TJ," he says again, amused this time.

"I'm not," I insist.

"You are. Want to know how I know?"

"Sure," I grumble.

Jude points at my face. "Your eyes lit up when I said, *cool new bands*. That's what you like, right? And you think if I play something you don't like, it'll make you stop thinking of all the presuming we're not doing."

I'm naked with him. "Why are you doing this?" I ask softly, feeling wobbly.

"Because I don't want you to hate me," he says earnestly. "I want us to be friends. Truly, I do. And the thing is, I'm rubbish with music. Maybe I can learn about your cool new bands, and you can learn about how delightful it is to have a shower curtain that's not boring." Jude pauses, then adds the clincher. "And I don't think disliking me is going to help."

He's called me out, leaving me with no choice but to try.

"Fine. Then how about this? I'll teach you about musical taste, and you can teach me about style?"

"That sounds so very friendly," he says.

This is my new world order in London.

I am no longer living in a rom-com.

I'm back to reality.

* * *

But first, tools.

The selection is downright abysmal in the tool aisle, and "aisle" is a generous term. It's more like one tiny sliver of a shelf.

"There are hardly any screwdrivers," I say.

"Do we need more than one?" Jude asks as if screwdrivers are a nuisance.

"Yes, and a couple of wrenches. The faucet on the sink is on the fritz. The pipes probably need adjusting. I definitely need a decent toolkit."

That seems to spark his interest. "Is that something you're good at? Fixing things?"

"I was the de facto handyman in my last apartment," I say. "And I've just always been good at it."

"That's kind of . . ." His eyes go a bit glossy.

All my instincts say *make a dirty joke*. Somehow, I refrain from asking: *Do you have a handyman kink*? "I just need to get a few tools," I say, keeping it on the level.

"Things I say every day," he says in a very flirty voice.

I shoot him the side-eye. "You're not helping."

Jude gives me a too-innocent look. "Maybe you could get a hammer, for instance. And some nails. In case anything needs to be . . . nailed."

Filthy images snap before my eyes. *Not helpful.* "Is this your definition of friendly?"

"Is it working?"

"Absolutely. I feel all sorts of buddy/buddy with you," I deadpan as I grab a basic tool set and we get the hell out of that aisle.

I don't trust my common sense anymore. It's haywire with Jude Graham. Black is white and up is down, and before I know it, tea will taste good.

But at least there are towels to focus on. Jude taps his chin thoughtfully as he checks out every style and color, asking my opinion on each set. It's both endearing and annoying.

"Are you prepping for a role as a towel inspector? And I mean that literally," I say.

"No, but that reminds me—I have to do a little prep work tonight. I'm auditioning for a role as a scientist who falls in love with a robot that he makes," he says brightly, like he's been looking for the right opening to share this news.

Jude's genuine enthusiasm makes me turn off my sarcasm. "That sounds cool. What's it for?"

"Do you really want to hear about it?" He sounds surprised like the default is that I wouldn't.

"I do," I say.

The giddy expression on his face is familiar. That's how I feel when an idea for a story zings *just so*—that magic moment. I hope it'll hit me soon, and I can start on my first novel. I've got a few concepts to noodle on. Maybe I can do that after work tomorrow.

"There's a studio here producing a new web series about robots and scientists in love. The head scientist falls for the robot he created. She's a perfect replica of a woman and even starts to develop sentient feelings and independent thought, and it freaks him out and thrills him at the same time. It actually sounds like a cool project," he says.

"It does. Do you have a script?"

"They sent over sides. Just a couple of scenes. I need to go over them tonight."

Jude sounds both nervous and excited. I should invent a reason to get out of the flat tonight, somewhere I'm far, far away from him, but I don't. "Do you want me to . . ." I clear my throat because this feels like a different sort of closeness. "Run lines with you?"

It's like I told him I'd clean the flat for a year. "Would you?"

"Sure. I like stories a lot more than shopping for towels. How about you pick a set right now, and when we get home, we'll run lines."

"I have to pick right now?" He sounds mildly aghast.

"You can do it," I encourage.

With a deep breath, he darts out a hand and picks a deep, dark blue towel. They aren't at all what I'd have thought he'd choose—they aren't perky. But I don't ask his reasoning since this selection gets us out of the store.

Which also puts us one step closer to the danger zone.

9

THE TIME I SWALLOWED A FROG

TJ

We stop in a grocery store on the way home, going separate ways, a reminder that we're not a couple shopping together.

Which is fine. Totally fine.

I wanted to meet a guy . . . to date.

I didn't come to London to meet a guy I'd want to shop for food with. I've got no interest in shopping for food with anyone. I didn't share anything but beer with my buddies back in New York. It was every man and woman for themselves.

And that's how it'll have to be with Jude.

When Jude and I are done, each man buying his own basket's worth of basics, we stop for sandwiches at a grubby corner shop, paying separately.

The opposite of where we'd have gone on a date.

The opposite of how we behaved last night when he paid for me.

Everything is the opposite. Especially this—when we're back at the flat, he hangs the bright yellow shower curtain, and I fix the sink.

We are just roomies doing chores.

Once we've put away the food and the towels, he emails me the pages, and we sit on opposite ends of the couch. "All right. Let's do this, Mister Rising Star," I say.

That earns me another smile. "From your mouth to God's ears," he says, then he clicks on his tablet.

His mouth tightens at the corners, his eyes turn down, dark, almost like he's possessed. He transforms into someone else. It's breathtaking to watch.

"But you're not real. None of this is even real," he says, utterly desperate.

"It's not?" I say as the robot woman, reading the lines to him. I am not an actor, so I don't try to play the part.

Jude, the scientist, sighs heavily. "Can't be. It just can't be."

"But how do you know what's real?" I ask.

"How do I know? Because real is this," he says, clutching his chest, as the stage directions call. "Real is what's happening here."

We continue through the scene until . . . oh, shit.

I swallow roughly, sounding like a real robot as I give him the last line of my dialogue. "Tell me if you think this is real," I say awkwardly, then I wait for him to speak.

Even though the robot is supposed to sashay over to her creator right fucking now. The script calls for a kiss.

Are we doing *all* the stage directions? A wild hope

moves through me—the wish for a stage kiss. Just to help him stay in character. So he can properly prep for his audition.

Want thrums through me, hot and greedy, but terrifying too. If I look up from my phone and see the same desire whipping through him, I'll lunge, kiss Jude recklessly.

I'd break after only one night in a long year ahead.

I have to stay strong. I *will* stay strong.

But when I raise my face, he's not looking at me. He's lost in thought. "Hmm. It's not clear if they want me to do the kiss," he says, studying the pages intently.

"It's not?" I sound like I swallowed a frog.

"Well, see, I don't know if they've cast the actress. Or if I'll just be reading lines with the casting director."

"Do you usually kiss in an audition?" A current of jealousy rips through me.

Which is dumb. Who cares?

"No. So it's odd they'd leave it in the sides," he says, and his methodical approach should be a relief. He wasn't even thinking about kissing me. He was simply analyzing the words.

"Maybe they just want *you* to know what comes next? They want you to have the feel of the end of the scene. So you know what you're building toward. Maybe that's why they left it in—so you can play the scene as you move toward that."

"Oh!" Jude's face lights up. "Yes. Duh. That's so obvious now that you say it, but yes, of course. You're quite astute."

"It's written in the script." I'm not taking the credit here.

"It *is* written. But you looked beyond the scene. You interpreted the intentions of the casting director, and you don't even know them." He leans forward, his eyes dancing. "That's the writer in you."

"Maybe," I say, trying to make light of it. I don't know how to take his remark.

"It's a compliment, TJ," he adds for clarity. "Truly."

"Thank you," I say, and I don't want to talk more about this. He doesn't know if I'm a good writer. Besides my work articles, I've only written in that travel journal, and he can never see that.

Ever.

Not even when I'm six feet underground.

Jude takes a deep breath. "So, how did I do?"

I'm not a casting director. I don't know that I can give him the answer he's seeking. All I can do is speak from the heart. "I believed you."

"Really?" It sounds like nothing could make him happier than those three words.

"I really did."

"That's all I can ask for." His eyes—it's like they're flickering just for me. It's heady the way he looks at me, but it's also tempting.

I've got to get out of his spotlight. It's too much. This moment is too close to what I want—art and creativity—hitting my heart in a way that makes me feel . . . seen.

I'm not sure I want him to see me. It's a relief to turn the light on him instead. "Tell me more about the show," I say.

As Jude shares the details, I listen intently—because I'm interested and because I'm a little bit selfish.

This could be useful. Maybe someday I'll write about an actor.

Yes, that's the trick!

The next year with Jude will be research.

That's how I'll classify this, and that will help me navigate three hundred sixty-five nights sharing less than a thousand square feet with him.

"Now, how about that music lesson?" he asks, bright and lively.

"No such luck, sweetheart," I say. "I have to be at work at eight-thirty. Raincheck."

"Of course . . . *sweetheart,*" he says, imitating me.

Is he teasing me? Or playing the scientist echoing the robot's lines? No idea. But if I stay out here, I'll get too lost in my head. I point to the bedroom. "I'm going to hit the sack."

And probably whack off.

"Me too," Jude adds.

The trouble is, once I'm in bed and he's in his room, I hear him shuffling around, opening drawers, one of which squeaks.

I push my hands through my hair, annoyed. These walls are paper-thin. Can't even fucking jerk it.

Sure, I can be quiet and all, but still. I don't want to let out a groan accidentally.

Well, the gods of horny men made showers for a reason. Swinging my legs out of bed, I head straight for the bathroom, shut the door and stand under the hot stream. I waste no time. I need to let go of all this tension.

I especially need to do it without thinking of my roommate.

I picture nameless, faceless men as I stroke.

Hard bodies. Broad shoulders. Mouths on cocks.

I close my eyes, grip myself harder, my breath stuttering.

The water skims over me as I hit the right pace, the one that makes my skin crackle, that gets me closer to release. As my fist flies down my length, I picture lips on me.

Yes, that's it.

Just a standard order blow job.

That's all I need to reach the edge.

I fight like hell to stay in that zone, seeing a generic face, a handsome man. Except my mind is a traitorous motherfucker. On an upstroke, the dirty images transform, and my fantasies are completely out of my control, like a runaway train.

Lush, full lips. Bright blue eyes that twinkle. Thick blond hair I twist my fingers through. And a willing mouth. Jude would take me deep, grin as he sucked me to the back of his throat.

The show-off. The gorgeous, filthy show-off.

With a grunt that's louder than I'd like, I come hard, panting too, and hoping he didn't hear me.

After I finish my shower and put on basketball shorts, I head to my room and flop on the bed.

That helped, and it also didn't help one damn bit.

When I turn to my side, I hear a sound. The bathroom door is shutting, then the creak of the faucet, the thrum of the shower.

I pinch the bridge of my nose, fighting a losing battle once more. I can't picture anything but him seeking release.

Needing it as badly as I did.

Or maybe that's just more of this foolish hope.

Tomorrow, I'll do better.

* * *

In the morning, I'm up at the crack of dawn, and I hit the pavement for a run. After I shower and get ready for work, I eat toast as I listen to Astronaut Food's upbeat mix of guitar and smooth vocals.

Jude strides down the hall as the song ends, yawning, hair I'm aching to touch sticking up in all directions.

The hair's not the only thing sticking up.

The bulge of his morning wood is like a target for my vision, and I can't look away from the shape of him in those soft gray flannel pants.

I try valiantly, pulling my gaze up, up, and away.

And my brain fills with static because he's shirtless and beautiful. Jude's smaller than I am, leaner than I am. His golden skin is smooth and makes my mouth water. He's toned in all the right ways, and I want to pounce on him, hold him down, and kiss every inch of him as he writhes and moans.

The entire image is too much. I'll combust if I stay here any longer. Somehow, I manage to take out the earbuds, just to be polite. "Good luck with your audition," I say, forcing my gaze away from him as I stuff my phone into my pocket.

"Good luck with your first day at work," he says as I reach for the doorknob. "By the way, I was right about the shower curtain, wasn't I?"

Right about what? Oh. Sure. He's into color. "Yeah, it's perky," I say quickly, opening the door, ready to bolt.

"It sure is. But I also meant the right one could make the shower more enjoyable. Wouldn't you say? At least, it was quite enjoyable for me. The sound of the shower and all," he adds.

Busted.

I close my eyes, let the embarrassment run through me, then I steal a glance at Jude. He heads for the kettle, and as he goes, I can see the hint of a satisfied smile.

I leave.

One down. Three hundred and sixty-four to go.

10

I'M ADDICTED TO THE GOAT'S NAVEL

Jude

Olivia is enjoying my personal hell far too much. The wicked minx cackles as I give her the roomie update as we walk down the street on Thursday afternoon.

"You're the worst," I tell her as we pass The Duck's Nipple, a pub that stocks some of the freshest new beers to hit the market. But it also reminds me of a band TJ sent me a note about this morning, saying, ***Check out this playlist. I challenge you not to become addicted when you listen.***

Addicted to The Goat's Navel? Is that a real name? I'd replied.

Don't judge a band by its name.

How else would we judge? I wrote back.

Just listen, Jude.

I've listened to the band, but I haven't replied yet. I don't want to seem overeager.

As we turn the corner, Olivia flicks her red hair off her shoulder. "Tell me one more time—how hard is it to live with the guy you want to shag?"

I roll my eyes. "The hardest. There. Does that satisfy your inner demon?"

The she-devil gives a too-big grin. "I'm not sure this tale will ever grow old."

"So glad I can entertain you," I say as I point to a café. "But I can't deny you. Let's get a cuppa."

"Always," she says. Five minutes later, we're parked outside the café, watching afternoon crowds flit down a busy street full of festive shops, including Out of the Closet, a thrift shop I like. I make a mental note to bring TJ there this weekend, perhaps—a fair trade for The Goat's Navel, especially when I tell him the story of the shop's name.

"So, tell me every dirty detail of this week," Olivia demands as she dunks a chocolate biscuit in her tea. "What have the last few nights been like?"

Surprisingly easy. "I thought it would be terrible. But I've been at the bookshop every night, and he works all day. I didn't even see him on Tuesday."

"Like, at all?" she asks when she finishes her biscuit.

I shrug. "Not once. And on Wednesday, I saw him for maybe five minutes at eleven at night. He came home then. Actually, I think he was home quite late on Tuesday too. Maybe after me."

She arches a brow. "Do you think he was out meeting less handsome men than you? I mean, obviously, they'd be less handsome."

"Obviously." I drink some Earl Grey to wash away

the thought of TJ meeting other men. "Anyway, I suppose he could be seeing other guys."

Olivia pats my hand. "Maybe he's just making new friends here. It's not a terrible thing if he is. I mean, it'd be good if you don't see each other more than you have to. I imagine you wanted to climb him like a tree during those five minutes of togetherness?"

"As a matter of fact, yes, I did. Thanks for reminding me, minx."

Another devilish smile. "So, when he came home late, did he look all freshly fucked?"

I groan at the image of a freshly-fucked TJ—though, I suspect it's the other way around, which works for me. "No. He returns with his laptop. So, I dunno—maybe he's just working, covering the markets. I suppose he has late story deadlines. Then he's up early in the morning. He goes for a run. And then he comes home and showers, and makes toast, and heads off."

"Hmm."

"What's that 'hmm' for?"

"For someone who's trying to be just friendly, you know an awful lot about his habits."

"Well, he is my roommate. I would hope I know something," I say defensively.

She tuts as she swirls the last biscuit in her tea. "You seem to know an awful lot about his habits in the morning when you're sleeping," she amends, then devours the treat.

"I hear him get up! I'm a light sleeper. Besides, are you trying to catch me in something? In still lusting after him? I fucking admitted I want him to bang me."

She laughs but then shifts gears, softening as she asks, "What's he like?"

That's easy. "Snarky. Witty. Likes to knock me down a peg. Also, helpful. He fixed the sink and the drawer in my dresser. It was squeaking on Monday, but the squeaking stopped Monday night, so he must have fixed it while I was out." I keep to myself that when I texted to thank him, he replied with ***Just call me Tool Johnson***.

"So . . . you like him?"

"What do you mean?"

She only arches a brow.

"What are you saying, Liv?" I press. I hate unsaid things. I hate when she observes me and doesn't just spit it out.

"I'm saying I don't think you just want to shag him, Jude," she says, uncharacteristically salt-free. "It sounds like you like the guy. You just told me how he fixed a drawer," she says, too bloody observant.

Good thing I didn't mention he sent me a playlist. Or that we texted about it.

I don't want to like TJ in the way she means. Not after my university ex left me, saying *I just don't feel the same way for you* as he walked out the door with a casual shrug while sawing my heart in half.

"I have no interest in liking someone after Robert," I say coolly.

"Robert was a twat," Olivia says.

"I know, but I'm the twat who fell for the twat."

"It happens to the best of us. It's not your fault."

"But it *is* my fault if I go out and get involved with someone else." I hear myself and shake my head. "What in the holy fuck am I saying? I'm not getting involved.

And I'm *definitely* not getting involved with my roomie. I'm not getting involved with anyone."

"Good. Then we can all go out sometime and have fun. As friends," Olivia says. "Let's get the crew together. Shane and Amanda and Archie."

"Yes, that sounds like a fantastic idea," I say. It's just the sort of activity to keep TJ firmly in the friends and roomies zone.

"Now, any word on scientists and robots in love?"

I frown. "Are you trying to remind me of all the things in my life that suck? I haven't heard from my agent about the gig, ergo I didn't get the job. The American is off fucking other men every night, and I have horrible exes."

She stretches an arm to ruffle my hair. "You are so dramatic."

"This is news?"

"Also, you're wrong," she goes on. "You not hearing from Harry means there's a chance you got the gig. If it were a no, you'd have heard as much."

My heart soars again with wild hope. "I really want the job."

"I know, love."

But she doesn't deny that the American might be shagging other men. And that bothers me—too much.

So much that I text him on my way to Cecil Court.

Jude: You were right. I'm addicted to The Goat's Navel.

TJ: Called it!

Jude: But you have to admit, that name sounds like a pub.

TJ: A pub I'd want to go to.

Jude: Have I mentioned I work near a pub called The Duck's Nipple?

TJ: That is a fantastic name. It's so good I want to steal it and use it someday.

Jude: In an article?

TJ: Something like that. Gotta go. Source is calling.

As I pass the kid's bookshop, I sigh, staring at the last message. There's something he's not telling me. I wish I knew what it was. I wish I knew why he wouldn't tell me.

I feel a little stupid, though, for wanting to know.

And that bothers me too.

But when he walks into An Open Book a few hours later, that doesn't bother me at all.

11

MYSTERIES CAN HAVE HOT SEX

TJ's Travel Journal
London, Day Six

After turning in my sixth article—count 'em, six—on Thursday afternoon, I took off for another research trip. I've spent all my evenings so far on a mission. Checking out moody places in London.

Because I've decided at last. At fucking last!

Here goes, Travel Journal. You're the first to know officially that . . . I'm going to write a whodunit. A race against the clock.

Whew. I said it, and I'm starting it tonight.

When I was a kid, I devoured Alistair Edwin's tales of the international teenage spy Rhys Locke as he cracked the case wherever there were jewel heists. Locke was the coolest hero, all steel and nerves, and just out of school. But I won't write a teenager—my hero will be in his twenties. Maybe there'll be some sex. Mysteries can have hot sex, right? Mostly there will be clues, and whodunits, and all sorts of wild plot twists.

A scene here at Aldwych station, an abandoned tube station that looks haunted.

Another at the Hardy Tree in a cemetery, where I went last night. Maybe there will be a chase there. An apprehension.

And I definitely want a scene in a creepy church like the one I saw on Tuesday.

I should pick up some Agatha Christies to get in the right frame of mind. *Murder on the Orient Express* makes my brain pop every single time I re-read it.

And, well, if I'm going book shopping, it'd be rude to go anyplace but Jude's store.

(Travel Journal, you weren't fooled by that excuse, were you? Yeah, me neither.)

12

AND THE CLUES ALL SAY

Jude

TJ looks freshly . . . showered. The ends of his hair are wet. He's wearing a plain white T-shirt. It's tight enough that I can spy the faint outline of his nipples. Dear God, did he wear that on purpose?

Well, of course, he did, you daft idiot! He didn't put on a shirt by fucking accident.

My roommate strides over to the counter. When he reaches me, I catch a faint whiff of aftershave. It's woodsy and clean. He wasn't wearing that on Saturday night when we went to The Magpie. Did he buy it here in London or was it in his suitcase that he retrieved on Sunday? And how much of a perv would I be if I nipped into our bathroom some night, uncapped it, and inhaled his scent?

The answer smashes into me like a wrecking ball—*a big pathetic perv.*

I straighten my shoulders. "Are you coming here to gloat about The Goat's Nipples?"

His brow furrows. "You mean The Goat's Navel?"

Shit. "Yes, that's what I meant," I say, trying to recover as if I'd merely dropped a line on stage. "The Duck's Navel, of course."

TJ grins slyly, his lips twitching. "It's the duck with the nips, Jude. You said so yourself," he says, waggling his phone. "You a little distracted, buddy?"

Did he come here to torture me with that shirt and that aftershave and that hair? When he squares his shoulders, making his chest look even sexier, I resort to a full-on rescue mission and save myself with a slice of the truth.

"Actually, yes. I keep checking my phone to see if Harry has gotten word on the audition." That's not a lie. I did check my mobile an hour ago.

TJ's face turns sympathetic. "Nothing yet?"

"Not a peep."

"Well, when you get the good news, we need to celebrate."

"How?"

"You know, get a beer or something. Something . . . *friendly*," he says.

"Was that irony?"

"Literally," he says with a smile. God, he has such a great smile, all straight teeth, and an easy grin. It's not a know-it-all grin like some men wield. It's a genuine one.

"Anyway, are you . . . looking for a book?" That's a logical question, even if I really want to ask *Where do you go at night and what do you do?*

"I am." He drums his fingers on the counter, then

glances back at the handful of other patrons in the shop. They're busy sifting through shelves, but I keep my eye on them in case they need anything. "Ever heard of this writer named Agatha Christie?" TJ asks.

I feign ignorance. "Not ringing a bell. Did she pen those bonkbusters about Hollywood royalty?" I snap my fingers. "Hold on, that's Caroline Vienna. Oh, I've got it! Did Agatha write those tales of the teenage spy?"

The gold flecks in his eyes brighten and flicker. "I loved the Rhys Locke books when I was younger. I devoured them all. Did I ever tell you I came to this bookstore when I was thirteen?"

"No," I say, surprised at how easily he reveals this and the gleeful look in his eyes.

"I spent hours here on a family trip. And you just named my favorite writers. Caroline Vienna and Alistair Edwin. I actually got a bunch of their books from this store," he says, with a faraway gaze like he's slipped into a memory—a very happy one. "So, it was . . . kinda interesting that you worked here."

"A little kismet," I say before I think better of it.

Because there's no kismet with us. And what the hell? I don't believe in kismet. I believe in work and putting in your time.

TJ gives a soft smile. "Yeah, it's kind of cool that you work in this shop."

"Are you going out tonight?" I blurt out.

His grin turns lopsided for the first time. His mouth is all kinds of crooked as he studies me. "I'm here right now. Why are you asking if I'm going out?"

I flap a hand at him. "Well, after you get your Agatha Christies. You look like you're going out." Ugh. I sound so flustered it must be obvious why I'm asking—because I'm a jealous, prying roomie.

"Nah. I just went to the gym after I went to—after I did some stuff." There he goes again—*not saying* what he's doing. "So I showered after I worked out."

Great. Now I'm picturing him at the gym, pumping iron, and getting all sweaty.

Everywhere.

Sweat dripping down that chest, between his nipples, then onto his navel, then his happy trail.

"Cool. Cool. I go to the gym too," I say.

Then I want to smack myself. *I go to the gym?* Have I ever talked to a man before? Let alone one I know? I need to lock up my mouth and throw away the key.

"Gyms are good," TJ says.

I've got to save me from me. I point to the mysteries near the back of the shop. "Let me show you the Agatha Christies."

"Thank you, but I don't want to keep you from work," he says, and maybe that's a hint he wants to look at them alone.

It's a reminder, too, that I need to do my job. As he heads to the shelves, I go to the other customers, helping them find some travel books, a photo book of London, and a cookbook.

I challenge myself not to steal a single glance at my roommate until I've rung up all the customers. Even then, I don't look. I march over to the romances and reshelve the books that some customers left on a nearby chair.

At last, my eyes stray to him.

Oh. I didn't notice he had on his laptop messenger

bag when he came in, maybe because I was too focused on that shirt.

I grab my phone from my pocket to have something else to look at, and check for messages from Harry while I'm at it.

And hello gorgeous.

An email from Harry flashes across the screen. The subject line makes my pulse spike—*Callback.*

"Fuck yes," I shout, reading the note quickly.

TJ spins around, then strides over. "Did you get a callback?"

"Are you a mind reader?" I ask, giddy with the news.

"The smile and the *fuck yes* gave it away," he says, then offers a hand to high-five.

"Monday at twelve." I smack his palm.

Before I can let go of his hand, TJ yanks me in close for a hug. "Congrats. I knew you'd crush it."

I say nothing because my throat hitches when I breathe in that aftershave. I shift my nose slightly, a thief nicking one more hit of that delicious scent.

With his arms around me, my mind races with after-dark possibilities. Bet he does too, because he murmurs something—something unintelligible. His incoherence makes the moment even sexier.

When TJ lets go, he's slow and purposeful, his hands sliding down my arms.

Or is that wishful thinking? My eyes drift to his hands to verify. But everything feels warm and hazy, and I don't know if he's touching me deliberately or just letting go slowly.

All I know is my insides are melting.

When he breaks the hold, he says in a rough voice, "Do you want to rehearse again? This weekend?"

"Yes. I do. How's Sunday?"

"Perfect."

Then, he smooths a hand over my shoulder. I blink, trying to figure out what he's doing.

"You just had a piece of something on your shirt," he says, with a lazy shrug.

"I did?"

His eyes darken as he stares at my lips, then glances back up. "I just wanted to get it off."

"Did you? Get it off?"

TJ shakes his head. "I don't think so actually."

"Better try again," I say, inviting him to touch me once more.

He brushes a hand over my shoulder, and it's maddening how good that feels. When his palm skims over me, my whole body vibrates.

"I think I got it," he says, all husky.

"Well, I don't know if you did," I whisper, mesmerized by his touch.

"You're right. I think I missed something here." He lifts that hand, brushing his fingers over my hair.

Sparks burst inside me. I haul in a gasp.

For long seconds, we stare at each other. I'm caught in the heat of his gaze, the way we subtly angle our heads to lean in for a kiss.

But the bell over the door tinkles, and I wrench away. I'm pained by the separation but grateful for it too. I was this close to demanding greedy, hungry kisses.

A woman in a red dress walks in. A young girl wearing a tutu skips beside her.

"I should . . ." I begin, my voice hoarse.

"And I should get these books," TJ says, sounding the same.

I head to the woman and child, letting them know I can help them if they need anything. I hope I don't bear the tell-tale signs of an almost kiss, but I suspect my face is flushed.

I return to the counter as TJ arrives, several mysteries in hand, and a London guidebook too. I ring him up, and he says goodbye.

When the store's quiet again, I still haven't come down from the contact high, so I send him a text. I need to know something. I just do.

Jude: Was that a new shirt you wore tonight?

TJ: No. I've had it for a while. I haven't shopped yet. I'm saving myself for you.

Jude: How sweet.

TJ: Well, I suspect I'll need to conserve all my shopping energy to keep up with you this weekend.

I should stop, but I don't. Flirting with TJ is the best time I've ever had.

Jude: I bet you'll love shopping with me.

TJ: As much as you liked my plain white shirt?

Jude: So you noticed that . . .

TJ: Let's just say it was as obvious as a duck's nipple. Also, I told you some things are good in white.

Jude: You were right.

* * *

Later, when I return home, he's not there. But the reader and bibliophile in me adds up the clues—the messenger bag with his laptop, the books, his unsaid things. I know what he's up to.

A pang of frustration wedges in my rib cage. I wish he trusted me enough to tell me. I wish, too, I understood *why* I so badly want him to admit his plans.

But rather than analyze, I decide I'll do my damnedest to get it out of him on Saturday.

13

MERIT BADGES

TJ

Today I earned my first official badge. The "I survived a week living with Jude" one.

Yay me!

Fine, technically, it's not a full week until tomorrow on Sunday, but these last six days feel like the longest test of resistance ever. So, there's that.

Can I last another fifty-one weeks? Yes, yes, I can.

Also, I totally said that last part in a ridiculous fitness class instructor voice in my head.

Because that's how I handle living with the swooniest guy I've ever known.

I finish the travel journal entry, shut the pocket-sized book, and slide it into the inside compartment of my messenger bag.

But, hold on.

I should know better than to keep an easily accessible record of feelings.

My next mission, should I choose to accept it?

Say goodbye to the pages in this journal.

I sling my messenger bag over my shoulder. It's Saturday morning and I've got a date with coffee and chapter two. I can't wait to dig into my book today.

I've already worked out this morning and showered, and since Sleeping Beauty is still snoozing, our first shopping expedition won't be till later.

I'm outta here.

I head to Coffee O'Clock, and when I push open the door, my new frenemy greets me. The inked barista in the leather apron holds out his arms wide. "Have no fear, Mister Coffee! The steam wands are thoroughly purged just for you."

Laughing at myself—*definitely at myself*—I thank him. "I appreciate that, William," I say, reading his name tag. "Now you know why the International Coffee Commission named me The Bane of Baristas' Existence."

"Shocked. I'm simply shocked. What's your poison this morning?"

I ask for an espresso, and as William grinds the beans, he tips his chin my way. "Have you been busy terrorizing other baristas this week?"

"All over the city, they duck and hide when they see me coming. At the coffee shop near my office, they try to lock the doors when I round the corner."

Shaking his head, William scoffs. "Not this guy. I love a good challenge. You, sir, are indeed a level ten challenge."

"Aww. I think that's the nicest thing anyone's ever said to me." I do my best to live up to expectations by peppering him with super douchey questions about the espresso machine. He answers them all to my satisfaction, then sets to work.

"So, are you a regular now in London?" William asks.

"I'm here for fifty-one more weeks," I say.

"That's specific," he says.

"Well, when you have a massive crush on your roommate and must resist him at all costs, you find yourself counting off every single day."

"Ouch. That can't be easy, mate."

"Not one bit."

"I've been into guys I couldn't have either. Probably always will," he says.

"Is that your curse?" I ask with a laugh.

"Seems to be. Probably will end up in therapy eventually. So, other than your shite romantic situation, how was your first week in London?" William asks as he pulls a shot.

I give him another honest answer. "Aside from The Roommate Resistance, it was inspiring."

"How so?"

Ah, what the hell. I've been bursting to say something to someone. "Everything snapped into place for the novel I'm writing. It's my first."

"You're a novelist. That tracks," William says drily.

"I am indeed a caricature."

"Nah. You're a character, but it works," he says, then serves the espresso. "I'm a bit of a writer myself. I write songs for my band."

"Awesome. What kind of music?"

"Alt-pop. We fancy ourselves a New Order," he says.

"I worship at the temple of New Order. One of my top five British bands. What's the name of yours?

"Lettuce Pray. And it's spelled like—"

"—the head of lettuce," I finish. "I love it."

"What kind of novels do you write? Wait, let me guess." He narrows his eyes, thoughtfully humming as he studies me like a science experiment.

Please don't say lit fic. I will die.

"Political thriller," he guesses.

Relieved he didn't pick the snobbiest genre, I square my shoulders. "Close. I'm writing a whodunit with a bit of a thriller feel. For now, I'm calling it *Only After Midnight,* but that's a pretty pat title, so it will change. It's set in London, and the young hero is determined to figure out who's behind a spate of murders at London's spookiest sites." Wow, that was a whole lot of info dump.

"Bet your research is fun. And creepy."

"A little of both," I say, feeling lighter. It's good to talk about the book with someone. Some of my wound-up tension slinks away.

"Be sure to let me know when it's out, and don't be afraid to put a barista named William in your story."

"It's a deal. And hey, let me know when your band is playing. I love to check out new music."

"Take our flyer," he says, then reaches under the counter and hands me a postcard with the info for a Lettuce Pray show.

"Excellent." I slap it against my palm then slide it

into my bag. Then I grab the espresso and a table, pop open my laptop, and execute my first mission.

I snap photos of each page in the travel journal, send them to myself, delete them from my phone, then upload them into a Word doc.

With that done, I dive into the scene at Aldwych station.

An hour and a half later, I've poured out some spine-tingling words, so I reason it's time to work toward my next badge.

The shopping merit one.

I'm a little tingly thinking about spending the day with Jude, but nervous too. I haven't seen him since I stopped by the store on Thursday. That's been deliberate. We were *this close* to kissing like crazy.

If we'd started, I'm not sure I would have had the will to stop. And then what? We'd wind up in bed? A few days or a few weeks later, we'd run out of steam.

I'd want more, and he'd want less, and I'd be the sucker who fell for the world's dreamiest guy and somehow, foolishly, thought it'd work.

Fuck that.

I'm a smart guy. I get how the world operates. Flings don't last, and relationships peter out. Beautiful, charming, utterly captivating men like Jude Graham are used to getting whatever they want when it comes to romance and then moving on.

No way could I stay in the flat afterward, so I'd be left to skulk around London, hunting for a new pad and explaining awkwardly to 24News that *Yeah, I can't live with the hot guy I banged because I developed all the feels for him.*

Pass.

At least today, when we shop, we'll be surrounded by people—a natural barrier to prevent me from acting on this unchecked lust.

I tell William goodbye on my way out of Coffee O'Clock, and then a block later, it's sayonara to the journal pages as I tear out the ones I wrote on and toss them into a dumpster behind a curry restaurant.

"Goodbye, disappearing pages," I say, then tuck the journal, now a little thinner, in my bag.

I'll keep the gift from my brother as a memento, but not as a record of my heart.

* * *

Back at our flat, I drop my messenger bag on the couch. Jude strides into the kitchen, dragging a towel over his hair. He's dressed in jeans and an aqua T-shirt that Eggplant Helen would surely approve of—nice and tight. It hugs his chest and snuggles his arms.

I believe the word for it is *scrummy.*

He tosses the towel on the back of a kitchen chair. "Good morning, TJ. Let me guess. You already went for a run, broke your personal best on the bench press, showered, shaved, and wrote a treatise on green energy."

I shrug, running a hand across my stubbly chin. "I didn't shave."

His eyes flicker, following my hand. "Keep that up," he says, and I make a mental note that he has a beard fetish. He puts the kettle on, then says, offhand, "So, you got a lot done while you were out of the flat?"

"I was at the coffee shop for a while."

How cliche would it sound if I said I was working on my book there? The most cliche.

But being a stereotype isn't my only reason for keeping my book a secret.

Spinning around, Jude lifts a brow in curiosity. "You were?"

"Well, treatises and all. Coffee shops are perfect spots for those," I say drily.

"Of course. All that broody energy," Jude says.

While he finishes making his tea, I dive into more of *Murder on the Orient Express.* When he's done drinking, he washes the cup and sets it down on the rack with a certain Jude-like panache.

"All right. Are you ready for the greatest shopping adventure ever?" Jude flashes a smile, and it's red-carpet-worthy. I could see him giving that to photogs and melting them with it.

Yup, that's the start of the answer to why I don't open up to Jude. His smile could devastate me. *He* could devastate me. So I protect my secrets from him and protect my heart that way too.

"As ready as I'll ever be," I say.

"Then, as our great leader says, 'In matters of grave importance, style, not sincerity, is the vital thing,'" he says.

"*The Importance of Being Earnest*?"

"Of course," he says as he opens the door.

It's a fitting quote for today.

14

THE SOCIETY OF OFTEN AND WELL

TJ

Out on the street, Jude waggles his phone. “Here’s the plan. I’ve mapped out my five favorite thrift shops in the city, plugged them into Google Maps, and designed an itinerary.”

I mime my head exploding. “I never would have pegged you for such a planner.”

“I’ve also planned for food. I included the best cafés near each shop and my favorite place for crisps in the whole city. Have I blown your mind even more?”

“My mind wasn’t the thing I wanted you to blow,” I say—low-hanging fruit and all.

“I think it’s a good thing when both cocks and minds can be blown. Wouldn’t you agree?”

Damn, this man. I have to work to keep up with him. “I stand corrected. Both should be blown. Often and well,” I say.

"Let's start a society with that noble goal in mind. We'll call it . . ." He scratches his chin.

But I've got this. "The Oscar Wilde Society of Often and Well. We can say that in polite company."

"Brilliant," he says, and he leads me down a few more blocks until we reach a thrift shop.

A sign swings above the door, spelling in bright pink and blue letters: *Out of the Closet*.

"I bet this store would want to be in our society," I say.

"As a matter of fact, there's a funny story behind it," Jude says.

I wiggle my fingers, a sign for him to serve up the goods.

"A married couple runs it," Jude begins. "Benji and Clive met at a party. In the coat closet. They were fetching their jackets at the end of the party, but their jackets got mixed up because they were so into chatting with each other, but both were a little nervous about making the first move. Since it was a phone-free party, they each had each other's mobiles in their jacket pockets when they left. And so, even though they went their separate ways, thinking they should have gotten each other's number, fate was looking out for them. They called each other, switched the mobiles, switched the jackets, and went home together."

"And they lived happily ever after out of the closet," I add, grabbing the door and holding it open for him.

Jude gives me an approving nod. "Such a gentleman."

As he walks in ahead of me, I take a moment to *ponder* how we're doing. If I were grading myself so far, I'd go with an *A*. Sure, Jude and I are flirting, but this level of flirting is safe. Despite one close encounter, we've made it through a week, and we can make it through fifty-one more.

Yup, I've got this.

Jude says hello to Benji and Clive inside the shop, then guides me to a rack of shirts. As he flicks through each one, he says, "I love thrifting. It's right up there with chocolate biscuits and a good book."

"I can tell you like it. Why, though?"

Jude swings his gaze to me, his blue eyes sparkling. "Thrifting is like a treasure hunt—finding just the right outfit. Something that doesn't look like it came from—" He stops, snaps his fingers. "What's that store in the States everyone loves?"

"Target," I answer.

"Exactly. When you thrift," he says, stopping at a black shirt with tiny skulls on it, "you can not only find bargains. You can also find something unique."

He yanks the black shirt from the rack then holds it against my chest. "Like this. I see you with a certain style. It starts with short sleeves. Something nice and tight in the chest. You ought to show off this body, but in a way that's not showy. That's simply . . . clever."

I love literally everything he just said. When Jude turns his spotlight on me, I'm helpless.

"Do you want me to try it on?" I ask.

"Yes. Fuck yes."

I get a breather in the dressing room, a minute or two to shake off the swoon as I try on the shirt.

I step out of the dressing room to a cheering squad.

Jude leads the brigade, but Clive and Benji are by his side, clapping too. "Hot stuff," the guy in glasses says.

The one with the shaved head wolf-whistles. "You look *fine*."

I dip my head, a little embarrassed.

"No, no, no, no, no," Jude says as he strides over to me while the two husbands return to the counter.

"No, as in, you don't like it?" I ask, unsure.

"No, as in don't be embarrassed, TJ. *This* is your style. This is you," he says.

Jude steps a few inches closer, adjusts my collar, then brushes his fingers along my shoulders, taking a lot longer than necessary to smooth out the fabric. "And I could see you wearing it while you're strolling around London, stopping at a park bench, reading Agatha Christie," he says.

Wait. What?

That's oddly specific. I try to figure out what he means, but I can't Inspector Poirot my way through this because I'm still sparking from his touch.

Instead, I say, "I'll take it."

* * *

After a quick tube ride and a detour for his favorite crisps that are "right up there with thrifting, biscuits, and a book," we swing over to a shop in Kensington. Jude hunts through the racks until he finds a short-sleeved green button-down with tiny eggplants all over it. He cackles in delight as he holds it up for me to inspect.

"Really?"

Jude rolls his eyes. "You're out of the closet. You can totally wear eggplants."

"That is not the issue."

"It's not too gay if that's what you're asking."

"Dude, that's not what I'm asking."

"Dude," he mimics. "Then what are you asking?"

"I meant *really,* as in, you really like it?" I ask softly, genuinely.

Jude parts his lips like he's about to speak, then he seems to think better of it, pausing for a few beats. "It's perfect for a writer. It's cheeky and a little sarcastic. Like you."

Perhaps he's right. When I look in the store's mirror, I look like who I want to be. Not just a financial journalist in staid blues and whites and grays, but a man who can create. A guy who can spin a yarn. The author penning his first novel.

Wheeling around, I meet his gaze. "You're right. This is my style. Thank you," I say.

He beams. The wattage on the spotlight goes up again, and so does the needle on the swoon-o-meter.

* * *

At the final shop of the day, I'm fading, but Jude possesses not only a second wind but a third and fourth, as well. He motors from rack to rack, grabbing a black shirt with cartoon cacti, a yellow shirt with a print of tiny green avocados, and one more with baseball bats.

"Yes! This one is perfect for my American friend," he says, thrusting the baseball print my way.

I smile. "It is. Especially since my brother plays Major League Baseball."

He blinks in confusion. "What?"

"I didn't tell you this?"

Jude scoffs. "You hardly tell me anything about yourself."

He's . . . not wrong.

But this is about my kickass brother, not a window into my heart's desires. "Chance is a relief pitcher for the Cougars—"

"The Major League Baseball team in San Francisco. That's amazing."

"He's got a killer cut fastball, and he's ice on the mound. I bet he's going to be their closer any day now. He's also my identical twin," I say.

Jude's jaw comes unhinged. "Your identical twin? You're taking the piss out of me, aren't you?"

"It's one hundred percent true."

He points at me. "There's actually another man out there this fine-looking?"

A smile takes over my face. "He's straight."

"I don't fucking care. That's not the point. The point is there are two fucking men on this planet who are, what? Six-ten, and built like hot redwood trees?"

"We're six-three," I say, but I can't shake my smile.

And since I don't want to turn off his spotlight, I decide to blow his mind some more. Grabbing my phone, I click on my photos and show him a pic I took of Chance and me at the airport a week ago. "We shot this selfie before I left New York for London."

Slack-jawed, Jude stares at the screen, shaking his head. "Dear God. You two must have been a pair of lady-killers and gent-killers growing up," he says.

"I was not. I assure you. I barely got any action in college."

"I refuse to believe that."

"It's the truth," I say, putting my phone away.

"Are you bad in bed?"

I snort-laugh. "No."

"Are you sure? Every man thinks he's good in bed."

There's a playfully dirty challenge in his tone. We are not in the safe flirting zone anymore. This is the red zone, warning lights flashing everywhere.

I race toward danger, ignoring the hell out of them. "I could prove it to you sometime," I say, feeling reckless thanks to that spotlight.

Then Jude does that thing. He scrapes his teeth over the corner of his mouth, and I go hot everywhere. "I wish you would," he says, all low and rumbly, driving me crazier than he did the night I met him.

Make that ten times crazier.

"Yeah, me too," I whisper, our eyes locked.

We don't move. We've reached a crossroads. Will I kick the flirting up another few degrees, yank him into the dressing room with me?

Or will he?

I do nothing, the standoff extending, the heat between us flaring until a customer wanders into the store, breaking the spell.

I grab the shirts from Jude, shut the door to the dressing room, and shove my back against the wood like I'm fighting off enemies outside of it.

The enemy is my own willpower, weak right now.

I breathe out, hard.

Holy shit. I was this close to dragging him in here, slamming him against the wall, and punishing him with a kiss to prove I could make his bones melt.

Because I could. I know I could. Because I want Jude Graham more than I've ever wanted any man. And I would kiss him and touch him and fuck him in a way that made him feel like the most wanted man ever.

And it would electrify him.

Like he electrifies me.

But the thing is—Jude does so much more than simply turn me on.

Thanks to his energy, excitement, and enthusiasm, this has been the best day I've had in ages.

That's why I won't tell him I'm writing a novel. I'd be exposing a piece of my vulnerable heart to him. Jude's already hellbent on figuring me out. He delights in it. He's been trying to get me to share writerly things with him today. Maybe even to admit what I did this morning at the coffee shop, why I read Agatha Christie, how I want to steal "The Duck's Nipple" to use it in my book.

But telling Jude my dreams is dangerous. It could lead to closeness.

He already knows my habits, what I eat, when I exercise, and yeah, what I sound like when I come in the shower.

He knows my taste in books, music, and home decor. He knows I had no style and that I like the kind he just found for me.

I'm sure he knows, too, that this is both lust and so much more than that for me.

If I let him into my head, I would become completely infatuated.

I prefer slightly infatuated, like I am now.

But Jude deserves something.

After I buy the shirts and we leave, I silently practice what I want to say. Something I once thought he'd have to get out of me with his tongue.

"Jude," I say, my tone serious once we're walking down the street.

He stops in his tracks. "Yes?"

I exhale and choose sincerity over style. "It's Terry Jerry."

15

WHAT'S IN A NAME?

TJ

Gotta give him credit—Jude hasn't erupted into peals of laughter yet.

We swing into a nearby pub, order two beers, and grab a booth.

Jude lifts his glass, tips it to mine. "Here's to you for saying that. I could tell it wasn't easy."

"Nope," I say, then drink some of the brew.

When I set it down, he does the same, then waits patiently.

Might as well serve up the whole enchilada. "It's officially Terry Jerome. For my mom's dad and my dad's dad. But they called me Terry when I was younger."

"Terry's a decent name for a bloke."

"I suppose, but it's not my favorite. It's kind of like Larry or Bob."

Jude arches a brow. "You mean, plain?"

"Yes, but when you put it together with Jerome, it's a living hell for a ten-year-old." The memory flashes bright and awful in my mind. "A couple of boys in fourth grade figured out that Jerome can be shortened to Jerry. And once that cat was out of the bag, it wasn't going back in."

He smiles sympathetically. "It was Terry Jerry all the way?"

"On the playground. In the halls. Every-fucking-where. All thanks to this punk—Robby Linden. And I think it goes back to the time our teacher praised me for writing a really creative poem, that, well, rhymed, since that was the assignment, and his did not. He liked to cough whisper *Terry Jerry* under his breath whenever I walked into class." I pause to drink some more beer for fuel, then say, "At the end of fourth grade, I asked my parents to change my name to TJ, since I said I liked my initials better. And they were super chill about it and told the school I was TJ. My brother asked me why I changed it, and I just said I preferred it."

"He didn't know what was going on?"

"No. He was an athlete by then, and I didn't want to be known as the artsy twin who needed his sporty brother to defend him. But I hoped things would change for good in sixth grade when we moved to a different section of Seattle. That I'd start over in middle school with a new name. My brother had already done that long ago with his given name – Chauncey for our mom's stepdad. But Chauncey was hard to say, so I started calling him Chance when I was two or three, apparently. And it stuck."

"So, he had the *cool* name sooner," Jude says, sketching air quotes.

"Exactly. But it was finally my turn. Except, guess who shows up at my school?"

"Robby the Wanker?"

"The one and only. And he decides to tell some of the other boys in sixth grade that my initials stood for Terry Jerry and that it would be fun to call me that, so he enlisted his dipshit friends in mocking my name." Another drink, then I soldier on. "But I ignored them. That was my new strategy, and that's why I never told my brother what was going on."

The way I saw it, I was protecting Chance from trouble. He'd have been pissed off—probably have confronted them. Maybe that made it easier to keep other things from him later on, like the nitty-gritty details of our parents' divorce. "Some things you have to handle on your own," I add, explaining my choice to Jude.

"I get that completely. My brother is nine years older, so we've always had to figure things out on our own," Jude supplies, and his reassurance that we're on the same wavelength feels good. "But what was Robby's deal?"

"I don't know how to say this without sounding like a complete douche, but he didn't like me because I was in the gifted track for after-school enrichment stuff, and he and his buddies weren't. And he liked to say, *Look, I can rhyme now too.*"

"What lovely lines did the wanker devise?"

"All sorts of catchy phrases like *It's Terry Jerry the Cherry.* Which was just dumb, so I didn't care. Then it was *It's Terry Jerry Who's So Hairy,* which felt more personal because I was starting to get a baby beard," I say, touching my chin. "I had to shave when I was twelve."

Jude's eyes pop. "That's young."

"It was. I don't mind the beardability now, though."

Jude gestures to my stubble and lets out an appreciative sigh. "I bet you'd grow a fantastic beard."

"I bet I would too." It's a little cocky, but I don't care —I earned this bit of cockiness the hard way. "But the name that bugged me the most was when they said *Terry Jerry the Fairy*."

Jude frowns. "Fucking pricks. Did they know?"

I shake my head. "I wasn't out, and I don't think they knew, especially since I didn't even really know I was gay till I was fourteen. But I was figuring it out in my head, and that's why it stung—not least because Robby's best friend was this really cute guy named Liam," I say, then slump back in the booth.

"That's such a classic cute-guy name," Jude says.

"Right? Anyway, even though I knew on an intellectual level that they weren't using a slur personally, I hated it."

Jude takes a long pull of his beer, then sets it down. "So what happened? How did it stop?"

"Research," I say, a small note of pride in my voice. "I knew the biggest advantage I had over Robby was my brain. So, I researched online how to deal with bullies. Most of the solutions—bring in an adult, tell the bully to stop, weren't my style. But *act bored*—I was really good at that. When Robby would start up, I'd just roll my eyes, open a book, do something else."

"Don't feed a fire," Jude says, delighted. "And it worked?"

"Over time. But the biggest thing that worked was me realizing eventually they didn't have any real power over me since I'd already renamed myself. Their stupid rhymes weren't going to last forever, but I had a name I finally liked. I had something that mattered to me."

"You did. You really did." Jude's eyes hold mine, and there's a new look in his—gratitude, maybe? A touch more vulnerability? It's hard to say, but whatever the emotion is, it brings that tingly feeling back to my chest for all new reasons.

Reasons that have nothing to do with my dick and everything to do with the organ in my rib cage—with what I'm feeling for the man across from me.

I might be more than slightly infatuated.

"Thank you for telling me, TJ," Jude says. "I couldn't figure out why you'd hate a name so much. I thought maybe it was that you simply wanted a cool name. But I get it now. I get you."

"I don't think I've told that story to a lot of people," I say, but that's not true. I *know* I haven't told anyone besides my brother. I didn't even tell him till middle school ended and I'd escaped the line of fire.

Jude gives a soft smile like he's glad he earned the tale. "Were you out in high school, then? Or did the name thing make it hard for you?"

"I came out to my brother when I was fifteen, then to our parents a little while later. They'd just gotten a divorce." Even though I poured out way more of myself to Jude than I thought I would, he's not getting the story of my parents' divorce. No one is. That goes to the grave. “I waited till the dust settled from that. And then I was pretty much out from my junior year of high school and onward. And no one gave a shit what my initials stood for. Everything else was more interesting, you know?”

“It ran its course,” he says. “But it stayed with you. It shaped you in unexpected ways.”

That’s one way of looking at it. “It did.”

Jude lifts his beer, clinks it to mine. “Cheers.”

“For what?” I ask, confused.

“For saying something hard. I know you didn’t want to tell me that.”

Funny how a week ago I wanted him to work my name out of me in the bedroom. I should keep that secret too, but fuck it. He’s easy to talk to. “Honestly, I’d been hoping you’d get my name out of me with your tongue. But now that I’ve given you the whole sorry story, I think I’m glad I didn’t say it in bed,” I tell him with a smile.

Jude pouts, all over the top. “Dammit. I would have liked to use my tongue for that noble purpose.”

“And that’s why you’re a member of The Oscar Wilde Society of Often and Well. Because you understand noble purposes for tongues.”

“I absolutely do,” he says, then drops the volume, sliding into a low, sexy tone. “I bet it’d have taken five minutes, tops.”

I smile wickedly. Shake my head. “Nah.”

“You doubt my tongue?”

“That’s not it,” I say.

“Then what are you saying, TJ?” He says my initials in his most seductive voice.

I lean a little closer. "I'm saying that with you, it would have only taken about one."

Jude murmurs appreciatively and stares hotly at me. Then, he seems to shake it off. "Incidentally, I've got a Robby in my past—although he went by Robert. He was, however, also a total wanker."

"Tell me about your Robby."

"My ex from uni. I was crazy about the twat. He dumped me when uni ended. Nothing but *I just don't feel the same.*"

"Ouch. He's a real top bloke."

Jude smiles at my attempt at an English accent. "A *super* dipshit," he says, emphasis on *super,* using one of my favorite adjectives. "But here we are, you and me, a couple of great dicks."

"We are." I smile and drink to that.

Jude pats his flat stomach. "I'm starving. Shopping makes me ravenous."

We order and eat, shifting to other topics, like his brother, who works in the London art world, and who loves books and theater too. Then, we make plans to run lines tomorrow, and Jude suggests we do it in Hyde Park. Works for me, since I want to see as much of London as I can. When we're done, I don't give Jude a chance to put down his credit card. "I got this."

"We can split it," he says.

"No, I want to."

He relents easily, tucking his card away.

And maybe, just maybe, that makes the whole damn day seem like we're both standing on safe ground and wobbling on terribly rocky terrain.

Date terrain.

16

HOLY BEARD-ABILITY

Jude

TJ's gone when I wake up on Sunday morning.

That's par for the course. But he's replied to the invitation I left for him on the fridge, the international location of roomie notes.

His reply is written on blue paper—the same blue paper on which he left his first roomie letter. The letter I tucked away in a book I was reading.

I read it as I walk to the stove.

Someone wiser than I am supposedly once said: "Practice precedes perfection." I've found Wilde right about nearly everything so far. See you this afternoon to practice your lines, so tomorrow you'll be fucking perfect at your callback.

I'm outta here now to do touristy things with another reporter. By the way, since you took me shopping yesterday, today it's my turn. Check out the band Lettuce Pray. Holy fuck. They're like Roxy Music meets New Order. Incidentally, both of those bands are on my Top Five Best British Bands Ever list.

Lettuce Pray is playing next weekend in Leicester Square. But so is Too Big For Their Britches. I might have to see both.

See you later . . .

I read it again as I put the kettle on, then once more as I drink my tea. When I'm done, I tuck the letter away in a book, then turn on my mobile, where I find a text from TJ. It includes a link to a playlist, and a note, ***Your homework***.

Because I'm a good student, I do the entire assignment, listening to all the tunes while working out at a local gym I just joined. I text Olivia about her date last night with a guy named George, who "might very well be royalty and also has a royally great prick."

After a stop home for a shower and a change of clothes, I meet my brother Heath for a cuppa at a café we like.

I give Heath a special-order book about art in the post-modern era—he has a collection from that period that he's selling through his auction house. He gives me what he always does—sound advice and sarcasm as I tell him about the auditions I've had.

"If I go on enough auditions," I say, "the odds will be in my favor. It's a numbers game."

His eyes say bullshit. "Right. I'm sure it's a matter of your lucky number turning up."

"What else could it be?" I ask, trying to stay cheeky and cool.

"Talent. Persistence. Luck. But first, talent. And you have that in buckets."

"Thanks." I needed to hear that. But I don't want today to be all about *me, me, me*. "Tell me more about that play you saw the other week."

And for a few short minutes, as he tells me about the theater, I don't think of my sexy American roommate.

Once I board the tube for Hyde Park, I reply to TJ's text about the music. ***I finished my assignment. I did it five times. Someday, when I win an Academy Award, I will thank you for teaching me about taste when it comes to bands. No more Zeppelin for this guy!***

His reply is swift. ***My work here is done. Also, when you get your Oscar, you will thank me for running the lines that got you your breakout gig. Though, sure, add in the music bit too. Why not make me sound even more awesome?!***

TJ's already wildly encouraging of my creative dreams. I suppose it shouldn't bother me that he hasn't told me he's writing a novel. Every man has to reveal himself in his own time and way.

When I exit the tube, there's a text from Olivia flashing at me. ***Where are you? I'm in the city. Just rode George and his royal package again. Want to get a tea?***

I call her back instead of texting. "More than anything, but I'm meeting TJ right now."

"Ohhhhhhhh."

"I asked him to meet me in Hyde Park," I add.

"How romantic," she says.

I sigh as I dodge past a pack of tourists wearing

matching Wicked T-shirts and doing their best to belt "Defying Gravity."

"We're meeting to run my lines and practice for my callback tomorrow. Did George's royal cock make you forget about me?"

"No, but apparently, thoughts of TJ's cock make you forget me," she counters.

I throw my head back, laughing. "Love, I could never forget you."

"And my other point?"

"I'm not thinking about his cock. Not much, that is."

"But enough that you asked him to run lines and not me."

"Well, he lives with me. And you live an hour away."

"Excuses, excuses. But why are you meeting him in the park instead of your flat?"

"I wanted to do it someplace with lots of people around, since that's how the callback will be," I say. "Lots of people."

"You creatives are so weird."

"Says my fellow actor."

"And this fellow actor thinks there's another reason you're meeting him in the park."

"And what do you think that reason is?" I ask, curious what she's getting at.

"Hmm. Shall I tell you? I think not."

"You're evil," I say.

"That is true. Have fun with your hot roomie and his hot accent and your filthy thoughts about his royal American cock," she says. "I bet it's as big as Texas."

"Ride 'em, cowboy."

After we hang up, her words linger—the ones about

meeting TJ in the park. Do I have some subconscious reason for meeting him here? If so, I'd quite appreciate it if my brain revealed it to me since Olivia didn't.

But those thoughts drift away into the afternoon air when I spot a familiar pair of shoulders above a park bench, just like I imagined yesterday when I told him I could picture him on a park bench, reading.

And wait . . . is that one of his new shirts?

Damn, I have good taste, in clothes and men.

TJ looks delicious, and my pulse surges when I get closer to him. He's reading *Murder on the Orient Express.* Looks like he's near the end.

"The butler did it," I call.

He turns around slowly, a sly grin on—

Holy beardability.

"Did I wake up a week from now, and you've got a full fucking beard?"

"It's just two days of not shaving," he says. "It's not a full beard."

I growl, low and guttural. That scruff. I want to feel the prickle of his beard on my face. My thighs. *Everywhere.*

"Two glorious days," I say, then join him on the bench. "That's like a week-o'clock shadow."

He rolls his eyes. "You have a thing for beards, manners, and handymen."

I waggle my brows, owning it. "I do."

TJ takes a deep breath, a thoughtful-sounding one. "Would it be easier—you know, for this whole roommate-friend thing—if I shaved?"

I slice that horrid notion off at the knees. "Do not ever utter something so blasphemous again."

"Noted," he says.

I tap the book. "So, I was right? The butler?"

He tilts his head. "Have you read this?"

I cringe. "Sorry. I should, right?"

"You should. It's the greatest mystery ever. I won't say another word, but it's genius." He hands me the paperback.

"Are you done with it?"

"I've read it five or six times. And yes, I just finished it. Again."

"That's quite an endorsement," I say, taking the book. "Thank you."

"You're welcome."

"But how do you read a mystery half a dozen times? Does your brain trick you into forgetting who did it?"

He laughs, shaking his head. "It's not about the ending. It's about how you get there. Every time, I find new details Agatha Christie planted. With every read, there's something to discover about how to tell a story."

That's today's reveal from TJ Ashford. I tuck it away for safekeeping. "I'll read it next. As soon as I finish Rob Lowe's memoir. I'm listening to that, though. That is, when I'm not listening to your music."

"You like celebrity memoirs?"

"The dishier the better," I say, wiggling my brows. "But I don't just listen for the salaciousness. It's good character work."

TJ's brow knits, and I can tell he's working out my meaning. "You mean you learn how to get into different characters when you listen to wild memoirs?"

I tap my nose. "Exactly. Learning about all sorts of backgrounds helps me. I've devoured stories from Carly

Simon, Patti Smith, Steve Martin." I rattle off the non-celebrity stories I've enjoyed, then shift back to his day. "How was your tourist time with a work friend?"

"It was good. Alex and I went to Buckingham Palace."

"Is Alex . . .?"

"He's a friend. Born in Kenya, raised in California, just transferred here from our Beijing bureau. Speaks about fifty languages. A real badass. He covers London tech. So, we geeked out as two non-Londoners."

I hide my smile as best I can. "Cool. The palace is cool," I say, and I'm not cool at all because I'm so damn happy Alex was not his date.

I hope TJ never dates a single soul the entire year he's here.

"It is. I like London. I've been checking out some fascinating places—Aldwych station, the Hardy Tree, the Greenwich Foot Tunnel—and it's been great," TJ says.

I think I understand him more now. I'd bet my call-back those places are part of his novel somehow. Maybe he's writing something about spooky London?

Maybe I can help him with his unsaid dreams. "The city has so many wonderful places to explore. Like Samuel Johnson's house. The writer. It's down a secluded alleyway," I say, then dangle an enticement. "Supposedly, he worked on the dictionary there." The gold flecks in his eyes seem to dance. "I knew that would hook you."

"It's only one of my favorite books."

"Of course it is," I say, then cycle through other places he might like. "The Vaults near us are great—

right under Waterloo station—if you're into the whole underground tunnel thing. There's some cool graffiti down there too. For us artsy types," I say with a wink.

"Thanks. I'll add those to my tourist list."

"I could take you some time," I volunteer.

"Yeah?" He sounds like he likes the idea.

"Of course. I mean, we can do London and bands and books and clothes." I dart out a hand and run my finger down the buttons on his shirt. "Nice eggplants, TJ."

He just smiles. Doesn't say anything more. But I know he wore the shirt for me.

"Let's rehearse," he says.

"Right." I get down to business. "You have the new scenes I emailed?"

"Got 'em."

He clicks on his phone and begins. We work through the first two new scenes easily, practicing a few times, then we get to the third.

TJ clears his throat. "So, what are you doing about this last part?" He sounds more nonchalant than I've ever heard him.

"Oh, the kiss with Lyra? My robot creation?" I ask, and wow, did my voice just pitch up or what?

"Last time, you said you didn't do the kiss. The scene ended right before it. But here, it continues. There are a few lines afterward. Do they want you to kiss the actress tomorrow?"

"Yes. I have to kiss the woman they cast as Lyra. They want to know if we have chemistry. But it's like a tease of a kiss. Full of restraint."

My neck goes hot, and it's not from thinking about robots.

"Okay. So we'll just . . ."

TJ doesn't finish. Instead, he reads her lines, and as we get closer to the kiss, he's slower with each sentence, more deliberate with every word.

"I've been thinking about the other night," he says.

"What do you mean?" I ask in character as the scientist, though I know damn well what my robot means.

"Our kiss. The one we never got to finish."

"What about it?" I ask, wanting the kiss but knowing how risky it is.

"What if it lasted longer?"

And this is when our scientist gives in to his desires. "I think about that too," I say, breathy and hungry.

And curious.

TJ's still looking at his phone, not at me. But I'm studying him. The way he swallows, his Adam's apple moving up and down, the stubble lining his jaw. I'm recording every detail, staring at the man next to me and wanting him so much.

TJ raises his face. "And then you kiss the robot," he says robotically.

"I do," I say, and my skin is on fucking fire.

He glances back down to the screen, licks his lips, and reads his next line. "I wanted to—"

I shut him up when I grab his face.

His eyes lock with mine. His brown irises darken.

"Practice precedes perfection," I whisper.

Give me your permission, TJ. I want it so badly. Want to kiss you so very much.

My roommate's quiet, just breathing as he looks at

me, my eyes, my mouth. He darts out his tongue, flicks it across the corner of his lips.

My breath catches, and I slide my thumb along his stubbly jaw. The scrape of his beard drives me wild.

He drives me wild.

Another few seconds tick by. He closes his eyes briefly, opens them, and angles his face.

Then, the American crushes his lips to mine.

It's not a chaste kiss at all.

It's full of passion, yet we don't even open our mouths. It's just his lips pressed hungrily to mine and mine locked greedily with his. His aftershave goes to my head. My body thrills everywhere at the feel of his mouth hunting mine.

Then it's his hand on the back of my neck, his fingers playing with the ends of my hair.

And still, we never part our lips. We never stroke our tongues together. We just kiss with so much restraint that the holding back makes it the hottest kiss I've ever had.

After ten, maybe twenty seconds, he lets go, breathing out hard. But his hand stays in my hair, mine remains on his face, and I don't want this moment to end.

"You should do that in the audition," TJ says, his voice full of gravel.

"Yeah?"

"That's how you should kiss your robot lover," he says emphatically.

"Like I've wanted nothing else for the last week?"

His lips twitch. He likes what I said. "Exactly. Do it

just like that. You'll capture the longing perfectly. I felt it."

I felt the longing fucking everywhere. In my bones. My cells. My dreams. I still feel it. "So, I should do it like I'm kissing the man I've been dying to kiss?"

He snaps his gaze away from me like eye contact is almost too much, and his breath shudders out. "You should. You really fucking should." Then he squeezes my thigh. "Let's walk around the park and run lines."

Olivia's words march from my subconscious to front and center in my brain.

I must have picked the park because I wanted to find a way to kiss him. I wanted to find the loophole in the roomie code. I wanted to practice.

And if we'd practiced at home, I don't know that I could have stopped.

But I know we *should* stop.

We really should.

17

IT WILL BE A WONDERFUL DEATH

TJ

I daydream more than I should the next few days at the office. Normally, reporting on the falling pound and the Bank of England's plans for interest rates keep my mind trained on the here and now.

Also, you know, deadlines.

But that didn't help me on Monday. Tuesday. Or today.

This article is due at four, and I'm only half done, and it's one-thirty. I need to call another source, but as the rain patters down on the city outside my office window, I'm someplace else.

I'm in the park three days ago, my fingers threading through Jude's hair.

I'm outside in the rain this afternoon, kissing him in an alleyway, up against a wall.

I'm at home in our flat tonight—

And I can't.

I have to shut down those thoughts. They've zigzagged through my head since Sunday.

I swivel my chair, return to my laptop, and crank up the music in my earbuds. I need to drown out the sounds of the office, of other phone calls in other cubicles, of reporters tapping furiously on keyboards, of editors barking out orders.

Need to focus.

I laser in on the next few sentences in my assignment. But one paragraph later, my fingers itch to recheck my phone. I give in and tap out a quick text.

TJ: Any word yet?

Jude: No. It's been eighty-four years, and I'm dying.

TJ: Don't die before you get the part.

Jude: It's no use. I've keeled over. It was lovely knowing you.

TJ: Does it normally take this long to hear about a callback?

Jude: This is a message from Jude in the afterlife. He says that waiting to know if you got a gig takes approximately a millennium.

TJ: Well, if you need a distraction, there's a band playing tonight at The Cat's Meow. The lead singer is in some show on the West End called *Wicked* (*shudders*) but when the theater is dark, she moonlights with her band, Ten-Speed Rabbit.

Jude: There is so much to unpack in that text that you raised me from the dead. First, is the band named after a vibrator? Second, YOU MEAN AMELIA STONE? Third, you don't like *Wicked*????????

I smile as I reply, the music ricocheting through my head—a sexy, dirty song from Ten-Speed Rabbit.

TJ: I hate musicals. And before you ask why, it's because no one breaks out in song in real life. And yes, it seems Amelia named her band for a very specific sex toy. I'm guessing because Sex Toys was taken, or maybe she went with Ten-Speed Rabbit out of cheek.

Jude: Never underestimate the value of cheek. But the flaw in your rationale for your dislike of musicals? International teenage spy Rhys Locke didn't actually rappel from buildings to save millions in stolen sapphires, and yet you still like those Alistair Edwin's novels. Since when did something have to be real for you to like it?

TJ: When music was added to plays.

Jude: I will never understand you. And yes, I would love a distraction, but I have to work tonight.

Jude's been working every night. I haven't seen him since Sunday—our schedules this week are the opposite.

Maybe that's for the best. Maybe I should stop texting him. Maybe that'll make me stop feeling things for him.

But before I set down the phone, he replies once more.

Jude: But do you want to go to the graffiti tunnels tomorrow evening? I'm not working Thursday night. I have some commercial auditions during the day and a voiceover thingy. But I could go around seven.

TJ: Yes. I want to go.

I'm grinning foolishly, and it's because of an outing with my roomie. When I set down the phone, I startle at the sight of Alex staring at me over the top of my cubicle wall, drumming his fingers on the divider and shooting me a *you're busted* look from behind his black glasses.

I take out my earbuds. "What's up?"

"What are you all smiles about? Let me guess. You're getting laid, you scored a scoop, or you scored discount tickets to that band you were telling me about?"

"Sadly, none of the above," I say.

"Dude, you need to change all of that. Stat."

"Don't I know," I sigh.

"So, then the answer is . . .?"

Man, reporters are persistent fuckers. "Just texting a friend." That's true enough.

Alex is not appeased. "A friend you'd like to yada yada with?"

I laugh, shaking my head. "You're a bold man, Alex."

He tilts his head. "And you still didn't answer me."

I huff, then relent. Somewhat. "A guy. Okay?"

He waggles his brows. "So, you *are* enjoying London?"

"Yes," I say. But that's all I'll admit.

"Cool. Want to go out with a bunch of us tomorrow night? There's a pinball arcade that has awesome cocktails."

I'm mildly tempted. "I love pinball. I am also fucking amazing at it, so I'd probably destroy all of you."

"So, you're in?"

I shake my head since even pinball can't tear me away from my plans. "Can't. I have a thing."

"With your *friend*?"

"Yes," I say.

"All right, Mister One-Word Answers. I can take a hint. This friend is the one you're daydreaming about?"

I jerk my gaze back to Alex. "What?"

"I saw you staring out the window. I don't think you were thinking about the London Stock Exchange. More like the London Sex Exchange," he says.

"Dude, you should be an investigative reporter."

"I'm pushy. I'm nosy. And I'm proud of it," he says.

"You are." It's nice to have this easy banter with him

—a colleague who's becoming a friend. "Hey, since tomorrow night won't work out, what about Sunday? I'm going to a club this weekend to check out some bands, and I'm trying to round up a group."

"I'm in," he says. "And now, I'm gonna pound out this story."

As Alex walks away, I spin toward the window and catch the outline of my reflection. Is it obvious I'm thinking about a friend?

I peer close into the rain-streaked glass.

It's painfully obvious.

* * *

That evening, I skip The Cat's Meow. Instead, I hunker down in Coffee O'Clock, trying to send my hero to the creepy church to investigate a clue, but he's delayed in the park.

By his love interest.

Our hero's been longing for this person for ages. He can feel it in his bones. My fingers tingle as I type, and something feels so right. Righter than it ever has before. When I reread the scene, my heart races. Yup. My book was missing a romantic subplot.

Like that, I write more. I pour all my rainy daydreams into the story, and suddenly, this whodunit sparks in a whole new way.

Finally, I feel a little obsessed with this story, and I half want to tell someone. But William's not here, and is he truly the one I want to share this realization with?

Later, when I return home, Jude's not there.

That's probably for the best. His absence saving me

from sharing more than I should.

* * *

When I leave work on Thursday, I'm jittery. I haven't seen Jude since Sunday night, but I'm meeting him this evening to go to The Vaults.

I could go straight to the tunnels, but they're close to our flat, and I wouldn't mind changing into something more casual, so I head home and take a quick shower to wash the day off me. But the showerhead is loose again, so when I get out, I wrap a towel around my waist and head for the kitchen to grab the toolkit.

The door swings open.

"I got the part!" Jude calls out.

With my hair wet, water droplets sliding down my chest, and tools in hand, I turn around. "Holy shit! That's amazing. I knew it!"

With his back to me, he shuts the door, then spins around. Like a cartoon character, his eyes pop out on springs. "Oh, fuck me." He holds up a hand. "I have to back away right now. If I don't, I will literally climb you like a tree."

Then, as fast as he comes in, he leaves. His footfalls on the stairs echo as I return to the bathroom and fix the showerhead.

With a smile I can't wipe off, I head to my room and get dressed. When I'm in jeans and the baseball-print shirt, I text him at last.

TJ: The coast is clear.

Jude: I have not recovered. I am dead again from the sight of you in NOTHING BUT A FUCKING TOWEL AND A TOOLKIT. DO NOT EVER DO THAT TO ME AGAIN. (UNLESS YOU WANT ME TO HUMP YOUR RIGHT LEG, YOUR LEFT LEG, AND YOUR THIRD LEG.) IF I SEE YOU LIKE THAT, I WILL HAVE A HEART ATTACK BUT IT WILL BE A WONDERFUL DEATH.

TJ: Sorry, not sorry.

Jude: I am at Angie's Vintage Duds. I had to go shopping to try to get the sight of you, wet, out of my head. And I mean my little head.

I laugh again, and I wish I weren't so fucking amused and delighted by him. I wish I weren't so attracted to him. I wish I weren't so close to wildly infatuated with him.

But I am.

I am all of those things.

* * *

When I push open the door to Angie's, Jude is chatting with Eggplant Helen.

"I could have sworn she was still with him," he tells her. "Well, it just goes to show you can't believe everything you read in the tabloids."

She laughs. "You can't, but it sure is fun to devour

every little detail about the royal family."

"Completely," he says.

Helen grins like a cat as she points from Jude to me. "So, you two found each other." She sounds as pleased as a cat too.

Jude swings his gaze my way, looking at me with a whole new kind of smile. It's dirty like he's still thinking of me in that towel. But it's also . . . private. Like he knows on some intrinsic level that I told Helen about him that first day because he enthralled me.

If he only knew I was so enthralled, a spark is sliding down my back from his smile. Yeah, it's devastating, all right.

"We did find each other," Jude says.

"I had a feeling you two lovebirds would," she says, singsong.

"It's not like that," I put in quickly, needing to dispel that for my own sanity. Hell, for my hold on reality.

"Yeah, it's not like that at all," he echoes, quickly too.

"Why not?" she asks in disbelief.

Jude drapes an arm around her, then sighs heavily. "We live together. TJ's my roomie," he says, and that warning is for her, maybe, and possibly for me, but mostly I can tell it's for him.

He's underlining the roomie rules we need to follow.

Rules I will follow because I care deeply about his dreams.

Helen sighs, aggrieved. "I can't listen to such rubbish."

Jude kisses her cheek. "Gotta go, love. Doesn't TJ look smashing in his new shirt?"

"He's the scrummiest," she says.

"I know," Jude says with a note of pride.

We leave, and once we're out on the street, I'm a little lost as to what's next. I want to hug him. I want to congratulate him. But I also don't want to fuck things up. Awkwardly, I offer a hand for him to shake.

He scoffs. "You want to shake my hand?"

"I'm congratulating you. I'm really fucking excited for you," I explain.

"Then congratulate me properly."

With a blow job, I say to myself. "With a hug?" I ask out loud.

"A hug and a beer and a dinner so fucking filling that it will take sex off my mind," he says.

Cracking up, I step in for a hug. It's thoroughly bro-dude style. A clap on the back. A pat on the shoulder. I do not linger.

I hope it takes sex off both our minds.

"Tell me everything about the gig," I say when I let go.

We walk, and he launches into the details. The shoot starts next week. The show is running on a streaming service that's gaining some traction. The actress is great. The director is too. "I'll be busy every day for a couple of weeks. And every night at the bookshop. And the pay is seriously not bad. Also, they said our chemistry was electric."

"Good," I say, and I don't push the topic. I don't ask if it's because he was thinking of me. I don't have to ask because I know.

And knowing does something to my heart that I haven't felt before. Not like this. Not this intensely. Or this deeply.

And definitely never this dangerously.

"So, this is a big break for you?" I ask, keeping the conversation only on work.

"It could be. I mean, it's not like I was cast in an American TV show or a BBC one. Or on the West End or in a Hollywood film."

I stop, put a hand on his arm. "Don't put it down. Don't compare it. It's amazing in and of itself. This is a big deal, Jude."

He smiles, his shoulders relaxing. "I'm really, really happy."

"I can tell."

"TJ?"

"Yes?"

"This is all I've ever wanted." We stop at the corner near Waterloo Bridge, waiting at the traffic light. "When I was six, I fell off the swing at a local park. Knocked out my two front teeth," he says, flashing a smile like he's showing me the missing teeth. His are perfectly straight.

"That doesn't sound like fun," I say.

"It took a while for my adult teeth to come in. But at that point, it was hard for me to say S properly. I had to see a speech therapist to learn to pronounce it properly," he tells me. "Her name was Alice, and she had three orange cats who roamed all over her house on the outskirts of London. She had me do monologues and recite poetry to work on my speech. And it was like . . . magic. I knew then that I wanted to perform."

Chills rush down my arms. His passion is infectious. "It's kind of amazing when something clicks, right?"

"It unlocked me," he says, and we cross the street. "And I felt alive and excited. I could see my future. I could feel it so deeply. I wanted this job so badly. Sometimes when I'm out with my friends, I don't always let on how much I crave the work. I try to act cool and casual. I even did that with my own brother the other day when we were having tea. But I'm not cool and casual about it. Not one bit. I just can't be."

"I understand completely," I say, and when we reach the entrance to The Vaults, I stop. "Jude?"

"Yes?"

Here goes. This feels like stripping naked, like showing him the most vulnerable parts of me. My hopes and dreams. But it also feels right to tell Jude before my brother, before work friends, before my friends back home. "I'm writing a novel."

His smile is like the sun rising in the morning. It's slow and unstoppable, and when it coasts across his gorgeous face, it lights up the entire sky. "Is that so?"

"What you just said, that unlocking—that's how I felt when I came to London when I was thirteen. When I went to the bookshop, that was my light bulb. When I knew what I wanted to do, that's why I visited all these places in London. For my novel," I say, and wow, that was hard.

But so necessary.

For a few seconds, Jude's lips twitch like he's trying to rein in an emotion that borders on laughter. But it's not a chuckle he's holding in. It's more like a look of utter delight.

Like he's even happier than he was when he got the part. "Let's visit all the places."

I revise my estimate to completely, utterly, absolutely infatuated.

18

THIS WILL SOLVE EVERYTHING!

TJ's Travel Journal
London, Day Fifteen

Dear Digital Travel Journal,

It's official. It only took two weeks for me to fall in love with London, from the sights to the rain to the music.

Don't get me started on the men, though. That situation is not what I expected. There has been no non-stop fiesta of dick.

Cue the sad wiener trombone.

But hey, I blame my roommate for that.

Jude takes up all the space in my mind. He makes everyone else look like a carbon copy of an already faded, old-timey, black and white photograph.

After the last week of getting to know him, I'm no

longer convinced I can handle fifty more weeks of living together with, let's face it, my dream guy. He's the swooniest man I've ever known, and my entire body vibrates just being near him. He's wickedly charming and ridiculously beautiful, and I am so far gone.

So, yeah, I'm pretty sure I'll melt into a puddle of unresolved sexual tension in a few more days.

And really, what use am I to the world in liquid lust form?

When I went for a run this morning along the river in the rain, I worked through the roomie quandary. I asked myself what I'd do if I were writing the story of a guy falling for his roommate who was stuck with a lease he couldn't break.

Two miles in, skin wet, shirt soaked, I formulated a badass plan to move Jude back to square one in the friend zone.

Let's call it Operation Wingman. All I have to do is enlist him as my comrade in arms.

19

THE ROOMIE PACT

Jude

My sex life is a whodunit, and I've added up the clues. A night of banging will solve the crime of too much horniness in 5E. Then we can focus on our careers and being the best roommates ever.

Now all I need is to find the right moment to present my solution to TJ.

My mission on Sunday afternoon, as we wander through Samuel Johnson's home? Keep the mood light to prime for the pump.

"Perhaps your hero needs to rescue a damsel in distress from a book thief," I suggest as we survey the research library.

TJ shoots me a side-eyed glance. "Is he *nicking* all her rare books?"

"Sure. Let's go with that," I offer playfully.

"Something to think about, that's for sure. But why

did you assume the romantic subplot involved a man and a woman?"

"Same reason my agent sends me out for auditions for straight and gay roles. I don't want to be pigeonholed early in my career. I want to play any part. I figured you'll want to make your mark writing both types of romance into your mysteries." I take a beat. "How did I do?"

He gives a small smile that disappears in a second. "You're right."

As we turn down the hall, TJ doesn't seem keen to continue this book talk. Weird, since he's been chattier after he shared the details of his novel three nights ago. Today, though, he sounds like he's elsewhere. I might have to table my proposition.

But as we head toward the door, TJ clears his throat. "So, when I went for a run this morning, I had an idea for you and me."

And we're back in business!

This could indeed be a perfect lube for my brilliant proposal. "I had an idea too. Something that might help our situation," I say, eager to make my pitch.

"Cool," TJ says, a smile on his face as we exit the house.

"I bet we're thinking the same thing," I say.

"I bet we are too," he says.

"So, tell me your plan." I'm dying to hear how deliciously it'll match mine.

TJ stops, straightens his shoulders like he's girding himself to say something hard.

But I'll help him along. "Why don't we—" I begin, right as he says, "We need to meet other men."

My head pops.

Wait.

What?

Did he just say *that*?

That terrible thing?

"I didn't mean to interrupt," he says, apologizing.

But thank God he did, or I'd have made a fool of myself. "No worries, mate," I say, then invite him to talk more. "So, you're thinking . . .?"

"I'm thinking. Clearly, we both need to get laid, right? It's not getting easier in our place. I mean, you avoid the flat even more now than you did when you first moved in."

Right, and my solution was to have you fuck me into the headboard. Yours is to fuck someone else.

"Sure," I say, so damn laid back that I'm nominating myself for an Academy Award.

"Let's wingman each other tonight. When we go to the club with our friends, we can help each other meet other dudes."

"It's not a gay bar, though," I point out.

"We could go to one after," he offers.

Oh.

Right.

He's thought this through, and I think I hate him now.

TJ stares at me, a little sheepish. "I mean, let's be honest. It's not really that easy to manage all this stuff," he says, gesturing from him to me.

You're right. It's not. So, shall I just hang a sock on the door when I'm shagging some American traveler who's not you tonight, you wanker?

But I'm an actor, so I throw on a winning smile. "That is brilliant. It's what I was literally going to say too."

TJ wipes a hand across his brow in mock exaggeration. "Whew. That's awesome."

"It's going to be great," I say, lying fantastically. "You should even wear that black shirt with the skulls."

Might as well torture myself. Call it an actor challenge.

"Sure. And you can wear anything. Because you look good in everything," he says, then offers a hand. "So, it's a roomie pact."

"It's a brilliant roomie pact," I say, shaking his hand as I wear a big, fat smile.

* * *

Olivia is in fine form tonight, entertaining the lot of us as we head toward The Cat's Meow.

"So, then the director said, 'Great, fabulous, but can you do that whole monologue again, but this time do it like you need to pee.' Isn't that mad?"

Alex raises a hand like he's in class. "Question. How does one do a bit like you have to piss?"

"Ah, let me demonstrate," Olivia says with a smile, then answers him with an encore of her audition.

TJ's workmate is a cool guy and one of the best listeners I've encountered. Good thing since Olivia likes to talk, and now she's telling him precisely how she redid the monologue as we weave through the thinning Sunday night crowds. "But I swear, shit is getting weirder in auditions. Like they're trying to test us in new ways. Don't you think, Jude?"

Ah, this is a perfect opportunity to stir the pot. If TJ wants us to wingman each other, he'll bloody well get it. "Absolutely. I ran into Trevor the other day at an audition, and he was saying the same thing. He's that gorgeous one I used to go out with—remember, Liv?"

TJ's shoulders tense.

"Aren't all your exes gorgeous?" she asks with a wink.

"You're right. It's hard to keep them separate when they're all so lovely to look at. But this might help—he's the one I said was the best kisser ever."

Olivia rolls her eyes, then pats Alex's arm. "Jude thinks a tiny bit highly of himself."

Alex laughs. "Self-confidence isn't a bad thing."

"So, what happened with this Trevor fellow at the audition?" Olivia prompts.

Oh. Hmm. That's a good question. I hadn't cooked up a story yet. But I was always good at improv. As I reach the door to the club, I say offhand, "Oh, he was just asking if he could join us later tonight. So maybe I'll text him."

There. Picture that, roomie.

With his jaw ticking, TJ heads to the ticket window. Olivia grabs me, tugs me out of earshot.

"What is your deal?" she whispers.

"Just having fun."

"You never talk about exes. They're all twats. And I have no clue who Trevor is."

"He's fake," I whisper.

She tilts her head, tutting me. "Be careful there. You're playing with his heart."

I scoff. "That would be impossible."

She wags a finger at me. "Don't be a twat."

I'm simply giving TJ what he wants. Me with another man. "I've got this under control," I tell Olivia.

We head inside, pouring into the crowded space, and soon the band begins. I'd like to say Lettuce Pray drowns out my thoughts. But it seems to stoke them. All these songs of longing have me imagining TJ kissing other men. Touching other men. Fucking other men.

Halfway through the set, TJ tells us he's going to grab a drink. I don't follow him. I dance with Olivia and Alex, and when Olivia spots her pretty blonde friend Polly, the four of us dance to the beat.

A few minutes later, TJ returns, but he doesn't join in. He nurses his drink, stares at the stage, and says nothing.

With every move I make, I fume.

With every shake of my hips, I seethe.

When the music ends, Olivia says the three of them are going to get a nightcap. Translation: Olivia is going to pitch a threesome to Polly and Alex.

"Cool. TJ and I are going to Wiseman," I tell her.

Out on the street, she pulls me aside once more. "What are you doing?"

I scoff, like none of this is a big deal. "I'm going to fuck someone else tonight."

She shakes her head, her eyes hard. "He's been staring at you all night with the most intense look in his eyes. He can't stop looking at you."

"I don't care," I spit out.

I don't care so much that when the three of them head one way, and TJ and I go the other, I stride right up to the bar in Wiseman and order two beers.

The bartender serves me straight away. I hand one to TJ, then lift mine.

"Cheers. To Project Wingman," I say, and yes, this is my best performance ever.

A resigned breath comes from him as he clicks his glass to mine. "Let's find you a man," he says, and when he sets down the beer, it is on.

20

MY KINGDOM FOR A DO-OVER

TJ

This was a rookie mistake.

Jude Graham is not only the most charismatic man I've ever known. He's the most charismatic man in all of England.

And I'm the dumbass who let him loose on the London population.

I wish I could reboot the last several hours. Erase them from existence and start over at Samuel Johnson's house.

Because my stupid idea led to *this.*

Men in the bar stare at Jude unabashedly.

The swoony Brit leans against the sleek silver counter, surveying a kingdom of cocks, ready for his choosing. He sets a hand on my shoulder, ever so casually. My skin sears from his touch. He gestures casually to a guy at the other end of the bar, a dark-haired dude wearing a tight white tank. Tribal tattoos circle his beefy arms. He's muscular—Jude's type. "What do you think about the guy over there? He's got *hot alpha* written all over him, don't you think?" Jude asks, charm dripping from his tongue.

I just grunt, *Sure*.

My wingman swings his gaze the other way, hums appreciatively at a group of guys, then whispers in my ear, "Check out the suit at three o'clock. He's perfect for you, TJ," he says, and his breath coasts across my skin sensually, but the knife of his words stabs my chest.

Where is a do-over button when you need it? But this is life, not a chapter I can start again. I can only get *through* this.

"Let's go for it," I rasp out, and I'm not even sure what I'm suggesting, that he talks to the inked guy or I talk to the suit?

But it doesn't matter because they're both heading our way. We are the hunted tonight. With his easy smile and casual pose, Jude is giving off all the *pick-me-up* vibes in the city. The tatted man licks his lips as he strides right up to my roomie.

"Hey there. Can I get you a drink?" the inked guy asks.

"As long as it's a martini," Jude says, flirting his fucking ass off.

"Anything for you," the man says, then sets a hand on Jude's shoulder and guides him a few feet away.

From me.

Jude leaves his beer behind, and it feels like a metaphor.

Great, now I'm comparing myself to a half-drunk beer.

Can this night please end, so I can go home and wallow in regret with my earbuds? I deserve a double dose of Zeppelin and The Allman Brothers Band.

I clench my fists, dig my nails into my palm. Breathing out hard, I try to get a grip on my emotions as the man in the suit comes my way. How can anyone be attracted to me tonight? Isn't it obvious I'm drowning in a boiling vat of self-loathing mixed with jealousy?

"Great bar, isn't it?" the suit says.

It's a decent opener since it's simple and not cringe-y. But it won't work on me because he's not Jude.

"Yeah, it's a cool spot," I say so that I'm not a dick.

And fuuuuck.

My mind lands on the great dick convo with Jude as the suit peppers me with questions.

Where are you from?

Do you like this song?

How's your night?

I respond half-heartedly with monosyllabic answers, sneaking glances at Jude the whole time. Swirling his martini, Jude laughs and smiles. It's a dance of seduction as the inked guy grins and runs a hand down my roomie's arm.

I burn everywhere. I want to throttle that guy touching Jude.

"Earth to the American."

I snap my attention to the suit. I'm an ass. "Hey. Sorry, man."

"Can I give you a tip?" the suit asks.

I brace myself for a cold send-off. I deserve it. "Sure."

The suit leans in, whispers in my ear, "You should just tell him you're into him, mate."

"Shit, I'm really sorry."

He smiles. "Been there. Just get your man."

"He's not mine . . ."

The suit lifts a playful brow. "Not yet." He drops a chaste kiss to my cheek and walks away.

Like acting on his advice is all too easy.

But I have to do this. It's necessary. As necessary as writing the next chapter in my book. Drawing a fortifying breath, I turn around, march over to Jude, and do what I should have done earlier today. Tell it like it is. "We're leaving."

Jude snorts. "But the fun just started, roomie."

The inked man drapes a possessive arm around my roommate and squeezes. "Don't steal Jude from me."

Yeah, some things *are* easy. Like this. "He's taken," I say to the guy.

Then I *take* what I want. *Jude*. I pull him outside into a stormy Sunday night in London. Fat raindrops pelt my head.

Jude stares hard at me. "What the hell was that about, TJ? This was *your* fucking idea."

"And it was the worst idea ever," I spit out.

"Maybe you shouldn't have suggested it," he counters, his voice full of fire.

"You're damn right I shouldn't have."

"You think?"

"Yeah. I do think that."

"So why the bloody hell did you?"

"Because I thought it would make things easier

between us," I say, or maybe I seethe. I'm still mad, but not at Jude.

I'm mad at myself.

For my supreme act of stupidity.

The sky flings water harder, and Jude slashes a lock of hair off his forehead. More drops slide down his face.

"And did it, roomie? Did it make things between us easier?"

"No, it made them harder," I say as I try to rewrite the ending to tonight.

"What a shock. I'd never imagined trying to hook you up with another man would be difficult."

I've got to break this cycle. I have to stop fighting with him. I have to say it. "I made a mistake," I mutter, starting down the path of honesty.

"I didn't hear you," he says as the rain lashes us, as cars rush by, as truths rise on the edge of my tongue.

"It was a stupid mistake," I say, louder, clearer. "My idea was a terrible way to deal with things." Admitting it lessens some of the tension in me.

"Then get a better idea," Jude huffs, locking his hard and fierce eyes on me.

It's time. I go for it. I close the distance in seconds flat, lift my hands, hold his face. "This is a much better idea."

I seal my lips on his, and I don't hold back. I pour everything I have into this kiss. It's like ten thousand kisses. It's all the kisses in the city. All the times I've thought of Jude. All the longing. All the desire.

With my lips, I tell him all the things I won't say out loud. The sentences form in my head.

I have a massive crush on you.

I can't get you out of my head.

I'm a little bit crazy for you.

He tastes like he's a little crazy for me too.

He kisses fearlessly, sweeping those lush lips over mine, nipping, biting, tugging.

Groans pass between our mouths like sips of a drink —a bottle shared back and forth for us to consume.

This kiss is everything we held back in the park. It's everything I wanted on that bench. On a rainy night in London, all the checked restraint washes away on the sidewalk as Jude wraps his arms around my neck and I hold his face in my hands.

We don't stop. We speed up, asking for more, throwing in the white flag of surrender completely.

I spear my tongue into his mouth, devouring his taste. My God, I want to claim him everywhere. Map his body with my mouth.

His tongue strokes mine and he tugs me against him, and we are unstoppable. I gasp into his mouth as our cocks rub together, rock-hard through our jeans.

My brain pops, and my skin sizzles, and somewhere in my mind, I'm aware that we're soaking wet on the streets of London after midnight, and neither one of us cares.

I never want to stop kissing him. But I do want to know all the flavors of his kiss, so I slow down, tug on his bottom lip.

And I shudder. Everywhere. *More, more,* my mind begs. *Don't stop*—my heartbeat echoes.

I downshift into a slow, indulgent kiss, and in seconds, he's moaning into my mouth.

His sounds electrify my senses as I take a long,

lingering tour of his lush mouth, lick the corner of his lips, then press a gentle, druggy kiss right there.

"Ohhhh," he murmurs and grinds against me, seeking contact. Seeking me. Inside, I smile wickedly. I'm kissing Jude, and he's coming apart under my touch.

I don't care about anything but getting him naked and into my bed.

We wrench apart. I stare hungrily at this man with the swollen lips and drenched hair. We're both soaking wet. "Have you seen my shower curtain? It's really perky."

Jude's smile is dirty and delicious. "Show it to me."

21

CONFESSIONS OF AN AFTERSHAVE THIEF

TJ

Wet clothes on your skin are not arousing. After a quick walk in the rain, we head up the five floors in our building, our shoes squeaking on each step.

Once we're in the flat, I pull him against me. Slide my hands through his damp hair. More honesty comes out when I say, "I want you naked. Want to do everything to you."

"Like what?"

I whisper filthy plans in his ear, then, since it's best to get this out in the open now, just in case we're not compatible in bed, I finish with, "And I really want to fuck you, Jude."

I wait, hoping he wants me that same way.

A breath staggers from his lips, and then he gives a slow, naughty nod. "Then you really should fuck me,

TJ," he says, squeezing my hard-on like he's checking the evidence. "Since it's clear how much you want to."

He smirks. The fucker *smirks,* then peels off his shirt, throws it on the floor, and heads to the bathroom, tossing me a *come-and-get-it* glance.

I follow him without question, unbuttoning my wet shirt, leaving it on a pile on the floor, then setting my phone on the table. Once he's in the bathroom, he unzips his jeans, but taking them off looks painful. They literally squeak. They're so wet.

"I'll help you," I say.

"Please do. That's really sexy," Jude says, laughing.

But when I sink to my knees and tug the cold, wet denim down his hips, he moans in appreciation. "Actually, it's ridiculously sexy with you like that, TJ."

With a smile I can't hide, I work his jeans down to his knees, then his ankles, watching his face. He grabs hold of the edge of the vanity, hopping for a second, nearly stumbling. I grab his hip to steady him.

"That was the hottest I've ever been, right?" he asks with another laugh.

I press a kiss to his hip with a soft murmur. His skin is cold, but I'm going to fire him up. "Yes, this is the hottest you've ever been because you're getting naked for me."

His grin burns off. "Been wanting to for so long."

We set a record as I help him get his jeans off the rest of the way.

I'm shaking with so much lust, so much anticipation as I check out his boxer briefs and the generous bulge behind them.

But also, the color. "Yellow. Your underwear is the

color of the shower curtain," I say, eating up this secret like it's candy.

"I told you I like color."

"You really fucking do," I say, my fingers trembling with wicked eagerness as I pull them down till his cock says hello.

My breath hitches. "Fuck, your dick is *nice*," I say in the understatement of the century. His cock is as beautiful as the rest of him.

"Bet it tastes better than nice," he says, threading a hand through my wet hair and guiding me closer as I push his briefs off the rest of the way.

My mouth waters. I wrap my hands around his ass and dip my head to his cock, swirling my tongue over the head.

The first heady taste of him lights up all the neon signs in my brain. The ones that say *touch him, taste him, please him.*

"Very, very nice," I whisper as I kiss the tip.

"Incredibly nice," he agrees, his voice thick with arousal even though I'm barely flicking my tongue along the crown of his cock.

Pride surges in me because I've longed to make Jude feel incredible, and now I'm doing it as I swirl my tongue down his length and curl my hands around his spectacular ass. He hums melodically in delight, and he's practically singing with pleasure already. But there's still one problem. His skin is cold and wet from the rain. I give a sturdy suck of his dick, hauling him deep and savoring the salty, musky taste, then pop off.

I stand up quickly, slap his cold ass. "That was the point of the shower. I want you all hot and bothered."

"Oh, I am. Trust me. I am."

"Get in there," I say, grabbing the shower curtain, holding it open.

He hops in then turns the faucet on. Water spews everywhere, this time from the tap instead of the showerhead.

"Fuck, fuck, fuck," he says.

"This shower has the world's worst parts. Hold on," I say as I spin around and head to the kitchen and grab the tools. I'm back in seconds flat holding the wrench.

Jude leans against the sink. His feet crossed at the ankles, and his hands pressed together in prayer. "I was such a good boy this year, and Santa is giving me a Christmas present early."

I laugh as I fix the tap.

Jude stares shamelessly at me, stroking his cock as I work the wrench.

"Yes, TJ, I have such a handyman fetish," he says.

"You really fucking do." And I love that I'm the lucky beneficiary.

Once I set down the wrench, Jude proves it, pouncing on me, tugging at my jeans.

Soon, we're both down to nothing, and when he sets his eyes on my naked body for the first time, I feel like a king. He doesn't seem to know where to look, except everywhere. His hungry eyes eat up my chest and stomach, and my dick, standing at attention for him.

"You," he says, all low and husky. "You are just . . . all my fantasies."

That's what tonight is. A fantasy. Nothing more.

I don't want to ponder too much on tomorrow—think about where this is going. If I do, the gears in my head will get stuck on the only answer—we're going nowhere.

Currently, though, we're on a path to the bedroom, and I want to savor every second of the trip.

Starting now.

I pull him into the shower. As the bathroom heats up and steam wafts around us, we make out like crazy.

Tongues, teeth, bodies. My hand wraps around his cock, and he grabs mine, and we both groan in tandem.

He slides a hand up and down my length like he's weighing my cock. Then he dips his face against my neck, presses a hot kiss to my skin. "I have to tell you a secret," he rasps out.

Hot and bothered?

More like molten and aching everywhere.

"Tell me," I demand.

He kisses my chin. My jaw. Then he draws a deep breath, inhaling me. "Your aftershave . . . I sniffed it the other day."

"On me?" I ask, shuddering as my hand coasts along his hard length. He does the same to me, and with his other hand, cups my balls.

Ah, fuck, that's good.

Letting go, I grab his hips and hold on for dear life as he toys with my dick and my mind.

He presses a slow, hot kiss to my lips, then whispers against them, "I steal hits of you whenever I can if I walk past you. If I get close enough."

I don't even know how to process this dirty confession. It's the sexiest thing anyone has ever said to me. It's the sexiest thing anyone has ever said in the history of sex.

"You want to know what else I do, TJ?" His voice is pure arousal.

"Yes." It comes out like a plea. It *is* a plea.

"Sometimes, I come in here when I'm alone in the flat. I open the bottle. Inhale the scent, close my eyes," he says, stroking me slow and sensual to the rhythm of his words.

This is unreal.

I ache everywhere for him.

I don't know how he does it, how he turns the tables. I'm supposed to be the writer, and he just told me the most erotic bedtime story ever.

"Do you jack off picturing me?" I'm not sure how I can even form the words to ask anything, but I've got to know the answer.

"I like to imagine getting down on my knees and sucking your cock."

I. Can't. Think.

I can only *do*.

Pushing his hand off me, I spin him around, shove him against the wall, and plant a bruising kiss on his lush lips. "But it's your turn, Jude."

Then I get down on my knees again, and I swallow his cock.

"Ohfuckohfuckohfuck." Jude grabs my head, yanks me against him. My face is up against his pubic bone, and his dick is down my throat, and I am so fucking turned on. I *need* to wind him up now. I have to show him I can make him feel spectacular. So, I give him even more. I slide a hand between his legs, press a finger against his ass.

He grips my hair. "You can't do that."

I believe in listening to a lover, so I ease off, slowly and torturously, my tongue flicking over the head as I go. "Which part? This?" I ask innocently, then tease at his hole with my finger, pushing the pad inside again. "Or that?" I ask as I draw the head of his cock between my lips once more.

A tremble racks his body. "All of it. I'll come on your face in seconds, but I really want to come on your chest."

There he goes again. Taking control.

We're dried off and in his room in two minutes flat.

When he falls snow-angel style on the bed, I'm pretty sure the only thing I'm going to ponder for the rest of the night is how to make him lose his mind.

I kneel between his thighs, spread them apart, and reach for the lube on his nightstand.

I've only thought about this five thousand times, and still I'm jittery, like it's my first time having sex.

But it's my first time with Jude, and that's all that matters.

Maybe the first of many times with him?

Nope. Can't go there, won't go there.

As I drizzle lube on my palm, I meet his gaze. "Show me what you look like when you're getting off to me."

Jude grabs his cock, stroking it for me.

I could watch him all night. I could stay in this front-row seat to his one-man sex show.

But it's not a solo production. We're in this scene together, and when I press a finger against his entrance, his mouth falls open. I slide my finger a little deeper.

"Yes, fucking yes," he moans, and my God, Jude is so

expressive. It's a gift to touch him, to be the man to earn these sounds.

He grips his cock tighter, twists his wrist.

I add another finger, crook both. His entire body jumps. And the best part?

He can't speak anymore. There are no more filthy confessions. He just grunts and groans, jerks and tugs as I open him up.

Then, everything happens in a red-hot blur. Jude bats my hand away, rises, and grabs a condom from the nightstand. "Lie down so I can ride your dick."

I thought I was in control. I thought I was topping him. But when I shift to my back, and he rolls the protection down my shaft, then straddles me, I know that was a lie I told myself.

I am only ever pretending to be in charge. He's got me in his hands.

All I can do is let him weave his magic.

And holy hell, Jude *is* magic as he presses my cock to his ass, then as he guides me inside.

His face is etched with intensity from the initial invasion. His jaw is tight, his mouth a straight line. Then, he lets out a sexy gasp, his gorgeous mouth parting as he sinks onto my dick with a heady groan.

"Yes, yes, yes," he murmurs, his eyes falling shut.

I can't look away.

When he takes me all the way, I'm not sure I can withstand the pleasure of fucking him.

But I'm willing to try.

I wait for him to give me a sign, letting him adjust. His shoulders relax, then his hands brace on my pecs. When he opens his eyes, those blue irises gleam with wicked delight. He bends closer to my face, his breath coasting over me. "Fuck me now," he demands.

Don't have to tell me twice.

I thrust up, pumping my hips, driving into him.

He fucks me right back, riding my cock, working his hips.

Soon, I don't know who's setting the pace or who's keeping the rhythm. But it doesn't matter. We're both in this. For several fantastic filthy minutes, we screw like that. He rides me, and I drive into him. We sweat and groan and get lost in each other.

When he wraps a hand around his length, stroking hard and fast, my mind spins faster.

I won't last much longer—not when he's jerking his cock with such purpose. Not when his potent need is written in every twist of his wrist, every swivel of his hips.

"Do it," I urge. "Come on my chest."

Seconds later, he growls and shoots all over me. Those neon signs in my brain go haywire. They light up the night sky.

I'm this close to the edge, and there's only one more thing I crave.

In seconds, I roll him, switching positions, so he's under me. Pushing his knees up to his chest, I sink back inside him. Jude slides his hands up my back and into my hair. "Kiss me," he demands like he knew why I did this.

Of course, he knew.

He knows I try to be in control.

He knows I want to kiss him when I come.

Smashing my lips to his, I fuck him hard as I chase my release.

I could drown in his kisses. Maybe I will tonight as pleasure consumes every cell in my body, and Jude fills all of my mind, till I reach the edge, gasping a string of orgasm-fueled curses as I come. For a minute, maybe more, my mind goes blank, spinning into a haze of bliss. And then, as my brain comes back online, into one shockingly stark awareness.

There is no *a little crazy for him*.

I'm just plain crazy for Jude, and I'm pretty sure all these emotions will devastate me.

And I won't do a thing to stop the ruin.

22

ABOUT LAST NIGHT

TJ

This is not my bed.

Which means I'm not near my alarm.

Which also means I conked out with Jude.

He's parked on his side, the sheets riding low on his back, his hair sticking up as he sleeps.

My heart gives a kick. I could get used to this view.

That's the trouble. Rubbing my eyes, I sit up and look around for a clock, but there isn't one.

I really hope I didn't sleep past seven-thirty. I need to be in the office by eight-thirty.

Quietly, I swing my feet out of bed, but the floorboards creak. I freeze in my birthday suit, stealing a backward glance. Jude rustles, flipping over to his back, and I stifle a groan.

He's hard, his morning wood tenting the sheets.

He sighs, stretches, and I'm sure he's going to open

his eyes, push up on his elbows, and then suggest I take care of matters south of the border.

I would.

But he stays asleep.

Maybe that's for the best. We might have to talk if he got up, and I still don't know what to say to him.

I pad out of his room, carefully snicking the door shut behind me.

I hunt for my phone, finding it in the living room on the coffee table. In three, two, one seconds, it will blast off.

But I catch the alarm in time, silencing it.

Good. Don't want to wake up Jude.

Though to be fair, my alarm beeps every weekday, and I don't worry about waking him. Today though? I definitely don't want him up because I don't know what to say about last night.

Hey, so that was amazing, and I want to sleep with you ten million more times. What do you say we bang our way through the next fifty weeks, seven nights a week, and in the mornings too?

Oh sure, I know it's a terrible, risky idea, and no way would it work out, but I'm insanely into you, and I promise I won't develop a smidge of feelings for you.

Well, nothing more than the smidge AND A TON AND A HALF I have right now.

Yeah, this won't be an easy convo, and we didn't touch it with a ten-foot pole last night.

After sex, we cleaned up, then when I stood in the hall, pondering where to go—because that's what I fucking do, I overthink everything—he just rolled his eyes, tipped his forehead to his room, and said, "Come on. I might want to suck you off in the middle of the night."

Well, I didn't turn that down. But he didn't blow me either. We both slept straight through.

And now it's tomorrow.

Talking about last night is inevitable, but the thought churns my gut.

I gather my clothes from last night, hang the still-damp ones to dry, then jam the rest into the hamper in my room before I head to the shower. Under the water, I try to make sense of what's next. I try to brace for whatever Jude will say. *That was fun, but let's move on now that we've got that out of our systems, shall we?*

My chest is a little hollow, knowing that once is probably all we'll have.

One time can be explained as a mistake. Or a necessity, what with hormones and all.

Anything more is deliberate. As deliberate as playing with fire and thinking you won't get burned.

* * *

When I reach the office, right on time, Alex waits for me at my cube. He holds up a hand to high-five, question marks in his eyes.

I roll mine. "I could ask the same of you."

He nods in satisfaction, then points his thumbs at his chest. "Oh, yeah. This American loves London."

"Get it," I say, then smack his palm.

"And you? Did you finally have that night at the London Sex Exchange with your"—he stops, clears his throat dramatically—"*friend*?"

As best I can, I rearrange my features, so they're stoic. I take my time, though, since I'm not sure how I want to answer.

In my silence, Alex leans closer, swings his gaze from side to side. "Dude, I know it's your roomie. You're so fucking obvious."

Are my feelings for Jude written in my eyes?

I try to fashion an answer that doesn't give anything away, but as I do, it occurs to me I don't want to tell Alex. I don't want to tell anyone. I want to clutch last night in my hands, keep it safe as a memory, save it for myself.

Once I share it, then I'll have to explain it. *Well, you see, I slept with my roomie because I'm falling for him, so yeah, sex seemed brilliant, and now it seems foolish, yet I'm dying to see him tonight.*

And tomorrow.

And the next day.

And I know this won't work, but so it goes . . .

"Last night was fun," I say evasively.

Alex arches a brow. "Got it," he says, then winks and heads to his cube.

I breathe a sigh of relief, but it hardly lasts when the news manager barks out my name in a gruff English accent.

"Ashford. Come to my office."

Like a good soldier, I follow him. Alex catches my gaze as I go, his eyes asking *what's up.*

No idea, I mouth.

When I head into Richard's office, he gestures to a chair across from his desk. I sit, nerves racing as he plops into his chair.

"TJ," he begins. "Your work here is excellent."

My stomach plummets. The only thing coming next is a *but.*

The trouble is, I can't figure out what I've done wrong. My stories have been great. My reporting is solid. My work ethic—top-notch.

"So excellent, I can't keep you," he adds.

That makes zero sense. "Why not?"

"There's an opening for a senior reporter. Turns out, our just-completed analysis of consumer behavior says articles on media and advertising fare better than financial pieces, and they want you for the promotion. It comes with a twenty percent raise and a gym membership since 24News just bought a chain of gyms. Must diversify these days. So, there you go. You're a very good writer, and you were a shoo-in. But don't let that go to your head."

"I won't," I say, though I'm stoked. *Very good* is editor speak for *head and shoulders above the rest.*

But that's not the most exciting part.

Not by a mile.

Since they're promoting me, I could maybe use that raise for a new place. I do the math quickly, and I'm guessing the extra might cover the three-month fee for breaking the lease. That way, Jude won't be screwed on the rent. My mind leaps ahead, picturing getting a studio in Bloomsbury maybe. A flat I can afford on my own with the raise. Closing out my gym membership and putting that money to rent.

Most of all, my mind jumps to the best part.

Seeing Jude on the reg.

Asking him to be my boyfriend risk-free.

My heart thunders so wildly, and I nearly set a hand on my chest to calm it down. Surely, Richard can hear it.

I smile, too big for work, but I don't care. This solves everything. This is the best news ever. There's only one question—Richard hasn't said when the new job begins.

"So, when do I make the change?"

He glances at the wall as if the answer resides on a clock. "Monday," he says evenly, as if he were giving me a deadline on a deep-dive piece.

Holy shit. I could be making more money in a week. I could have enough to pull this off—romance and work.

Sex and a career.

Jude . . . and me.

"So, I'll work out the week in finance, then I'll move desks on Friday," I say, trying but failing to hide my enthusiasm.

This is some kind of luck. This is like finding Jude on Cecil Court. This is rom-com meet-cute fate.

"No. You can have the weekend off to pack and unpack, of course," he says.

"Pack?" I don't have that much on my desk. What's he talking about?

"Oh!" He chortles, like I'm a silly boy. "The job's in New York, TJ."

Ohhhh.

Right.

My shoulders sag.

"Media and TV and marketing. That's a New York post," he says, like *duh. How did you not know this, you idiot we just promoted?*

"Yes. Of course," I say lightly, swallowing past the knot of disappointment lodged in my throat.

"We're sending you back to New York," he adds. "On Friday. So you can start Monday."

The floor drops from under me, and for a few seconds, the office spins. My head spins. The whole city whips on its axis. "This weekend?" I repeat.

"Yes. Friday is this weekend," he says, clipped, like he doesn't have time for ridiculous questions.

Understandable.

"What happens to the job here?" I ask, and I'm not sure why. It's not like I'll beg to stay. When you're twenty-three and get a big, fat raise, you follow the job.

You don't follow the man.

"We're going to outsource your post to a freelancer. The New York bureau is eager to have you back. HR has all the details. Hope you enjoyed your time in London. Be sure to go to Fortnum and Mason before you leave."

I'm dismissed in a daze, and the HR woman waits for me in the hall, then takes me to her office, and we review the details. My flight to New York is Friday night. The company will cover the lease here for three months, as per the contract, and 24News will help me find a new place in the city.

That's all.

Like a zombie, I walk to my desk, sink onto the chair, and stare out the window.

I'm not daydreaming this time.

I'm freaking out.

On the one hand, this is great news. On the other, this is also awful.

There will be no more Jude after this week. There

won't be any more weeks to get through. There won't be any merit badges to earn.

There won't be a London romance.

And I won't fall in love for the first time in my life.

Instead, I'll be gone.

Maybe there's one silver lining, though.

23

AN ANALYSIS OF PET NAMES

Jude

I stare at my phone during a break in rehearsal, like I can will a reply from TJ through sheer mind power.

Unfortunately, the trick doesn't work, and it's been three hours. He hasn't responded to the text I sent this afternoon. Maybe I should have been more . . . definitive. More demonstrative?

But I'm not keen on relationships, and I've no fucking clue what's next, so I figured a sexy, ***Thanks for last night, stud*** was a good jumping-off point.

Into what, though?

Into more epic, mind-bending, knee-weakening sex?

That was so much more than sex, you daft idiot.

"All right, everyone ready to tackle scenes five and six?" the director calls out, and I tear my gaze away from my phone, powering it off as I return to the studio. This is where my focus should be.

Not on my roommate.

I give robots and scientists my all for the next few hours, loving every second of rehearsal.

* * *

When seven rolls around, my phone takes pity on me. Right as I leave the rehearsal studio and hit the pavement, a message flashes across my screen.

TJ: Hey . . . any chance you'd want to get a beer at The Duck's Nipple? We never made it to that place, and I figure we should.

That's oddly . . . unspecific. Is this a post-sex discussion? A post-sex date? Beer with the roomie? I can't tell, but saying we never made it to that place sounds like he's ending us before we start.

But we can't really start anything. And what would we start anyway? More sex? That feels insanely risky because last night was already so much more than sex.

Except, risks are in my nature. My job is the definition of risk. I want another night with him. And then more after that.

Call me greedy.

I write back immediately, and we make plans to meet in thirty minutes.

* * *

Twenty-nine minutes later, I turn off Rob Lowe and walk into the bar, nerves racing in my chest. Telling myself I'm in a play where I'm a fighter pilot—the epitome of cool.

Settle down, nerves. Just tell the man you want more.

I find TJ at a booth. He catches my attention with a quick wave. I stride over to him. Do we hug? Kiss? Shake hands?

But TJ answers that for me when he slides out of the booth, stands, and yanks me in for a hug. It's not dude style. It's definitely I-know-what-you-look-like-naked style, and his aftershave enhances it.

That potent woodsy scent, chased with a hint of soap, smells like a secret he's wearing just for me. I dip my nose, drag in a whiff of him, and I'm instantly aroused.

That's not surprising since the scent has turned me on since I first smelled it.

But I'm also feeling . . . a little floaty—a little warm. Like I want to get close to him. Snuggle up against him, run my fingers through his hair, kiss him at the bar like he's mine.

"Mmm," he murmurs.

Yes, he did this on purpose, slapping on that aftershave.

And I'm caught up in him. I also now know what tonight is—a date.

But when he takes a seat and I sit across from him, he looks like he's got something on his mind. Something big. "What's going on?"

TJ doesn't answer at first. Because, of course, he

doesn't. He just seems to weigh the question, stroking his beard, sighing heavily, but maybe happily too?

"So, this is kind of crazy," he begins, and holy fuck.

Is he going to ask me to keep this up? Screw the risks. I'm all in. "Yes. Just yes."

He laughs. "You don't even know what I'm going to say."

"Right, sorry."

"So, the thing is," he says, and I wince. This is bad news. "I just got a promotion."

"Oh, that's great. Congratulations," I say, still trying to figure out what's happening on this maybe-date.

His gaze levels mine, and before he speaks, I see the truth in his eyes. I won't like what he's going to say. "It's in New York, Jude. They're sending me back to New York. Even if I had a choice, and I don't, they decided to freelance my beat here. It's both a great opportunity and the only opportunity."

Wow. That's a twist I didn't see coming. And frankly, I don't care for it.

"I return to New York on Friday," he continues, his tone heavy, then business-like as he explains that 24News will cover the lease.

But my head pounds.

My ears ring.

TJ is leaving.

I knew he'd go eventually, but I didn't think too hard about what that might feel like. Now, the idea consumes me. And it's like a bowling ball, dropping in my gut.

I desperately want him to stay. My chest actually aches at the prospect of opening the door to the flat and seeing . . . some random person.

That seems horribly wrong.

"Would you stay and write your novel?" I ask, a note of wild hope in my voice.

But the question lands like a thud on the table. He doesn't even have to answer me.

I know what he's going to say.

He can't stay to write a book. We aren't rich. We live hand-to-mouth. He's not independently wealthy. He's young and scrappy like me. He lives paycheck to paycheck.

TJ shakes his head. "I can't, Jude," he says, then he gets up, comes around to my side, slides an arm around my shoulder.

He buries his face in my neck, the prickle of his beard chasing the ache in my chest away, soothing it until my bones start to hum.

He kisses my jawline, the corner of my lips, my cheek. His kisses are a little sad, a lot poignant. "But what if we make the most of the next four days?"

* * *

On Wednesday night, making the most of it looks like this.

I'm kneeling on the floor of the living room, indulging in my favorite treat.

TJ's cock.

We're setting records. Since Monday night, it's been nonstop. Plenty of sex, lots of blow jobs, a handful of hand jobs, and some dick-to-dick action, when I learn something new about myself—*that* becomes my new guilty pleasure, and I don't even know why, it just works spectacularly well with TJ, and I tell him as much when we're naked and grinding together.

We've done other things too. A few beers in Chelsea, a music club in Leicester Square to see a Brit-pop band TJ wouldn't stop telling me about, then an at-home reading of the best lines from *The Importance of Being Earnest* before we shagged last night.

And now *this*. Blowing TJ is the sexual equivalent of unlocking the man who takes so long to share *anything*. It's the antithesis of all the secrets he keeps. When I have him in my mouth, he is helpless, and he is vocal.

With his legs spread and his head thrown back, he ropes his hands through my hair. "Your mouth, Jude. Fuuuuck. Love your mouth. So fucking much."

His praise inspires me to take him deeper, suck him harder. I swirl my tongue up and down his length, having a party with his dick.

But right when I have him pulsing in my throat, I relent, letting him fall out of my mouth.

I slide my hands up the coarse hair on his thighs, and he whimpers. "C'mon," he says, gripping himself, offering his dick to me again. "It's so fucking good."

I lick the tip, teasing him, playing with the head, lapping up all those drops of arousal.

"Take me deeper, baby," he pleads.

That's what I wanted. I've never been one for pet names, but the way he says *baby* drives me wild. It's so unlike him. It's such a surprise. I don't even think he's aware he says it in the throes of passion.

He never says it outside of the bedroom.

But when we're naked, when he's undone, he doesn't think. All the time he usually takes before he speaks vanishes. In bed, he babbles and grunts. He whispers and begs.

I savor all the things he says as I draw him back into my mouth, lavishing attention on his thick, hard shaft. Things like . . .

You.

You're incredible.

Want you so much.

Want this.

Want us.

Those last two words send my mind to dangerous shores. To impossible futures. They remind me cruelly and beautifully that making the most of these four days isn't only about sex.

I close my eyes, suck him deep, and revel in the taste of him. I like the pet names because I like him so fucking much.

So much that it feels like falling.

So much that I shove my hand into my boxer briefs, stroke my aching cock, and wish I could have him and us for longer. A lot longer.

"Jude, fuck, baby. That's so hot. So fucking hot, we need to stop."

Letting go, I pout. "Why do we need to stop?"

"Get up here." He pats the couch, stretches out on his side, then tells me to fuck his face.

Well, what the gentleman wants . . .

A minute later, we're tangled up together, my face between his thighs, his between mine.

We are loud and messy. Slurps and sucks fill the air and mix with his playlist of Brit-pop sex tunes that make me even hotter for him.

Make me hot and bothered and thrilled to have him in my life.

In my head.

And, as we go to town on each other's bodies, I'm pretty sure he's in my heart too.

But soon, he'll be gone for good.

All I can do is enjoy every second of these last few wonderful nights.

Pleasure cascades down my spine, coils in my belly. My legs shake, and I let him fall from my mouth, grunting out, "Coming . . ."

I'm seeing stars, trembling all over, and I want to give TJ the same thing. I'm right back on his dick before the aftershocks have finished.

I'm on it, loving it, sucking, and wishing this could happen next week, next month, maybe even next year.

But he'll be gone in less than two days.

Some stories just play out that way.

24

THE CASE OF THE DISAPPEARING PAGES

Jude

I'm not counting down.

There's no point.

Life goes on. But it's Thursday evening, and TJ's flight departs tomorrow. And even though I'm secretly hoping it's delayed another day and that we get a reprieve, I'm also realistic enough to know that it won't happen.

I rearranged my schedule at An Open Book, taking shifts on Friday, Saturday, and Sunday so I could spend this last night with him.

We go to The Magpie, settle in with a beer, and just like that first night, we talk. Even with the looming departure, the connection between us is still strong. TJ cares about my dreams and I care about his too.

"Robots and scientists . . . Does it have a name yet?" TJ asks.

"It has a working title. I don't love it though. *Machine Love*."

"Yeah, that's a little cringe-y. But I say this as someone who has a cringe-y working title for his book."

"You still won't tell me what that is?"

"It's bad, Jude. It needs a good name. Just like *Machine Love* does."

"I know. Hopefully, the writer will change it," I say. "But you know how writer types can be. So pig-headed."

"Writers are the worst. Well, after actors," he says. "You still love the show, though?"

"I do. We started shooting today, and it was . . . everything. You know what I mean? It makes me feel alive. Energized. It makes me feel like I've found myself."

"The artistic impulse," he says, getting me completely. "You *have* to create."

"*I* do. *You* do." I gesture to the man across from me. The man who's become a friend, a lover, and the human I'll miss more than I imagined I could miss a person. And this shared passion is such a big part of our connection that I almost want to ask if we could stay in touch. If we could be the actor and the writer who have an international friendship. That could happen, surely.

But *should* it happen?

Sitting here with him, sharing freely at last—this doesn't feel entirely like friendship. It feels like fire, and heartbreak, like the start of a new obsession. It feels like something I could get lost in.

But I can't, so I focus on the practical part of the future. "Will you finish your novel in New York?"

"I better." Then he laughs. "I mean, how cliche would

that be if I leave London with an unfinished novel and an unfinished . . .?"

He doesn't complete the thought.

An unfinished romance.

I slide a hand across the table, link our fingers together. "Don't forget the romance in your book, TJ."

"I won't," he whispers, dipping his head.

"I mean it. I bet you'd be really good at it. At writing that," I say, squeezing hard.

He squeezes back. "I bet you'd be really good at playing it."

My heart thumps harder in my chest, and it hurts. But it feels good at the same time. "I want to read your book."

He licks his lips, takes a very TJ-like beat, then blows out a breath. "Do you want to read what I have so far?"

Fireworks burst inside me. "Fuck yes."

We fly out of there.

* * *

To say he's a nervous wreck is an understatement. TJ's fingers slip and slide as he flicks open his laptop. His breath comes hard through his nostrils.

He clicks on the keyboard and curses. "Shit. Wrong file," he mutters.

Next to him on the couch, I drop a kiss on his scratchy cheek. "You don't have to show me."

In slow-motion, he turns his gaze to me. "I know I don't. But I want to, even though it's not easy for me."

"I know it's not easy for you," I say, though I have no idea why he struggles like this. Maybe it's a writer's dilemma. Maybe he can *only* live in the interior. As an actor, perhaps I have no choice but to live in the exterior.

Or maybe there's more to it for him. Maybe it's rooted in something long ago. Either way, I'm grateful for all the times he has opened up.

He returns to fighting with his computer while I return to kissing his neck.

TJ groans softly, stretching his neck, inviting more kisses. "Maybe we should just spend the whole night having sex instead," he murmurs.

"If you want, that can be arranged," I say, closing my eyes as I nip on his earlobe.

Another moan. Another sigh. "I do, but I also really want to do this."

He takes a deep breath, hands me the laptop, and stands. "Listen, I'm going to go for a walk. I'll drive you nuts if I stay here. And I'll just pace like a caged lion, so I'll get a coffee."

"It's eight at night."

He grins wickedly. "Coffee O'Clock caters to hyper-caffeinated Americans at all hours."

"Go, go, go," I say, shooing him away.

A pang of missing lodges in my chest once he's gone. I shift my focus to the laptop, and the story opens in front of me.

Except, this is a piece about . . . bond trading.

Ugh.

This is dreadful.

I mean, it's nicely written and all. But blah, blah, blah.

He must have opened this file by mistake, so I navigate, searching for his book. Except the sneaky fucker won't tell me the title.

I poke around the desktop, hunting for it. Maybe this is it. *The Case of The Disappearing Pages*. It's not a terrible title, like he said, but the man is harsh on himself.

I click it open.

My breath catches.

This isn't his novel.

The hair on my arms stands on end. Chills sweep down my body. But they're weirdly good chills as I stare at a few sentences from . . . a journal.

After the last week of getting to know him, I'm no longer convinced I can handle fifty more weeks of living together with, let's face it, my dream guy. He's the swooniest man I've ever known, and my entire body vibrates just being near him. He's wickedly charming and ridiculously beautiful, and I am so far gone.

I swallow roughly, my throat going completely dry.

Holy shit.

My fingers tremble.

This is wrong. Looking at this is so wrong. I have to stop. I will stop.

I do stop. I close the file straight away.

Then I exhale the biggest breath in the city as I sink back into the couch cushions, processing what I just read.

Tingles rush down my body. They sweep through my chest as his words intoxicate me.

I'm thrilled that he's as fucked up about me as I am about him.

But I can't let on I read even three sentences. He'll

die of embarrassment. I shake it off, so I can pretend it never happened and tuck this moment far, far away. Then, I groan, laughing at myself.

The fucking book file was opened right behind the article. Thanks, Microsoft Word.

I dive in, and I have chills in a whole new way as I read the first four chapters of his book.

The man can write.

When I'm done, I grab my phone. A text blinks at me.

TJ: It's been twenty minutes, and I'm dying.

I laugh as I tap out a reply.

Jude: Get your arse back here so I can tell you how bloody fucking good it was.

TJ: You're just saying that so I'll give you a blow job.

Jude: Pretty sure I don't have to say anything but 'Get down on your knees now,' for you to suck my cock.

TJ: That is true. Also, can I tell you that everything you say in your accent is hot, but I draw the line at arse. Ass is hotter. Can we agree ass is better in all forms? An end to arse.

Jude: WHY ARE YOU TELLING ME THIS NOW?

TJ: I'm a dick ☺

Jude: OMG, I DIDN'T EVEN KNOW YOU KNEW HOW TO FIND AN EMOTICON!

We text like that till the sound of footfalls hits my ear, then his key rattles in the lock, and he walks in with two cups in his hands and happiness glittering in his brown eyes.

TJ hands me a tea, sits next to me, then says, "Well?"

I tell him all the things I love about his story. Especially the longing the hero feels in chapter three.

"You're very good at writing longing," I say, then take a drink of the tea and put it down on the table.

"Thanks." He just shrugs, then says softly, "Write what you know and all."

I melt a little more. He takes another drink of his coffee, then I reach for the cup, set it down too, and take his hand.

I tug him up from the couch and bring him to my room, and we undress each other, probably for the last time.

Soon, we're in our element, naked and breathless, our skin hot, our mouths searching and finding. We come together, and it's sexy and dirty like it's always been.

But it's also a little bit sad.

Especially when he kisses me with so much longing

that I'm pretty sure I feel the same as the guy in The Case of The Disappearing Pages.

So far gone.

The next morning, he packs his bags, and we walk along the river for the first time and the last time.

25

SOME OTHER GUY

TJ

Maybe someday I'll write a guidebook about how to spend three weeks in London. But it won't be after this trip.

I can only imagine the conversation I'll have with my friends when I return to New York this weekend. I'll grab beers with the crew from college, and they'll fire off the usual litany of questions to a returning young traveler.

How was Big Ben? Did you see the Crown Jewels? Ride the London Eye?

My answers will be something like this.

Big Ben was very large. Extra, you might say.

Not only did I see the Crown Jewels, I felt them too.

As for the London Eye, why yes, I did, only it's not the London eye you're thinking of.

But it has an eye, for sure.

Right now, I'm savoring the last few hours in this city, looking over the Thames with the guy I'm *this close* to falling in love with.

There's no way I'll tell Jude that. There's no point. But some part of me wants to acknowledge what happened here in this city. I give it my best shot, though it's terrifying to say.

"I'll miss London," I say to the river, managing to get the words past the tangle of emotions in my throat.

I wait, dreading that he doesn't feel the same, hoping that he does, and wishing for him to understand what I mean.

His hand glides up my back into my hair, plays with the ends. "I'll miss it too," he says, and I shiver.

But that's as close as I'll come to telling him how I feel. "I can't believe I'll be in New York tomorrow at this time," I say, shifting.

"Tell me all your big plans for your first weekend back. Will you gallivant around the Big Apple? Go to Central Park? Catch a musical?" he asks, rubbing his palms together, putting on a very excited air. Even though Jude is a good actor, I can see through his facade. This is a distraction tactic, so we don't talk about what happens when I get on that plane.

I don't want to talk about it either. Mostly because I don't want to deal with it. But I also don't want to go home with any expectations. We'll have to bite the bullet of the goodbye rules, and we'll have to do it soon.

"Yes, I have front-row seats to *Wicked*," I deadpan.

He curls a hand around my shoulder. "I knew you were a secret musical lover. Soon, you'll be sending me links to Amelia Stone tunes you found on Spotify."

That's as good an entrée as any. With a queasiness in my gut that won't abate, I bite off the uncomfortable question. "But is that what you want?"

Jude's expression transforms from a cheery bloke to a serious man. "Spotify links from you, you mean?"

I swallow roughly. "Yeah. That."

He stares at the river, sighing deeply, then looks back at me. "I mean, we could. We could stay in touch. I could see how you're doing with your book . . ."

"And I could watch *Machine Love* when it premieres," I offer, even though I don't know if that would help me live without him or make it harder.

"And I could send you links to fantastic styles of shirts, and you could hunt them down in New York," he says. "And you'd let me know how things were going with your career."

"And you'd do the same. Because I'd want to know," I say, and I do want to know, but this sounds like an unsatisfying outcome. This sounds like the tale of two young guys staying in touch on only the most superficial level.

Because there's no other way for us since the inevitable will happen when I leave, and he stays. Our lives will go on. My world will spin into new stories, new opportunities, and new romances.

His will do the same.

He'll meet someone. He'll date someone. He'll fall in love.

And the mature, caring, thoughtful part of me does want that for him. I want all the good things for Jude.

If we cling to three weeks in London, neither one of us will ever truly live.

We'd check in every few months, we'd wonder what might have been, and we'd never let go.

Never move on.

We'd be stuck in the past because soon, very soon, that's what this present moment that feels like *everything* will become.

"We could do that," he says, but his tone is resigned.

"Yeah, we could," I say, my voice matching his. "It's an option. It's an idea."

Someone is going to have to say the hard thing. Someone is going to have to lay down the rules for goodbye. "But is it a good idea?"

He shrugs helplessly. "Probably not," he says softly. "So, what do you think we should do? How would you write this in a story?"

I stare at the river, let the scenes unfold, imagine the words on the pages. I turn to Jude, run a hand up the front of his shirt. "I would write a different ending. These guys, they'd go their separate ways. They'd focus on their careers. That's what they should do, right?"

"They should," he says, underlining that new rule.

"The one guy should become the actor he longs to be," I say, hoping he feels as strongly as I do about this.

Jude nods several times, clearly getting it, clearly agreeing. "The other guy should write and write and write."

But I can't shake the possibility of a happy ending. And I can't leave without trying to write one for us. Far into the future, I imagine a wildly unlikely scenario. But one that's too alluring to ignore. "Let's make a deal," I say, buoyed by this outside shot I'm taking.

He arches a brow. "I'm listening," he says, then he

does that thing. He drags his teeth across the corner of his lips.

"You know that drives me crazy," I whisper.

"That's why I did it."

That's also part of why I can take this chance. Jude and I didn't hurt each other. We didn't choose this ending.

I grab his face, run my thumb along his bottom lip. "Down the road, when we've made it, if you're ever single and in the same place . . ." I pause to make sure I'm saying this the right way.

But Jude doesn't miss a beat. "You want me to look you up?" He sounds enchanted by the idea. The smile that spreads on his face reaches deep into my heart, maybe touching the last part of it, the only part that hadn't quite fallen all the way yet. That last piece of me tips into his hand.

"I do," I tell the man who didn't audition to become my first love. But he got the role anyway. "Someday, I do."

"I will, TJ. I will definitely look you up." He cups my jaw, presses a confident kiss to my lips that leaves me woozy. "And you better do the same, TJ Ashford. You really better look me up too. Make it a promise."

"It's the look-me-up promise," I say.

"Now that's a good title for a book. *Look Me Up*."

"It's not bad," I say, and I make a mental note of it, then shift gears back to teasing. "But I have to tell you something."

"Yes?"

"No one in New York calls it the Big Apple."

He rolls his eyes. "If I bring my big eggplant to New York, I bet you'd call it the Big Apple for me."

I crack up. "I probably would. But we both know I'm a sucker for your big eggplant." For his charm too, so I give him one more promise. "Someday, when I become a famous novelist, I'll be sure to write a hero named Jude. And give him a big cock."

Jude covers his face with his fingers, laughing into his palm. He shakes his head, then pulls his hand back, flashing me a grin that's going to grace billboards someday. That damn smile melts me. Bet it will melt millions someday soon. "That's all I want, TJ. To be the inspiration for your big-dicked protagonist," he says.

That's fitting. He's already been the inspiration for so much else. But I keep that to myself.

Some truths don't need to be spoken. Some secrets you should protect.

Like the fact that I fell in love with Jude Graham in three weeks in London.

When I buckle into my airplane seat a few hours later, the last twenty-one days already feel like they happened to some other guy.

26

YES MAN

A month later

TJ

The New York Comets slugger comes to the plate. I have no choice but to boo the hell out of him.

"You're going down, Brady," I holler from the third-base line seats.

"Get out of here, Bozo," the guy behind me shouts. "We don't want no stinking Cougars fans here."

I whip my head around. "Do I look like Bozo?"

"You will soon if you keep that up," the New Yorker taunts.

I shrug, water-off-a-duck's-back style. "Cool. I have no problem with clowns." Then I turn my attention back to the action on the diamond. Chance goes into the windup and fires off a beauty of a fastball.

Brady swings and misses.

"Yes! That's how you do it, Ashford!"

My buddy Nolan shakes his head, laughing lightly. "TJ, you are playing with fire."

I know, and I don't care. I'm at the New York Comets Bronx ballpark, and I'm rooting for the enemy, and I'm good with that. I've got on a Cougars jersey and a ball cap too. Take that, home team. "It's just a game," I tell Nolan.

"And fifty thousand Comets fans are sooo rational," my friend mutters.

But I'm not rational right now either. How could I be? My brother is pitching at the bottom of the ninth. I cup my hands around my mouth. "Strike 'em out, bro."

"How 'bout we kick you out?" the New Yorker behind me suggests.

"That won't be necessary when my brother closes this game," I say because trash talk doesn't scare me.

Besides, this game is my brass ring. I've been counting down to it since I flew across an ocean thirty days ago.

This is the goalpost I wanted to reach.

It's the one-month post-London mark.

The first few days back were the hardest. I met up with some of my college friends. They all asked about London. I didn't mention the guy who captured my heart and mind.

Once I put Jude out there for my friends to analyze, someone will tell me to call him, text him, or worse, FaceTime him.

And I might be tempted.

More than I am already. At some point each day, my fingers hover over his name on my phone.

But I haven't caved. I won't cave to the Comets fans either. Rooting for the enemy in the home team's ballpark is my little act of defiance, and it makes me feel good.

Three batters later, my brother strikes out the side. "The Last Chance Train is pulling out of the station," I shout, jumping to my feet, punching the air.

"Yo, Bozo. You want to take it outside the ballpark?" This offer comes from Mister New Yorker.

I spin around one more time, give the guy a sympathetic look. "Thanks for the offer, but I'm already seeing someone. I'm not interested."

With a reined-in laugh, Nolan grabs my shoulder. "Dude, I fucking missed you. It is good to have you back."

"I'm glad to be of service as your entertainment," I say.

We meet up with Chance and grab some post-game burgers and fries in Manhattan.

It's the first time I've seen my brother since I returned to New York. That'll be good—another few hours where I don't have to think of Jude. We can talk about baseball and other shit.

Chance sweeps a fry through his ketchup, then brandishes it. "Tell the truth. Fries are better than chips, aren't they?"

Spoke too soon. I'm thinking of London again. "Of course, fries are better," I say.

Chance peers closely at my shirt. "Are those cacti on

your shirt? What happened to Save Ferris? No Name Band? Pinball Wizard?"

Nolan gestures grandly to me like he's presenting me on a game show. "TJ went to London and got style."

"Evidently. How the fuck did that happen?" Chance asks.

I grab a fry and chew, stealing time to think before I speak. This is the moment. I could tell both of them. I could reveal the biggest thing that's happened to my twenty-three-year-old heart. Crack it wide open and serve it up to two guys I trust to the moon and back.

I could tell them, and they'd understand me completely.

But then, keeping things to myself got me through my parents' divorce. Before then, it helped me navigate the shitstorm of middle school. Now, keeping Jude locked up will probably help me get past him sooner.

I shrug. "I guess London rubbed off on me," I say, snickering privately over my own dirty joke.

Chance taps his chin. "You know what I'm thinking?"

That I just lied by omission to you?

"No, my twin-tuition is on the fritz right now," I say.

"I'm thinking this new look of yours will make it easier if we ever need to switch," he says.

"You guys do that?" Nolan asks like this is the coolest thing ever. "You pretend to be each other?"

"We have," I say. "We did growing up."

"His beard would make it hard right now," Chance says, pointing at me.

I rub a hand along my jaw, and that makes me think

of Jude too. I go hot all over, remembering our nights together.

That's the true reason I say nothing. I can't feed this fire inside me by talking about him.

If I say nothing, the fire of Jude will eventually die out.

* * *

But not quite yet. Two months later, I watch *Machine Love* when it premiers online, retitled *The Artificial Girlfriend*.

It's a test of my willpower. Will I tell Jude I saw it? I want to since he's incredible in it, completely becoming the scientist and falling madly in love with his creation.

The kiss scene lights me up from head to toe.

I'm more tempted than I've ever been to contact him.

I make a new vow. I won't follow his career. I won't look him up on social media or Google him.

I won't give the fire any oxygen at all.

* * *

Several months later, I finish my first book, but when I reread it, the best part is the love story.

I don't have to show it to a writers' group to know what I need to do. Shelve it. Turns out I like reading mysteries, but I don't want to write them.

I start all over again.

The following year, I work on my first romance. I

don't call it *The Look Me Up Promise*. It's not about Jude. I *can't* write about Jude.

Instead, I write a whole new story, one straight from my imagination. I call it *Yes Man*. It's about a brash, sarcastic lawyer who's got a big mouth and tells the senior partner he works for that he has a date for the firm's weekend in the Hamptons barbecue. But oops, the perennially single dude doesn't. So he convinces his quirky, cute next-door neighbor to be his pretend girlfriend. The story is chock full of sexual tension until they finally bang.

Spoiler alert: They screw a lot, fall in love, and live happily ever after.

It doesn't matter that I've never been with a woman. I know what it's like to fall. I know how infatuation feels. How desperate it makes your heart. How intensely it consumes you.

The rest is body parts and choreography.

Two years after I leave London, I find an agent and a publisher. This dream comes true while my dream guy becomes a distant memory.

27

MY LITTLE OBSESSION

The Night of *The Artificial Girlfriend* Premiere

Jude

Olivia pushes open the door to Sticks and Stones, whips her gaze back and forth, then declares in her big, brash voice, "Star, coming through."

I slap a hand over her mouth. "You're the worst, woman."

She bites my palm.

"Ouch," I say. "That smarts."

"Taught you to silence me then, didn't it?"

"I learned my lesson."

With a smile, she points to the back of the pub. "All right, let's go to the party room, shall we?"

"We could have done this at my flat," I say, except of course we couldn't.

My new roommate is a stick in the mud. Fine, he's queer-friendly and a non-smoker, but he also doesn't like noise, music, or people.

In the plus column, I don't want to shag him, hang out with him, or share all my hopes and dreams with him, so there is zero chance I'll fall arse over elbow into an endless well of feelings.

Or, I should say, *ass.*

In honor of a certain someone.

Someone I wish were here.

As we weave through the pub, Olivia nudges me. "Practice your red-carpet walk."

"You practice your red-carpet walk," I retort. "It's not even like anyone here is looking at us."

"They're not today. But mark my words, Jude Graham, they will be soon."

Though I'm realistic enough to know I won't be recognized from a web series, I cross my fingers. Sure, advance reviews have been fantastic, but it's not as if Hollywood is beating down my door. Harry is still sending me out on commercial auditions.

Though, I did nab one a few weeks ago.

I nearly texted TJ to tell him I'll be the face of a British menswear brand. And that I also landed a couple of voiceovers. One is for a music streaming service, and I wanted to say *Maybe you'll hear me in the States when you hunt for new bands, and by the way, have you heard the new Ten-Speed Rabbit single and isn't it fantastic?*

I didn't tell him, though. Instead, I called Olivia and blurted out, *I'm telling you because I love you, so I'm not tempted to tell TJ.*

Her response? *Use me anytime. That's what I'm here for.*

I'd be a right mess without my best mate.

When we reach the back room, my jaw comes unhinged.

Olivia invited everyone. My brother, some of his friends, lots of our mates from uni. Even Alex is here. So is Polly. Sometimes the three of them hang out. Sometimes Polly hangs out alone with Olivia. And sometimes Olivia goes out with Alex.

It all works, as she says. That's Olivia. She makes things work.

William is also here since the inked barista by day and Lettuce Pray singer by night has become a friend.

He offers me a clap on the back. "Congrats, Jude. I pretty much told everyone at the coffee shop for the last few weeks to tune in. So really, I consider myself responsible for your sure-to-be-smashing numbers."

He's teasing, of course, but I'm still totally grateful. "Every little bit of buzz helps. Seriously."

"I'm excited to see your show," he says with a genuine smile. "I bet TJ is too."

Did he tell you that?

I'm dying, fucking dying, to ask William that, as well as the other questions about the guy who hasn't left my head.

How is TJ doing? How often do you talk to him? Did he finish his book? Does he miss me as much as I miss him?

Instead, I smile and give William an offhand shrug. "Wouldn't that be something?"

Olivia pulls me aside, whispers out of the corner of

her mouth, "Are you okay? Do you need to text me and tell me you hope TJ's watching it?"

I give a small laugh, wishing it weren't so obvious, but glad I have someone to talk to. "Do you think he's watching it?"

"Oh, love, you don't want me to answer that."

"But I do," I say since I want her to say, *of course, he is.*

She shakes her head. "But I won't, and that's what you really need from me."

"I know," I say with a sigh. "I hope he's watching it."

Mostly, I hope he's still writing his book. When I'm at the bookstore, I check trade reports in the publishing business to see if he sold his book even though I know it's too soon. Still, I do it anyway.

And I read all his articles, though I don't give a flying fuck about media and marketing conglomerates and holding companies and agencies and blah, blah, blah. I read them anyway, just to know what he's up to. Reading his pieces makes me feel connected. But that's part of my problem. My little obsession.

"Time to watch," Olivia calls out.

I settle into the booth. The pub has arranged to stream the show on a big-screen TV so we can watch the first episode together.

"Go, Jude! Go get your android," Alex calls out during a flirty scene between Lyra and me.

A little later, William gets in on the cheerleading. "Give her some tongue, mate."

"Are you blushing?" Olivia asks, swatting my shoulder.

"Maybe a little," I say.

"Snog her, Jude! Snog her so hard," Olivia shouts,

whistles at the telly, then turns to me with an evil grin. "Did that make you blush more?"

"Nothing you say makes me blush."

"That only makes me more determined to try," she says, and when I return my focus to the show, everything feels surreal.

All I want to do is reach out to TJ and tell him about tonight.

It happened, stud. It really happened, and I'm fucking proud of it, and I hope you are too.

But I don't do that.

On the way home, I'm a little quiet. Olivia links her arm through mine. "Hey."

"Hey you."

"I hope he watched it too," she says.

I give a faint smile. "Thanks. I needed that."

"I know. I can tell you miss him extra tonight. Makes sense and all. He helped you get the part."

"He did. And I want to thank him." It feels good to admit that.

"I bet he'd appreciate it. I bet he'd love hearing from you."

My heart beats a little faster. "He would. That's the problem."

She squeezes my arm like she's giving me a shot of her own strength. "But you're not going to reach out. Right?"

"I want to. But if I do, I think I'd get obsessed again, Liv."

TJ made my obsession easy with his wit, his brain, and most of all, his unwavering support. He could have been my rock.

Maybe that's the real heart of the issue.

I go home to my stick-in-the-mud roomie, and I spend an hour typing and erasing messages to TJ.

Can you believe it?

How the hell are you?

You helped me get this role, yes, I thought of you when I kissed her, and yes, I think of you every day.

But right when I'm this close to hitting send on all of them, my agent emails with a note that says, *Booked you a small part on a TV show!*

That feels like a sign.

Go forward, not back.

And so, I do.

I stop reading his articles. I don't check the trades. Then, I do the hardest thing—I delete TJ's number. It's too tempting having him on my phone. I know myself. Some night, I'll have too much cheap champagne. I'll get the grand idea to say hello. I'll act on the impulse to contact him.

I have to save him from me. And, most of all, I have to save myself from me.

Soon enough, all that cold turkey does the trick. I move on.

Fine, fine. I don't always make the best decisions when it comes to my heart over the next seven years. Or my career.

But I do one thing exceptionally well—I stop chasing the past.

PART TWO

Seven Years After London

And then he looked me up . . .

28

PRETENDING TO BE WICKED

Jude

I can't possibly keep all these books in my little flat in Bloomsbury. But I can damn well try.

My brother has other plans. Heath hunts through my shelves, grabbing friend after friend. "Seriously, do you truly need this copy of a Rhys Locke book you've read fifty times and also own in e-book?" He grabs the delicious mystery of the stolen sapphires.

"That's my comfort read. I do too need it," I point out, then grab the pristine paperback, wrench it away from him. I hold it close, precious thing that it is.

Heath shakes his head and grumbles. "I'm gifting these to the library. Rhys Locke is popular, and you're obsessed with keeping his books in perfect condition. Ergo, they'll make a lovely donation. So will most of these."

I sink onto the couch, flinging a hand over my eyes. "Just take all my darlings. I can't even look."

"Excellent." He chuckles without remorse, then riffles through some of my absolute favorites.

"You can't possibly need three copies of *The Importance of Being Earnest*. Plus, don't you have it memorized? You played Jack Worthing once."

True, but that's not why I love that play. "I like Oscar Wilde. A lot."

"Understandable. But you don't need this in triplicate." Heath crooks his finger on another copy, the one with a man in a suit on the cover.

"That one is fine to donate," I say, watching his every move.

He reaches for the edition with the two men in top hats. I shake my head vehemently. "Take the red and white one instead."

I grab the book with the top hats. "I'm keeping this one."

Forever.

If someone wanted to take it, they'd have to pry it from me in my grave, and I'd fucking haunt them for the rest of time.

Heath lifts a very brotherly eyebrow. In that arch, he asks a silent question. *Why is this one so special*? Then he makes a guess. "Did Arlo give this to you?"

I shudder, like a wave of nausea rolls through me. "No. Arlo did *not* give me books."

"Reason number seventy-eight why he's an ex," Heath says drily.

"Please. There are easily more than one hundred reasons why he's history," I say.

But really, a few big ones. The bastard of an ex-boyfriend used me to get my agent and then slept with him.

Harry was very nearly headless when I found out. Arlo too. But that's not the worst of it. The worst of it was how I handled the two years that followed.

I don't even like to think about what went down then.

Heath waves the book at me. "Then is this edition the one you used when you performed it in uni?"

"No. Someone gave that to me," I say quickly, darting up to reach for the copy I've kept with me for seven years. TJ gave it to me on his last night, told me to read it now and then, that he'd underlined his favorite passages just for me. That book had lived on my shelves in that Waterloo flat for two years with Sir Boring, then a place in Bankside when I roomed with William and Olivia since she finally moved into the city when she became the queen of voiceover work. And now, the book has its home here with me.

When I flop back onto the sofa, I flip to the page my long-ago American lover read to me in bed years ago. *I hope you have not been leading a double life, pretending to be wicked and being good all the time. That would be hypocrisy.*

Then, the words he whispered to me next. *Always be wicked, Jude.*

Running my finger over the line, questions race through my head as they have many times before.

What is he up to now? The occasional glance at his social media reveals only the basics—he still worships at the altar of caffeine and seeks out new music like it's a religion. But does he still despise rubber ducks on shower curtains and write his romances mostly in coffee shops, like he did when he was here?

Then comes the question that always jostles its way to the front of my mind.

Is he single? Or has he met someone new to whisper Oscar Wilde to? I asked Google about TJ a year ago, and the tight-lipped search engine didn't say a word about his *relationship status*.

Heath breaks my trip back in time with an amused glance. "What's that smirk for? A line you loved saying under the spotlight?"

Good thing I'm trained at feigning emotions. "Just thinking of all things wicked," I say since that's true enough. Then I tuck the copy safely back on the shelf and nod to the door. "I need to take off for curtain. And you need to drop my darlings at the library. Give them a good home. I insist."

He smiles. "I will."

We leave, and after I say goodbye to my brother out in front of my building, I head to the Garrick Theatre, an intimate West End playhouse. For the next two and a half hours, I perform *Pillow Talk* to a packed house, bow at the end, then search for a familiar face in the crowd and blow a kiss when I spot her.

After I change out of costume, I meet up with Helen outside the theater.

"Fancy meeting you here," I say, then kiss her on the cheek.

"As if I'd miss it," she says, then swats my shoulder. "I can't believe you made me cry."

I give a devilish smile. "Nothing makes me happier than audience tears or cheers."

"Well, you earned both. Thank you for inviting me."

"Thank you for coming. It means so much."

She waves a hand dismissively. "You've always been so good to my store over the years. Before it was *my* store," she says, since Helen bought the shop when Angie retired several months ago. "I mean, you sent that scrummy American to me all those years ago. Did you know he still shops here? He's one of my best customers."

I startle, my spine straightening. What in the bloody hell? "He's in London?" TJ's in my city, and he didn't look me up? The rat bastard. "Does he have a boyfriend now?"

Helen chuckles, shaking her head. "Sorry, sorry. I didn't mean it like that. He shops online. I sent him button-ups to New York, including a shirt with dinosaurs he wanted for a recent press appearance. And God no, he doesn't have a boyfriend. You didn't hear?"

This I have to know. "Hear what?"

When she tells me, I race home, curiosity fueling my every step.

It's one thing to delete someone's number. It's another thing to resist the impulse to follow his career.

After my initial year-long TJ detox, I gave in to my natural curiosity. Looked him up online from time to time. Smiled at his pen name, then filed away a memory.

But now *this* nugget from Helen?

And on the very same day I re-read one of his notes to me? I've always believed in signs, and this feels like a big one.

My skin prickles with possibility as I head up the steps to my flat, unlock my door, toss the keys on the table.

The second the door closes, I plug the American's name into Google, and the search engine serves me the Wikipedia details I already know. As a bestselling romance novelist, he's written ten books published in the last five years, including *Yes Man, Mister Benefits, Happy Trail,* and *The Size Principle.*

Ah, but this next detail is news to me—both the book and the reception.

With a falling-for-his-best-friend's-brother storyline, the author's newest release, Top-Notch Boyfriend, *became an instant bestseller.*

I click on the second search result—a YouTube video from *Trish's Morning News Show*. It's a segment from last week titled *New York Power Couples.*

A pang of jealousy zips through me, but I quash it because the subtitle is *Ouch, that's gotta hurt.*

I brace myself as I hit play.

The camera pans in on my one-time roommate-turned lover. TJ's lounging on a red couch under studio lights, looking incredible in trim burgundy trousers, and a black shirt with a tiny dinosaur design on it.

Too bad he's seated next to a fellow with a man bun, who looks like he's swallowed an egg. I hate him on principle.

The camera swings to the host, a woman with a

blonde bob, of course, since that's the required haircut for hosts. "I'm here with one of the city's newest power couples—the bestselling novelist and the rising star chef. Flynn, your new pop-up rotisserie chicken café boasts lines around the block. And your beau's breakout book is the toast of the book world, having become a number-one bestseller in the first week of its release. Now, let's be honest. Did Flynn inspire this new romance, TJ?"

TJ dips his face, a little embarrassed, but smiling too as he reaches for Flynn's hand. I burn a little seeing that, even though I know what's coming.

"I never kiss and tell," TJ says, and my God, that's such a TJ answer. Then he winks at the host and whispers, "the good parts."

Cheeky fucker.

Trish turns to the long haired man. "Flynn, how does it feel to know that you're the muse behind the book that's been dubbed the *it* love story of the year? Bet you gained a few thousand new follows from that. Am I right?" she asks with a knowing nod and a smile to the audience.

"Well, I *thought* it was great," Flynn says, but he pulls his hand away from TJ to adjust his own shirt, but his shirt didn't need adjusting.

Oh hell. It's like watching a car crash in slow-motion.

But Trish doesn't seem to pick up on the hand cues. She simply waggles the red paperback around. "Personally, my favorite part in the story is when the hero says, 'After all these years, do you have any idea what it's like to fall madly in love with the one guy you thought you couldn't have? It's awful and wonderful at the same time. But that's what love is—awful and wonderful.'" She clutches her chest. "Flynn, did you love that part when you first read it?"

"When I first read it, I *did* think it was great," Flynn begins, then pauses, his brow knitting. He's quiet, and there's nothing worse on live TV than silence.

"And now it must be incredible. What with the book topping bestseller lists and helping bring those huge new crowds to your café?" Trish prompts.

More silence.

TJ sits up straighter, fear flickering in his brown eyes, awareness registering.

Oh, shit.

Flynn looks down, grabs the mic from his shirt, tugs at it, irritated. "Now, it's just awful. I've been turned into a laughingstock—a circus sideshow. I only want to make the chicken, cook for people, and get great reviews. But that hardly matters anymore. I'm just some novelist's trophy boyfriend." He turns to TJ. "It's all been about you—your coffee shop writing and your punny titles that you ask my advice on. But you can't do that anymore—because we are over."

Flynn storms off the set on live TV, but the camera doesn't leave TJ. His gorgeous eyes are etched with utter shock. He mouths *what,* and I fill in the rest—*what the hell just happened to me?* I feel his pain in the way my chest clutches, my stomach curls, and I wish I could kiss it away.

Dumped on TV by a wanker who's trying to get press for a chicken café?

And I thought the shit Arlo did was bad.

This is infinitely worse.

* * *

During the performance of *Pillow Talk* the next night, I pour those heartbreaking emotions TJ must have felt into my performance. The audience gives me a standing ovation.

I relish every second of their cheers. Especially since I know what it's like to hear silence. To wander past theaters and wish I were part of the cast. To flip through channels and long for opportunities to leave it all on stage.

A few days later, the director gathers us backstage. "Good news. We had some American producers at our Sunday night show. Later this month, they're taking *Pillow Talk* to Los Angeles for a limited run with the original London cast."

I freeze, letting the enormity of the news sink in. That's almost too good to be true. "Are you serious?" I ask.

"Completely," the director says, filling me with the hope of breaking out of this plateau where I've been the past few years. This is my chance to finally reach the next level.

My castmates and I cheer, then indulge in a long group hug. I'm the last to let go. As the director shares more details, I feel all fizzy inside.

I've never been to the States. I haven't had the chance to court the star-makers in Hollywood yet, having only now and then nabbed small parts in American flicks shot in England.

Something else appeals to me about America. Sure, Los Angeles isn't close to New York, but it's a whole lot closer than London is, especially when you're both single and made a deal on a bridge seven years ago.

29

THE DATING VACCINE

Some weeks later

TJ

I should be better at this breakup shit.

Considering all the imaginary people I've tortured. I've written ten romance novels, so I've eviscerated twenty fictional hearts. Often, in all sorts of terrible ways—from a dead girlfriend, to a six-time cheating boyfriend, to an awful liar of an ex who stole money, drugs, and diamonds. And in the ultimate shitty ex backstory, I gave one of the heroes in *Top-Notch Boyfriend* an ex who ghosted him by taking off for New Zealand, faking his death along the way.

Incidentally, that bit was pure fiction. To all the critics who claim *Top-Notch Boyfriend* is ripped from the headlines of my life, I say this: "Go show me my ex who faked his death."

Wait.

Shit.

Hold on.

Do I have an ex who's faked his death to get out of seeing me?

Actually, I'd rather not know.

Point is, I should be better at whizzing through all this heartache stuff and getting to the other side, since I had to fix those twenty imaginary hearts and architect all their happy endings.

Instead, I'm still in a funk. Partly because someone is staring at me at this coffee shop in Chelsea, and it's not my friend Hazel across the table. The gawker stands next to the counter, a college-age guy with electric-blue hair, a nose ring, and an OMG expression. Lifting his phone, he whispers to a girl next to him in goth gear, whose jaw then drops to the floor.

Turns out, I'm actually the circus sideshow.

I wave. "Yup. It's me. I'm the one you're thinking of. *Trish's Morning News Show*," I say, and if I could hunker down and write at home, I would. But I'm a coffee shop writer, as Flynn so thoughtfully pointed out, so I'm here.

The guy's smile ripens, like he can't believe his luck. Stepping closer, he clears his throat. "We're on Team TJ. Flynn is such a fame monger," he says, raising a fist in solidarity. "We boycotted his chicken café."

"And we left one-star reviews for it on Yelp," the girl adds.

"Work it," Hazel chimes in.

Then, the strangers snap a pic of me. I manage a small smile.

When they walk back to the counter, I slump in my seat, plant my face on the wood table. *Portrait of Modern Dating Carnage*—that's what they'll call this photo if anyone else snaps the shot of me while walking past Big Cup Coffee on Thirteenth Street.

A soft hand pats my hair. "The number of sightings is way down," Hazel says.

Right after the breakup video went viral, people recognized me every day—as I got on the subway, went to the gym, grabbed a coffee. Now, more than a month later, it's down to a couple times a week. The Internet moved on to fresh clickbait—a former child star turned out to be a secret cult leader, a woman found a turtle in a hamburger shop and adopted it. Named it *Lunch*.

"Yay, me," I tell Hazel. I'm nearly yesterday's news. I only need to ride this spotted-in-the-wild phase a little longer.

My friend strokes my hair. "You okay?"

"Fantastic. Never been better."

"Ah, let me get out my decoder ring and translate that."

That piques my interest, and I lift my face an inch. "I want to see this ring."

The redhead across from me taps her temple. "I store it up here." She shifts into a coolly robotic voice. "Target acquired is one TJ Hardman. Defeated, beleaguered wordsmith who hasn't written a single word all day."

Hazel shuts her laptop then clicks the screen closed on mine, a satisfied glint in her eyes.

"I didn't save what I was working on," I protest as I sit up.

"TJ," she says pointedly. "You weren't working."

Fine, fine. Why does she have to be so right? "I wrote a Twitter post."

"I know. I saw. It said *Coffee is life*. We need to jump-start you, stat."

I stare through the window at the New Yorkers streaming by after work while the sun dips low on the horizon. "Why am I such a mess? I don't get it. I don't even miss Flynn."

Turns out it's super-easy to get over someone when he jerks the rug out from under you in front of, oh, say, everyone in the world.

Everyone as in . . . Jude?

My stomach plummets as I ask myself that question yet again. Trish's show is the most popular in morning news, and the video has been viewed online more than five million times.

Is one of those viewers a guy in London with a smile that flipped my heart? With eyes that saw through me. A guy who's visited my thoughts more than I'd care to admit to anyone but a barista, cab driver, or airline rep I've never met before?

Fine, Hazel knows.

But she worked out for herself that I was not pining —but not *not* pining—for a man abroad. When I confessed the details, it was cathartic. Especially when I confided how I was tempted to reach out to Jude a few years ago.

I'd been watching *Our Secret Courtship*—had seen every episode featuring his recurring character. But when he stopped appearing and another guy took over the role, I figured that wasn't the time to DM him with a: *Hey, what's up, guy who got away? Want a visitor?*

A deal's a deal, and our terms were very specific—*when we'd made it*. Something happened in Jude's career. I don't know what. He went quiet, so I didn't reach out, knowing that wasn't what he'd have wanted.

One day, more than a year ago, Hazel mentioned him. Said he was back at it, snagging parts in plays off West End, in more commercials, and then in a popular British TV show. He was making things happen again, but I was seeing someone, so I saved the Jude update for a rainy day.

Now? Sure, I want to look him up once more, as per our deal. I *am* very, very single after all. But what if I put his name into Google and find pictures of him traipsing all over London with some other man?

A guy like Jude won't be single for long, as Helen once told me.

I focus my attention on my *work wife*. Hazel and I write together most days, working on our respective books but helping each other plot when we get stuck and stalking hot models on Insta for cover pics. My job doesn't suck. "If you were writing this story of a private guy who got dumped in the most public way, what would you do to jump-start him?"

She hums thoughtfully, taps her chin. "His favorite things. I'd take him to play pinball, to see a cool new band, and to go thrifting—especially since I have a date this weekend and I need a new dress."

"So, my funk works for you too," I tease.

"And so does the cure. But first, I'd arrange a happy-hour intervention. Gimme ten minutes," she says, then whips out her phone.

How sad is it that an intervention is the first thing that's sounded fun in many days?

* * *

If I've learned anything from writing both gay and straight romance, it's that no matter the orientation, a night out with friends is like a necessary booster shot. It helps the vaccine work. I've taken my I-won't-date-assholes-ever-again medicine in the form of that viral video.

This *intervention* will protect me for the long haul.

When Hazel scurries me into Gin Joint in Chelsea an hour later, she points to a table. Nolan and his brother, Jason, are in town, waiting with beers and an old-fashioned. Hazel says she's going to freshen up in the ladies' room.

I join the guys, and Nolan slides the cocktail to me. "Figured you'd need this."

"Real friends know your drink order," I say, lifting the glass and knocking some back.

"And they also know what you need," Nolan adds, wasting no time. "Listen, I've been thinking about your problem."

Wow. Okay. Someone's direct. "Which one?"

"The big one," Jason puts in, an intense stare in his eyes like he probably gives when he's about to take the snap on any given Sunday during football season.

"That doesn't narrow it down," I say. "Do you mean the fact that all of New York knows I'm radioactive?

That my publisher wants me to start my next book and has a hundred-thousand-print run already slated for it? That I love my privacy almost as much as I love sex and pizza, but I only have one of those three things now? Or that I wake up each day feeling like a complete and utter fool for dating the *World's Meanest Man* who makes the most average chicken in the city?"

Nolan smiles sympathetically. "All of the above."

Jason leans closer. "But I have the solution. There's a time-honored tradition when it comes to getting dumped. You need to get back on the saddle, my man."

I shudder. "I'd rather drink turpentine. No way am I dating again," I say, setting down the glass with a loud *clack*.

"Ever?" Nolan asks, arching a brow above his eyeglasses.

I consider that question. Then consider the number of views on the video. "Sounds about right."

"Dude," Jason says, calmly, "no one suggested a date. You're constantly one step ahead of everyone else, telling us how things would play out in a story. What's next in *your* story?"

"A Kevlar vest? I think I might pick one up at the armory on my way home. Protection from any post-breakup shrapnel."

Nolan cuts in. "Listen, I've been friends with you since college—more than ten years. I've always been direct with you. So, let me spell this out in no uncertain terms." He cups his hands around his mouth, making a megaphone. "You need to get your dick wet."

But dicks are usually attached to dudes who kick you in the balls on TV.

"Pass," I say.

Jason's eyes pop out. Like, they might hit the floor. "Do you like sex?"

"Obviously. It's only the greatest thing ever invented. But pizza's close, so I'll keep sublimating with that, thanks."

"Don't you have a craving for something other than a cheese and mushroom pie?" Jason asks.

With a sigh, I sink back into the chair. "Yeah, but sex is a social activity and I'm on hiatus from socializing."

"Grindr." Jason waggles his phone, showing me the app on his home screen. "You don't have to say a word to anyone."

I give him a dead-eyed stare. "I know how Grindr works, thank you."

"Or you and me could hit The Lazy Hammock—the new gay bar that opened a few blocks away," Jason offers.

"I want to go too," Nolan says, like a puppy dog. Then tilts his head. "Do you think anyone would hit on me?"

I roll my eyes. "You give off straight vibes. No offense."

"None taken. I am straight. But I still want to go and cheer you on," Nolan says.

I love my friends, truly. But this is not gonna happen. "Guys, I appreciate this. But I can't handle a pity fuck right now, and that's all it would be. I *will* get recognized at The Lazy Hammock as that romance writer who was dumped on TV. People at coffee shops recognize me. Dudes on the subway check me out. But not for me—because they hate what Flynn did to me. Let me show you." I whip out my phone and click on my Instagram DMs. "*I don't kiss and tell either. So, if you let me kiss your dick, I'll keep it a secret.*"

Jason laughs, but I think he's embarrassed for the sender.

"Or how about the guy at the gym who, while I was on the treadmill, said, 'Fuck Flynn. Fuck me instead'?"

Nolan reaches across the table to pat my shoulder sympathetically. "You win. That *does* suck."

"I'm going to stay off the radar for a little while longer," I say as Hazel returns and flops into the seat next to me.

"Any luck?" she asks our friends.

"We tried valiantly," Jason says. "But no dice."

"Your efforts to get me laid are noted. And they do not go unappreciated," I say. "But listen, why don't we all play pinball and get pizza and enjoy the hell out of the McKay brothers being in town? How about that? Let's just have a Friends in New York weekend."

Hazel twirls a strand of red hair. "Can we still please go shopping for my date tomorrow?"

"Yes, take me thrifting, Hazel," I tell my friend, and I vow that will be the start of me moving the fuck on from the chicken guy.

Then, I order a cheese and mushroom pizza for dinner.

* * *

The next afternoon, I meet Hazel at a consignment shop in the Village. Our good friend Jo is there too, and the ladies grab dresses so fast I can't see what they picked.

"I need to know if this makes my butt look good, great, or super-hot," Hazel says, rushing into the dressing room.

A minute later, she steps out, modeling a Pepto-Bismol pink dress with lime-green polka dots.

Is she for real? I look to Jo for a clue. Her blue eyes say *what the hell,* but aloud she says, "Your butt looks good." Jo always was the nice one.

Fuck diplomacy. "Hazel, your ass looks great. But that dress needs to go unless you're planning to peddle hand jobs on the street corners of Candyland," I say.

Hazel marches over to me, slams her hands on my pecs. "I was right!"

"About the dress?" I ask, confused.

"About your need to thrift. Your sarcasm is, like, ten times stronger than it was yesterday."

"Maybe TJ's starting to get his groove back," Jo says suggestively.

"See? Doing your favorite things is like giving you an injection," Hazel says. "Maybe you need other injections too?"

Ugh. Not again. Shaking my head in amusement, I point to the racks. "Focus, ladies. Hazel has a date. Pigs are flying."

My friend swats me. "You dick."

"I'll consider that a compliment," I say, reining in a private smile. I spot a dress that's perfect for her—a swath of blue that shimmers like a jewel. "Try this."

As she movie-montages through more clothes, I feel a sliver of something like *drive* again—maybe a touch of inspiration—topped off by the satisfaction in being right because she tries on half the store and then picks the sapphire-blue dress.

I go next, combing through short-sleeve shirts until Jo grabs my arm and thrusts a shirt at me. It's light blue with pinprick illustrations of yellow rubber ducks.

The design shoots me back in time to the night I shopped for shower curtains with Jude.

This shower curtain is the opposite of what you'd think two young blokes would have in their flat.

His voice feels as close as yesterday. What would it be like to hear him again next to me? To cash in on that promise we made on the bridge?

If I'm being analytical, I'd say I've met all the conditions of that promise. Seven years later is definitely "down the road." I've made it as a writer. I'm absolutely single. Hell, I could go to London tomorrow. Get on a plane like that. Stay in a sweet hotel. I'm not twenty-three and broke. I'm thirty and successful, a self-made man.

Who just got dumped on TV.

I groan to myself.

Maybe now isn't the best moment to reach out to my London romance to see if he's single too.

I snap back to the present, where I'm staring at the ducks.

"It's very you," Jo whispers.

I'm not sure I'm ready to wear it, but I buy it anyway. When I hang it in my closet that night, I make a new promise to myself.

In a few more months, once the breakup stink wears off completely, I'll put on this shirt and reach out to Jude.

* * *

If you want to have killer arms, you keep lifting weights.

So I lather, rinse, repeat for the next several days.

I play pinball with my friend Easton and help him prep for one of his epic matchmaking parties.

I scope out new restaurants with Nolan for his food show.

And I work out with Jason before he returns to California for the football pre-season.

At the gym, we finish a set on the bench press, and Jason takes a swig from his water bottle then says, "You doing okay, man? I know it's not easy when you have to deal with romance shit in public."

"It's not. But I'll be fine. Especially since my agent emailed this morning to say my publisher's putting out feelers, trying to land a celebrity narrator to do my next title and rerecord this one in audio. They want Christian Laird." I shrug. The chances of landing an A-lister are slim to nil, but a guy can hope.

"Sweet. I loved his last flick. That dude is funny and hot."

"And gay," I add.

"Yes, I'm aware," Jason deadpans.

"Anyway, it's all because my book's selling even better since the video. Like, double the sales, and it was selling great before. So, there's that," I say and offer a fist for knocking.

He knocks back. "That's a helluva silver lining."

Later that day, I go to a coffee shop to meet Hazel, and I write, and I write, and I write. It's the first day since the breakup that I've made progress, and it feels damn good.

On the table, my phone pings with a notification. I check to see if it's Mason with another yummy update on my book's sales.

But it's a DM from Instagram, and the handle is JustJude.

30

THE REUNION GUIDEBOOK

TJ

The hair on the back of my neck stands on end.

My Jude wasn't JustJude when I last checked him out on socials. Ergo, JustJude is probably some random guy. Maybe the newest pity fuck. Still, I click that profile so fast. Just in case.

And . . . holy fucking dream guy.

I gawk at the phone, then glance around the coffee shop. Can everyone tell what just happened to me? That I got a message from the guy who got away?

No one's looking at me. Everyone's in their own world, chatting about yoga and mindfulness, ROIs and business plans.

Hazel doesn't even look up. Meanwhile, my pulse spikes to the sky.

The second I click on the profile pic, my breath catches like it has every time I've watched his shows.

He's still somehow more beautiful—and I have no idea what kind of sorcery this is—than when he was twenty-three.

At thirty, he's matinee idol gorgeous, with any trace of early twenties innocence all gone. He's matured in the best of ways. His blue eyes are more smoldering. His lips are more biteable.

Most of all, his charisma is rocket-fueled. Wow. He's sooo . . .

Wait.

I bet this is just a fan account. Yup. That has to be it.

But when I scan the info, it's blue-check verified. Holy shit. This is the one and only Jude Graham, who's no longer Graham.

A smile spreads to the edges of the city as I read his new stage name. A quick search tells me he changed his name a couple of years ago, and he goes by Jude Fox now, but the handle is what gets me.

Could this really be an homage to the day we met? *If I'd told you I was Jude the Third, I doubt you'd have come looking for . . . all the Wildes. Besides, I'm just Jude.*

Oh, but he was never *just* anything. He was the only guy who ever made me this light-headed. This . . . *happy*. He was the only one who never hurt.

I scroll to his feed and a pic of him on stage in a play. He's laughing, looking like sunshine and sex and every queer man's wet dream. The next image is from *Broadway World*, a close-up of a news tidbit from a few weeks ago. *The West End production of* Pillow Talk *is traveling to Los Angeles to open at the Mark Taper Forum for a month-long run. Buzz swirls around the play and its star, Jude Fox.*

Chills.

I have chills.

Not only did he debut on the West End at last, as I believed he would, but the show is coming to America. Mark Taper is big-time in the theater world. I knew he'd make it.

I click on another shot. He's on set in *Afternoon Delight*, a British TV dramedy, the one Hazel mentioned. Looks like he's had a recurring role for the last few seasons. "As the show's heartthrob," IMDb informs me. No shit, IMDb. As I check out a few more pics, my skin tingles everywhere.

I'm floating outside my body, watching this moment play out for some other dude as my finger hovers over the DM link.

He's probably just saying hi. I'm guessing he saw the video and is offering a pat on the back. That sounds like him. Jude never laughed when I told him the story of my name. He didn't laugh when he read those chapters of my trunk novel. And he didn't laugh when I shared all my dreams.

This is merely a friendly check-in. That is all.

I scrub a hand across my jaw. Take a breath. Swallow down my hope, then open his DM.

Hey roomie,

It's been a while, hasn't it?

Seven years, but the years have been good to you.
As luck would have it, I'm wrapping up a play in LA, and I'm

going to stick around for a couple days to take a few meetings. I know you're in New York and I'm all the way across the country, but LA is closer than an ocean.

Maybe I'm crazy for reaching out to you after all this time, but I'm positive we're both single, and that seems as good a reason as any to extend you an invitation to the other side of the country. Are you free at the end of the month?

As Jack Worthing said, when asked what brings him to the country: "Oh, pleasure, pleasure! What else should bring one anywhere?"

Pleasure indeed.

Jude

For once, I don't analyze. I don't break it down in my head. I don't do a single thing except buy a ticket to Los Angeles for next weekend.

* * *

There's a difference between a pity fuck from a stranger and an offer from the guy you had it bad for once upon a time.

The difference is *everything.*

I count down the hours till I leave. I keep busy in every possible way. I pop into my favorite bookstore, buy a book for Jude, pack it, then unpack it. I'll wait and see what the vibe is before I give him a gift. After a week has passed since the infamous DM, I head to JFK on a Saturday afternoon and send my suitcase through security.

On the other side of the turnstile, the security agent pulls my bag aside. A sturdy woman with a long braid unzips the toiletry kit as she tosses me a stern look, one that says she takes her job seriously. I cross my fingers she doesn't give a fuck where, when, or how my laundry was hung up to dry for the masses to see. Nope, all she seems to care about are the rules of size and liquid, since she's fondling my ACURE shampoo and reading the bottle. "Ooh, I like this brand," she says.

"It's cruelty-free," I say.

"Cool. I'm vegan," she says, then picks up a travel-size container of lube, gives it a curious once-over.

"And that's cruelty-free too," I add.

She blinks, her lips parting in question.

"In fact, it's cruelty-free in all the ways, if you know what I mean," I add.

She's quiet, and I watch as her brown eyes process the full meaning. I just smile when she gets it.

"Umm. Have fun," she says awkwardly.

"Oh, I will. I definitely will," I say.

This guy is getting his groove back.

* * *

But the plane is not.

Seven hours later, I am still not in Los Angeles. We're flying over Who the Fuck Knows Where. Someplace not close to California, and I am not anywhere near on time.

At this rate, I won't be at my hotel till after midnight.

Eventually, the plane touches down around ten, when it was supposed to land at eight.

When the wheels touch the tarmac, the frustration that's buzzed through my body dissipates. This is real. I'll see Jude in mere hours.

But since we're not sharing a hotel, will he still be in the mood to meet up tonight after his performance? He might be done for the day. When I text him as we taxi, I keep it thoroughly casual since I don't want to presume.

Plane just landed two hours late. Gonna catch a Lyft to the hotel. See you in the morning, I presume . . .?

When I walk off the plane a few minutes later, there's a message.

You'll do nothing of the sort. I am a night owl, and if I get my sexy ass to your hotel, I presume you'll be one too.

That answers one question—Jude texts just the same way he did seven years ago. With so much flirty charm.

Luck is on my side when I score a Lyft in five minutes, sliding into the backseat. The driver is chatty, asking me what I'm doing in LA as he turns down Check Your Ego, streaming through his speakers.

"Seeing someone for the weekend. He's performing in a play. Closing night is tomorrow," I say, and I don't try to be casual. I'm legit thrilled to see Jude on stage. "I have front-row seats."

"That's awesome. You sound stoked," he says.

I smile as I stare out the window. "I am." I'm beyond stoked, and I don't want to scare off Jude by telling him that his invitation to meet up and then see his play is kind of like a fantasy.

And it feels too good to be true. So good that I need to settle down. I gesture to the radio. "Love this band."

"Me too. Saw them the other week at Whisky a Go Go and they killed it."

"No kidding? That's a great club."

We talk some more about the Los Angeles music scene, and not once does he ask if I'm the guy who was dumped on TV. The front desk clerk doesn't do a double take when I check into the hotel an hour later. No one stares at me, and it's awesome.

New coast, new city, and I feel like a new man.

After I head into my room, I shower like the wind, get dressed at the speed of sound, then head downstairs to meet the guy who looked me up seven years later.

Nerves fly through me as I try to picture the scene. What to say. How to act.

I want to put on my best face for Jude. No way do I want to be the guy in a funk in a coffee shop.

I want to be the guy who's on the other side. Someone who's witty, clever, confident. The guy who helps his work wife find the dress of her dreams. The dude who entertains a security agent. The man who chats with a Lyft driver about new tunes.

That's a start, but is it enough?

Pretty sure there's no guidebook for how to act when you see the guy who got away.

Except, maybe there is.

Maybe I've been writing the guidebook over the last several years, for all intents and purposes.

As I push the stairwell door open and head to the

lobby bar, I ask myself who I want to be tonight when I see Jude in a couple minutes.

Easy.

I'm gonna play this reunion like I'm one of the heroes in my books.

31

ALL THE WORLD'S A STAGE

Jude

I've always believed in luck.

Signs, even.

Helen coming to see my play was one of those signs.

Almost like the universe said, "All right, you served your time. Learned your two-year lesson. Here's your reward. The man from your past."

But one big question nags at me—will TJ like who I am now? Years ago, we connected because we were both questing. But we aren't in the same boat anymore. He's a big-deal bestselling author, and I've yet to earn a starring role in a film or be cast as a lead on a TV show. I don't want him to be disappointed in me.

Maybe for tonight, it's best if he sees me as the guy he fell for so many years ago. I've never forgotten his private words: *He's the swooniest man I've ever known . . .*

Clearly, I'll have to be so damn charming, he'll be blown away by how worthy I am.

The scene will open like this. I'll wait at the bar. I'll order us both drinks. I'll have a witty word at the ready.

As I near the glass doors of the hotel, I practice possible opening lines.

My shower still needs fixing. Know a handyman who can help?

Is there a meeting this weekend of The Oscar Wilde Society of Often and Well?

Hello, Great Dick.

Trouble is, they all sound like I'm trying too hard.

I'll go for simple instead. *Hey there. Thanks for coming. You look incredible.*

There. That's settled.

But once I head into the lobby bar, his dark eyes lock on me and the power of the past throws me off. All my instincts say to wrap him in a warm embrace and demand he enthrall me with every detail from his life over the last seven years.

As TJ strides over and I get a good, long look at the man I once lived with, my mind pings with hope, and my body lights up with possibility. My grin might be too big, and I kind of don't care, especially when he wraps one strong arm around me, then pulls me close, his beard whisking against my cheek. "You were great in *The Artificial Girlfriend*. I've been wanting to tell you for almost seven years, Jude."

That's his opening line? Talk about knowing the way straight to my heart. I want to say *Thank you, I'm so fucking happy you saw it, and I was dying to reach out to you and ask you a million things.*

But I keep my cool since I know something too—the path to his writer's brain. "And you were right about

Murder on the Orient Express. I've read it twice," I say, since that feels like a fair trade. Starting where we left off in London with things we shared.

He separates his chest from mine but doesn't let go of my arm. His lips twitch in a grin. "So you read it again, even though you knew who did it?"

"Exactly. As someone once told me, *With every read, there's something to discover about how to tell a story*," I say, though that's not why I re-read that mystery. I read it again because I was missing him. The second time around, the story made me feel connected to him across an ocean. Every night, I puzzled over what details delighted him the most.

"I'm really glad you read it, Jude." He chuckles softly, the gold flecks in his dreamy brown eyes flickering. "Jude Fox is the perfect stage name. I'm just jealous that I didn't get to help pick it. It's so good, I almost wish I could steal it for a hero in one of my books."

"Oh? You haven't written about the big-cocked Jude yet?" I ask playfully, though I know the answer, and it's a no.

He shrugs, all inviting and flirty. "Maybe someday," he says.

I like the sound of that someday. Better me than that twat of an ex who didn't deserve to be immortalized on a bathroom wall. Fuck Flynn and his chicken.

"Well, let's start with The Duck's Nipple then. Did you ever get to use that?" I ask, though I know that answer too. It's a pub the hero and his friends frequent in his third book. But I don't want to let on yet that I've read most of his books. Don't want to look too eager to impress.

"I did. It's in *The Size Principle*," he says.

"Then you could write off all those beers we had long ago," I tease. "Must have made the whole trip to London worthwhile."

"Yes, that's what made it worthwhile. The tax benefits," he deadpans, then gestures to the bar. "Beer, champagne, Negroni?"

I tilt my head to study him since that's quite specific. "Those are all my favorite drinks, but we only ever drank beer."

His smile is full of satisfaction. "So, what'll it be, *Just Jude*?"

"Well, *Troy Jett*, I'll have a champagne."

"Then I will too," he says, and that kicks up a sense of déjà vu, like I've heard him say that before, but maybe it's just the déjà vu of him and the nickname game.

After he orders the drinks, the bartender pours quickly, then hands him two glasses.

"I reserved the table in the corner," TJ says.

I follow as he heads for a small, curved booth in a private spot. "So, how did you pick those three drinks? Did you read my diary?"

"I like research," he says, drily.

"You always did. You liked to go around London, researching places. Did you research a certain person and his favorite drinks?" I ask, and I'm dying to know if he's been following me.

"When you DM'd me, I scrolled through your feed, naturally," he says, and maybe he hasn't been following my career like I've followed his. Perhaps he only checked me out after I messaged him. That shouldn't bother me. Really, it shouldn't. "You posted a picture from your brother's birthday last year. A shot of you toasting *the old fucker.* Your words. In your hand was a bright red drink. When I saw the orange peel, I deduced it likely wasn't a vodka raspberry but a Negroni. Was I right?"

"You're correct."

"And of course, we always ordered beers."

We. My stupid heart likes that he remembers our times. "We did, but I don't think there's a photo of me having a champagne on my feed," I say, like I've caught him in something.

He smiles. "Sometimes you have to go out on a limb. I rolled the dice that you liked it. Good guess?"

I lift the glass, bring it to my lips. The man always loved my mouth, so I glide the rim of the glass right along my bottom lip for a second.

He breathes out hard, shuddering lightly.

"A very, very good guess," I say, then clink the glass to his. "I'll toast to writers who do their research."

TJ clinks back, his voice all warm and rumbly as he says, "To actors who act on an impulse to look someone up."

I have so many more questions for him: Now that you've conquered the book world, do you have new dreams? Does music unlock you? Does coffee make you happy? Does wandering the city thrill you? Do you still take your time before you speak like you're writing the words first in your head? Do you still know how to say just the right thing when a guy needs a supportive word? Most of all, do you still feel the connection too?

But any of those would reveal too much, and once you reveal yourself, people have a way of betraying you.

Instead, I play the catch-up game. We talk about Olivia, and I tell him about her voiceover career, how she's spending time in New York now. He tells me about his brother, who's become one of the top closers in the Major League.

"I watched the last game of the World Series," I say, and this topic feels a little more real, since he was always so proud of his brother. "Saw him strike out the Miami Ace batter in the final at-bat."

"That's so cool, the idea that you were watching it, Jude," he says, his voice rising in excitement. "Did I ever tell you I used to catch for him in the backyard when we were growing up?"

Yes! This is working. *We* are working. I feel like we're thrifting again, and it's the day he told me he's an identical twin. The day he opened up for real.

"No, you never did."

"I spent hours upon hours catching fastballs. When he signed a new contract a few years ago, I teased him that he should give me ten percent of his salary. He joked that I should give him some of my royalties since he used to listen when I read him stories."

I am ravenous. This is what I want from TJ. This side of him, when he shares his true heart. "You read him stories growing up?"

"Sometimes. When I came home from London the first time, I wrote a couple stories after we visited Buckingham Palace. One was about the queen's late-night antics, plotting heists as she ate Cap'n Crunch. I read him that one. Others I didn't read to him, like the one where the prince was having an affair with one of the palace guards in the library."

I laugh. "The prince dallying with the guard. You were writing a forbidden romance back then."

"And a royal one too." He smiles. "I haven't done that yet. Written a royal hero."

"Do you want to?"

"Maybe I do," he says, sounding enthused, and I kind of want to talk shop all night, find out what inspires him these days.

"Then you should. But it better be hotter and dirtier than what you wrote when you were thirteen. Incidentally, I love that you had gay affairs in your stories way back when."

He gives me a curious look. "You knew I was thirteen when I wrote that?"

Did I reveal too much? That I remember so many details? Fuck, this is exhausting, playing a part with him. "You told me that you were thirteen the first time you went to London," I say plainly, since I can't dance my way around this with flirt.

He lifts his champagne, takes a drink, but I swear he's hiding his smile around the drink. Why is he doing that? Is he glad I remembered but won't let on? But when his smile disappears, I wonder if he's holding back tonight too?

Maybe we're both putting on a show. I want to be real with him, but for now, I stay on safer shores—talking about other people. "I watched the World Series with Olivia and William. He was in London then."

"He's made it big time, hasn't he? I love their new album, and I love that Lettuce Pray is all the rage," TJ says, a note of pride in his voice over the barista who made good.

Does that matter to him? Is he looking for a man who's his equal in success? "Do you keep in touch with him?" I ask, keeping it light, though I don't feel light at all.

He doesn't say anything at first, just levels me with his deep brown gaze. Studies my eyes. The gears are turning in his head as he looks at me, and I have another answer to one of my many TJ questions—he still writes in his head before he speaks.

"We text from time to time. William's a *friend,* Jude," TJ says, emphasizing that last word like he wants to impress this key detail on me. "He's only a friend."

And I've gathered all the necessary intel. TJ's still into me. And I'm so fucking into him. So much that I want to get to his room, unlock him with touch, and break down his walls.

"Good," I say, and it feels like the most honest thing I've told TJ all night. "That's really good."

He runs his finger along the base of his glass, looking at me the whole time, his gaze darkening. "Jude?"

Hope rises in me, as well as desire. "Yes?"

"I don't want to talk about William," he says, and he sounds just like he did that night in London when it rained hard and he kissed me on the street in the storm.

I seize the chance, reach for his hand on the table, cover it with mine, then ask him a leading question. "What do you want to talk about?"

32

THE GOOD TIMES ZONE

TJ

It's hard to think when Jude touches me, and I'm pretty sure he just asked me a question.

What do I want to talk about? I want both to talk and to stop all this talking. I want to rip off this mask and keep wearing it too.

I want to say *You make me feel so good and I can't even explain it. I can't even rationalize it. Except, I picked champagne because that's how I feel every time I'm with you.*

Trouble is, I don't know what Jude wants from me beyond his text earlier tonight—that he wants to get laid. I don't truly know if he wants me the same way I want him.

But the last person in the world I want to experience an ounce of rejection with is Jude since he's never hurt me, and I like it this way. We only ever make each other feel good.

That's the zone I want to stay in. The *good-times* zone.

I keep things firmly centered on him when I glance at his empty champagne glass, then answer his question at last. "You. I want to talk about you. Do you want another drink?"

"Do you think I want another drink?" he counters.

I look at his hand on mine, and it's proof. "No. I don't think you do."

"A drink isn't what I came for, TJ." He slides the pad of his thumb slowly, ever so slowly, between my thumb and forefinger. This should not be so erotic, but the burn in his eyes and the ownership in his touch heats me up.

I turn my hand over, curl my fingers through his, cataloging this moment, how it feels to touch him again. It feels incredible. "I didn't come for a drink either. Want to get out of here?"

His smile is slow and dirty. "I thought you'd never ask."

The hotel room is very Santa Monica. An orange wall. A teal-blue bedspread. A glass brick wall separating the bathroom from the rest.

But it's too quiet, and that's no good for setting the mood. I borrow a move from Hudson, the hero in *Mister Benefits,* who always had a playlist before sex.

"Let me put on some tunes." I hit the playlist I made an hour ago, then set my phone on the desk. Like one of my heroes, I grab the collar of Jude's shirt as a sexy number plays, but I don't make a move yet to kiss him.

I want to take my time.

Savor every single second of the anticipation.

Let the years melt away in our gazes then drive him wild with my lips, and my—

Thump!

With a quickness I didn't see coming, Jude's grabbed my shoulders and slammed me against the wall. His hands spear into my hair, and he seals those lush lips to mine.

Yessss.

I just . . .

Wow . . .

His lips are feisty, and he kisses like he talks, playful and clever, darting his tongue into my mouth then tugging on my bottom lip—turning the tables on me with a kiss that makes my body feel like warm honey.

Everything in me just . . . glows.

I bathe in endorphins, splash around in the best feel-good drug anywhere.

Jude.

His fearless kisses are dizzying. His touch turns me inside out, from his hands in my hair to his tongue, teasing and toying and making me groan with desire. Making me forget how I planned to seduce him.

My heart hammers painfully from the utter rightness of our kiss. This is happening. The guy who got away is kissing me madly. He doesn't even stop kissing to toe off his shoes. I kick mine off as I bite his bottom lip. He grabs my shirt and walks backward, keeping me in his grip as he regards me wickedly.

Holy fucking yes.

Jude is worth every sighting, every coffee shop photo, every annoying comment on Twitter.

When he pulls me onto the bed, it still feels like a dream, an escape into a world where nothing can go wrong. He falls back on the mattress with a grin, an invitation for me to climb on top of him. Bracing myself on my palms, I stare down at the face that can charm millions.

But the look in his eyes is for one person only. *Me.*

And I have to keep my cool. Be the hero of my own story. "Want to know why I ordered champagne?"

He bites the corner of his lips, and I shudder. Already, he's got me by the balls. "Because you wanted to know how it tastes on my lips," he whispers.

I blink. Swallow. Realize I didn't even get to deliver the line because he saw right through me. He knew what was coming.

"Am I right, TJ?" he asks, running his tongue along his teeth.

"You're right." I nip his mouth. "And you're doing that thing where you bite your lip. You love to toy with me. You always did."

"I do—because getting you worked up is such a turn-on."

"Everything about you is a turn-on," I blurt. There's nothing seductive in my voice now. Nothing sexy as I give up the plain truth.

He grabs my face and consumes my lips. Maybe I don't need to play tonight like it's a scene. The truth seems to spur him on.

We kiss harder, deeper, and with so much passion.

Maybe I shouldn't be surprised at how natural this feels with him. But I am. Every touch is so real. Every touch reminds me of what I've been missing over the years—*this connection*. I've only ever had it with him.

As we trade kisses, my head feels lighter, my mind freer. The kiss downshifts as we take our time, our bodies rubbing together, my cock grinding against his through all these damn clothes.

Too many layers.

As we wrench apart, I gaze at my once and again English lover, then I groan as I drop my mouth to his collarbone. We come back together like we did in our flat in London. Scraping my beard over his skin, I whisper, "You feel so good. Want to get you naked, baby. Want to feel you against me."

Jude's hand snakes between us as he works open the button on my jeans. "Let me give you what you came for."

You. I came for you.

But that's not entirely true.

I'm here to feel good again for me. He's the one person who can give me that. Jude and I, we have no hurt. We have no pain between us. We never split up; we never broke each other's hearts. Distance ripped us apart, but never words, never deeds.

He can only be good to me. And I can be great to him.

Grabbing his waistband, I yank him up with me. Then I get busy getting busy, unbuttoning my shirt, jerking his off.

"Look at you," I groan when I stare at his chest. His pecs are smooth, his muscles trim and lean. He's toned for the camera, but not action-hero level, and that suits me just fine.

"Like what you see?" Jude sounds vulnerable, as if he truly needs my heartfelt yes. His tone reaches deep into my heart.

"I do. You're the sexiest man I've ever known. Seen. Met." He seems to bask in the compliment, to light up.

"Same. Same with you," he murmurs, and I doubt that's true, but I don't care because he's here, turning his spotlight on me.

In no time, our jeans are off, then I push down his boxer briefs, and his cock greets me.

My mouth waters.

It's borderline embarrassing how much I want him. Maybe even a little crazy how attracted I am to this man. But then, I always have been, from the second I met him.

Jude stares at my hard-on. "Get. Your. Boxers. Off."

I hook my thumbs into my boxer briefs and try to seduce him with a striptease like a guy in total control would. But once my clothes are off, I can't maintain anything but this pure, true lust. I can't pretend to be one of my heroes for a second longer.

I can only be me, the guy who wants Jude. The guy who needs Jude. When he returns to the duvet, I crawl over him, straddling him. But he shakes his head. "Get on your back. Now."

Oh, hello. Commanding Jude is in the house.

With a smile and seven years' worth of anticipation, I do as he requested. He settles between my legs, pushing my thighs apart. My breath comes in harsh pants, and I don't even have time to think before his mouth is on me.

"*Fuck yes.*" He kisses my dick, and it's pure indulgence. It's better than any scene I've ever written.

I ache everywhere. *More, more.* I just want more, and he gives it to me, drawing me in, moaning and murmuring against my shaft.

His mouth is heaven, and I don't want to leave. I slide one hand into his hair. The other coasts between his shoulder blades, pushing him deeper onto me. When he swallows my cock, I tremble from head to toe.

I can't hold back. "Yes, yes, God, yes," I groan.

Jude hums around my cock, his eyes locking with mine, looking so fucking filthy and satisfied, like this is all he wanted tonight.

For a few mind-bending minutes, he sucks and licks, and I am lost in the sensations. But when my balls tighten, I stop him, gently tugging him off.

"Together. I want to come together," I say, and it's the most honest thing I've said to him tonight.

If one weekend is all I get, I want to be close to him in the same way he's close to me. He pops off, climbs up me, then drags his hand along his cock, squeezing out a drop. When he slides his thumb into my mouth, I unleash a carnal groan, then I crush my lips to his, tasting me on him, tasting him, the flavors of us colliding into a cocktail of lust.

I flip him over.

That's how he likes it. Wrapping my arms around his shoulders, I clasp him hard, so we're chest to chest, cock to cock. Electricity shoots down my spine. He thrusts his hips against me and our dicks rub together. Sex doesn't always have to be one of us inside the other. This drove him wild, made him come harder than other ways. And so, I love it too, and I surrender to the feel of our bodies reunited.

There's so much I'm dying to say. So many sentences forming in my head. *This is soooo good. We could be so good together.*

I can't give my whole heart away, but we've always communicated well in bed. I can give that much. Open that far. "Can we fuck later? Right now, I want to finish like this," I say, and it feels like serving him a piece of my soul.

Jude shudders, grabs my face. "You know the answer," he says.

I reach for the lube I left on the nightstand, drizzle some into my palm. I rise on my knees, push his legs open, and grip his dick.

The second I touch him, he arches into my hand. "Yesssss," he moans, thrusting into my fist.

He's so sensual, so easy in his body. The way he gives in to pleasure is a thrill to experience. Jude turns his face to the side, bites his lip, and breathes out hard. He stays like that for a minute as I stroke him, savoring the feel of him in my hand again.

Then he pushes up on his elbows. "Get back on me," he rasps, a sexy order.

I do as I'm told, and it feels so good as we grind and rub. But soon, lust crackles down my spine, my body warning me it's go time.

I get a hand between us, reach for our dicks. Grasp, stroke, jerk.

He shakes his head. "My turn. I want to finish us off."

Jude swats my hand away, then works us together, his slick hand jerking us in tandem. Lust coils low in my stomach, a tight, hot knot. It gathers speed and intensity till my legs shake.

His hand flies between us. I am a ticking time bomb, and I'm going to detonate any second.

"TJ," he growls. "I fucking want you so much."

That's it. That is all.

His words launch me into blissful oblivion, and I shoot all over his golden skin, groaning savagely, the world blinking off.

He's right there with me, coming hard too.

When he lets go, I collapse onto him, our orgasms smearing together on our chests. All the evidence that past Jude and present Jude are here with me.

And maybe, just maybe, there's a new future with Jude too.

It starts tonight, as we stay together in bed.

Only, in the morning, he's on his phone, his eyes glued to the page.

What is he reading so intensely?

A glance at the screen gives me the answer.

He's figured me out.

33

JUST CALL ME DETECTIVE

Jude

As the sun rises, I jolt awake.

His books.

Holy fuck. That's what he's doing. He's playing his heroes. Last night, I had a feeling he was putting on a show for me every now and then. Certain phrases tickled my brain.

Well, two can research, TJ.

I confirmed he's been giving me lines with a quick scan of his books on my e-reader. As he sleeps next to me, I hunt through his stories. No wonder I had déjà vu. Last night, he played Hudson in *Mister Benefits* with a touch of Tanner from *The Size Principle.* I read a few reviews of those titles—they're considered his coolest, most alpha heroes.

I shake my head, but I'm not annoyed, per se. I'm damn curious *why* he'd need to do that.

A few minutes later, TJ stretches, yawns, then opens his eyes. I don't think before I speak. I dive right in. "Have you heard this scene from *Mister Benefits*?" I clear my throat and read from his novel. *"I had a feeling you'd want champagne, so I ordered it for you."*

TJ's eyes go wide.

I jump ahead to the next spot I bookmarked. *"Why did I get you champagne? Because I want to know how it tastes on your lips."*

TJ swallows, then mutters *shit* under his breath.

"Hold on, stud. I've got one more. Ahem. *Let me put on some tunes.* Then Hudson plays a moody, sexy number."

He pushes up in bed, holds up a finger. "In my defense, that's not a unique move during sex. A lot of people play music when it's business time," he says.

I roll my eyes. "Fine. That's true, but what the fuck, TJ?"

He sits, drags a hand down his face, sighing heavily. "My heroes also always brush their teeth first thing in the morning since they hate morning breath as much as I do. So, can I please do that first?"

I laugh. "Funny, but I knew that too. That you hate morning breath." I flash my pearly whites. "I brushed mine already."

He gives a sheepish grin. "You remembered."

Last night, I barely wanted to admit how much I remember. Now that I've learned he was secretly trying to impress me, I don't mind admitting the truth I didn't speak last night. "I remember a lot of things, TJ."

He licks his lips. "Me too."

Then, he swings out of bed, pads to the bathroom. I

watch him go, admiring the curves of his strong ass. I do enjoy his devotion to the gym. A few minutes later, he returns to bed, flops down. "So, you busted me, Jude."

I shift to my side, prop my head in my hand. "You're not even going to protest? Try to deny it? Dance around it?"

He shrugs. "First off, I'm not a good dancer. Second, what's the point? You figured it out."

But I didn't figure out the reason, and the only way to know is to ask. "Why did you do it?"

TJ stares at the ceiling for a few beats, breathes out hard. Then he looks at me. "Imagine how you'd feel if you made a deal on a bridge to see this guy again. This guy you don't see for seven years. Don't talk to or text for seven long years. And then boom. He reaches out, he invites you to see him, he gets you tickets for his play, and you're like *fuck yes*. And you see him again after all that time. How do you think you'd *act*?"

I don't have to imagine. I did the same thing he did, for all intents and purposes. I acted. "Touché," I say, even though his *fuck yes* makes me feel like gold.

The intensity on his face tells me this isn't easy for him, but he's doing it anyway, like when he told me about his name. I give him all my focus as he talks.

"Jude, I got off that plane, and it hit me. I was seeing *you.* And I didn't know how the hell to act with you. I just figured I'd act like a guy who knew what he was doing." He scratches his jaw, shakes his head like he's annoyed. "That sounds dumb now that I say it."

"No, it doesn't. Look, I didn't know how to act with you either," I confess, since finally, fucking finally, we're getting somewhere. We're getting to the truth. That's where I hoped the bedroom would lead us. Maybe our intimacy paved the way.

"Yeah?" he asks, with hope in his voice.

"I wasn't sure how it would be to see you," I say, but that's only the start of it. "I didn't know if we'd still vibe, so I . . ." But am I ready to tell him how I felt walking into that bar? Not good enough? No, I don't think I'll say that. "So I tried to be cool too."

With a smile, he shifts closer, runs his fingers through my hair. "Jude Fox," he says, like he has a secret. "I saw you before you came into the hotel last night."

I blink. "What do you mean? Where?"

He points to the window of his room, gesturing to the ocean beyond. "Outside the hotel. The lobby bar has a view through the glass wall by the lobby. I swear I saw you practicing lines."

It's my turn to groan. I've been completely busted now.

TJ moves in a flash, pinning me, his hands on my wrists. "Was I right? Were you putting on your big-time actor charm for me? Like you do when you think people are watching?"

"Do you think pinning me down is some kind of torture? I quite like this position."

He laughs, rocks his pelvis to mine. "Were you trying to charm me?"

I let out a soft moan as he presses harder. "Is that what I do? Charm you?"

He rolls off me, running a hand down my chest as he goes. "Yes. Do you have any idea how you come across? How captivating you are? When you smile at me, it's like the world disappears and I'm caught in your spotlight."

My body likes the sound of that, every inch of my skin warming up. My heart likes it too since it thumps harder. But still, I doubt him. Because I doubt me. "That sounds like a line."

He holds up his hands in surrender. "Trust me, that doesn't come from any of my books. It's just true. I've always felt that way around you. You have charisma, Jude. You have so much of it. It's like an overflow. You're the sun. You're the center of the world. You warm anyone who comes near you. And last night, you wanted to do that to me."

"Maybe I'm not such a good actor. Because I did want that," I admit, half wishing I wasn't so easy to read, but half glad he saw through my charade.

He pokes my chest with his finger. "You're a great actor, and I can't wait to see *Pillow Talk* tonight. But I figured out what you were doing because it's my job to read people. To understand their motivations. To look beneath the surface. And I'm pretty sure you wanted to charm me," he says, reading me like an open book. Then he spreads his hand across my pecs, stretching his fingers over my skin and gliding down my chest, over my abs. "But don't you know? You already did."

My pulse surges, and I go for it. Jumping. "Maybe I wanted to keep charming you last night."

TJ locks eyes with me. Holds my gaze. Then he asks, in measured words, "Do you? Do you want to *keep* charming me?"

There he goes again. Speaking in subtext. I know what he's asking, and I was worried yesterday because I didn't know if he'd feel the same way, or *want* with the same passion I do. Now, after a night with him, I know one truth—the years didn't erase this thing between us.

"I do want to," I say, and it's as much of an admission as I'll make.

It's not a commitment. It's an acknowledgment of the here and now.

His lips twitch in a grin. A devilishly satisfied one. "Then let's do London again. This weekend."

"London in Los Angeles?" I ask with a laugh.

"Let's be who we were. No bullshit. No trying to impress each other." He holds my gaze, asking with his eyes for me to be honest too.

"I hope you know, way back when, I was trying to impress you in London," I admit. "I totally wanted to get in your pants."

He laughs. "Dude, it drove me crazy every day how much I wanted you. But you know what I mean. Let's be ourselves. Like how we were when we went thrifting, when we went out for beer, when we went shopping for the shower curtain."

I fling a hand to my head dramatically. "The awful day I learned you hate rubber ducks," I say.

He grabs my waist, hauls me close. "Some things change over the years. Maybe I don't hate them anymore."

I arch a brow. "Do you have a rubber duck fetish now?"

TJ dips his face near mine, then drops away from my lips, dusting a kiss to my jaw. "I might." His lips travel along my chin. Then under it. Then along my neck. "I have to tell you something."

I tense, worry flashing through me. "Okay?"

His soft lips return to my neck, coasting near my ear. "You were also really good in *Our Secret Courtship*."

I flinch. "What? You watched the show?"

He pulls back, looking a little sheepish. "I watched every episode. The ones you were in, I watched maybe five times."

Who's the sun now? I'm hot everywhere. "You really did?"

He nods. "I kept hoping there'd be a scene with you and that stable guy. But then, I also *didn't* want to see a scene with you and the stable guy, if you get my meaning."

"Oh, I definitely get it. I was terrified to read your first gay romance. Terrified but secretly turned on."

"So you really read my books?" He sounds shocked, maybe a little awed. Which is odd since I just quoted him back to him.

But then, this fits the TJ I knew. The TJ who had to leave the flat when I read his chapters. He's never quite believed in himself. "Most of them. Not the most recent one."

"Good. Don't read *Top-Notch Boyfriend*," he says quickly, like he needs to cut that notion off at the knees.

"I won't," I say, since I can't stand the thought of reading something that chicken peddler inspired. "But I loved *Happy Trail*. I wish I could play a rancher getting it on with his rival. Holy fuck, those scenes at the lake were scorching."

"I seriously can't believe you read that book. Or any. I just . . . can't."

"Why are you so surprised? I just recited lines from

your books. Did you think I just found them on the Internet this morning to call you out?"

He shrugs, like he can't quite believe it. "Kind of?"

"You really thought I googled them?"

He holds up a thumb and forefinger.

"You're ridiculous. You watched my shows. Why wouldn't I read your books?"

He looks away, and I know he's weighing his words, deciding what order to put them in. He returns his gaze to me. "I just didn't let myself think you had. That's all."

I lean across the bed, grab his face. "Like I said, the lake scene was totally fucking hot. When Clint gave Nick his first taste of cock, I had to leave the park where I was reading so I didn't wank off in public. But first, I had to wait for my dick to deflate."

TJ cracks up. "That's how I felt when I thought of you and the stable guy."

"Want me to let you in on a little secret now?"

"Hell yes."

I lean closer, whisper near his cheek, "I wanted that for my *Our Secret Courtship* character too. I always imagined Victor was bisexual."

TJ's eyes sparkle as he pumps a fist. "I knew it! I could tell he liked dick. But I still liked your secret romance with the countess too. You two liked to get it on. In the drawing room, in the parlor."

"In the library, in the gardens," I add, thrilled that he remembers the details of my character's trysts. But I hope he doesn't ask what happened to me next after my character was written off. I don't want to lie about those two years that followed, but I will. I absolutely will.

"Don't forget on the piano," TJ adds, kissing my neck.

A dart of pleasure radiates in my chest, spreads through my body. "You saw that scene too? That was like eight seconds long, and at the end of my last season."

His full lips coast along my neck, on a journey toward my ear. "More than five times, Jude. I watched it over and over. It reminded me of the robot and the scientist."

I sigh, greedily taking more of his kisses, lapping up his attention. Most of all, the admission that he didn't forget me over the years. That he didn't simply say a few weeks ago *Oh cool, glad that guy reached out so I can fly across the country for a good fuck.* Instead, he followed me as I did him. He didn't lose track of me. He stayed close and connected in the only way he could.

Like I did for him.

TJ sucks on my earlobe. "But I was pissed when your character disappeared. When that other guy took over."

You have no idea how pissed I was.

But I don't want to go there, so I try to stay calm as I say, "All good things come to an end."

He pulls back, his dark eyes glimmering. "Do they though?"

We aren't talking about our work anymore. The episode review is over. The book report is through.

"They can come to other ends," I say in a low and husky voice.

His hand travels down my body, on a fast track for my cock. "Jude, come in my mouth."

Fuck talking.

"Make me come," I tell TJ, since he loves orders.

Seconds later, he's between my legs, his mouth worshipping my dick, his hands squeezing my ass. It doesn't take long till I'm moaning, groaning, spreading my thighs. Then begging him. "Put your fingers in me."

He lets go of my dick, reaches for the lube, then returns to me. There's a click, then a squeeze of the bottle. His lips wrap around my cock again. His tongue flicks along my shaft as his fingers press in.

Sensations whip through me. The dark, dizzying pressure inside. The lush intensity of his mouth. My desire for more gathers like a storm.

More contact. More him. Just . . . *more.*

My hands wrap around his head as he draws me deep. I gaze down at the sight of him, his beard brushing my thigh, his lips stretched wide, my cock filling his mouth.

All while he fucks my ass with his fingers. Adrenaline pulses everywhere inside me. And still I want more.

"Get in me," I demand.

TJ slows and lets me fall from his mouth, and when he does, I grab a condom and open it quickly. As he rolls it down his length, I get on my hands and knees.

He palms my ass, squeezes hard. "Yes. Fucking yes. Need to be in you now."

Seconds later, he lines up, and sinks inside. I catch my breath, gritting my teeth as I adjust.

Soon enough, the hint of pain abates, and it's only good.

Only lust.

Only the best sex I've ever had as I tell him what I want, when I want it, how I want it.

As I order him around while we fuck, I ask for everything I crave, and he gives it. His hand on my cock, his body covering mine, his arm wrapped like a vise around my chest.

When I demand he get me there, he does. Oh yes, he fucking does, with his fist shuttling along my length till we both come hard.

Once again.

Then, we shower, dress, and head out for breakfast. It feels like the start of a perfect day.

34

THINGS I'VE DONE

TJ

There's a lot to learn.

For instance, I never knew Jude liked kale so much. But he's actually eating it for breakfast, along with his egg-white omelet.

"I feel like you were a toast guy before," I say as I dig into eggs and potatoes.

He groans. "Do not mention that four-letter word."

"Toast is five letters, honey," I tease.

"C-A-R-B," he says as the sun streaks through his hair at the sidewalk café.

"Ah," I say, after I finish a bite. "Let me guess. You're not allowed to eat anything except kale, eggs, mangoes, and chia seeds."

He points dramatically with his fork. "Blueberries! Do not try to take my blueberries away from me. I can eat those too."

I take another bite of my eggs. "I almost feel guilty about the pizza I had in New York before I left."

He growls, his eyes narrowed. "I warned you. Carb is a dirty word. I must pretend pizza doesn't exist."

"I'm pretty good at putting my head in the sand, but there's no way I could even imagine a world without pizza," I say, as I wave my fork at him and his toned physique. "But I get it. You probably have to maintain a strict regime and whatnot."

"I do," he says, but shrugs happily. "It is what it is. I kind of did a whole reboot a couple years ago, and that was part of it."

He must mean those two years when I didn't see him in anything. "Do you mean after *Our Secret Courtship*? What happened there with your character?"

His expression shifts, a hard edge in his eyes I'm not used to seeing. Then it disappears, replaced by a breezy grin. "Creative differences," he says, like it's no big deal. "But by reboot I meant I switched agents. I'm with the Astor Agency now. And when I signed, we went over everything I needed to do to get to the next level. All the things, from kale to auditions."

"Was the other guy not cutting it? Harry, was it?"

Jude frowns. "Harry and I didn't part on the best of terms."

I don't like the sound of that. "What did he do to you, and do I need to take out a hit on him?"

He sets down his fork, sighing, then glances around. The café is bustling. At the table behind us, a woman in pink yoga pants slips a piece of ham to a chihuahua in a handbag. By the door, a pair of young moms try to get a toddler to eat eggs. Jude lowers his voice. "Look, I know you'll understand because of the whole chicken cook wanker." Normally, I don't like to be reminded of Flynn. But if Jude's gearing up to tell me something, it's probably something I want to know. Since, well, I want to know *him*. "My agent screwed this guy I was seeing. It was a whole terrible mess."

Good thing I'm not eating this second because my jaw drops. Anger courses through me. "I'll take out a double hit then. That's terrible."

"It was. But here we are, you and me, a couple of great dicks," he says, a call back to the night I told him about my name, when he then told me about his college boyfriend. This time, his words mean even more. The two of us have this second chance because we dated jackasses *and* because we're no longer dating jackasses.

"Here we are," I echo, but I don't think he wants to linger on his exes or mine, so I shift back to shop talk before I take another drink of my coffee. "The new agent? Is he or she better? I hear good things about Astor so it sounds like a good move."

"It feels like a partnership so far, so that's good. I have a film and TV agent there, Holly. And a theater one, Kenta. They're both great. And yes, I do the whole actor watch-what-you-eat thing. It's just part of Hollywood, I suppose. Which is what I want."

"To work in Hollywood?" I ask curiously.

"Yes, TJ. Of course. Hollywood's the top of our business." Jude says that like it's obvious, and I feel a little foolish for not gleaning that as soon as he said it.

"Why do you say it like I should have known? Not everyone's goal is to work in Hollywood. It's not mine," I say, especially given what my agent told me when *Top*

Notch Boyfriend shot up the charts. *Everyone from Hollywood is nice to your face, but when you turn around, you should trust no one as you smile and wave at the sharks while they swim by.*

"Look, London is great and all, but the action is here," Jude says. "I want jobs in America. Or Canada, or Georgia—wherever they're shooting."

Ah, that adds up. "So you'd move *here*?" I privately cross my fingers. If he were in Los Angeles instead of London, I could see him even more easily. Fly here on weekends. Or weekdays. My schedule is my own. I could make a go of it.

Except I'm getting ahead of myself. No idea if he wants that.

"If the opportunities allow," Jude says, thoroughly business-like.

And that's my reminder to get a grip. We haven't even been together for twenty-four hours yet. I should not get ahead of myself. He hasn't given any indication that he wants to do this, whatever this is.

Best to focus on what I know—that this man is a star. "They will. You're opening a show at Mark Taper. You opened in London. Jude, you're a big fucking deal."

"TJ, you don't have to suck up to me."

I crease my brow, confused. "What do you mean? I'm not just saying it."

"Look, you're further along than I am," he says, and it almost sounds like he's biting out the words.

"That's not true," I protest.

"Please. It totally is. You have ten bestsellers, including a huge breakout hit. You're a big fucking deal. You've done everything you said you'd do in London."

"And you had a role on TV. You did the West End. You're performing at Mark Taper," I point out, all while trying to shut down an unpleasant idea that pops into my head. Is this Flynn 2.0?

"And I'm thrilled about that. But it's not all sunshine and roses. I have a long road ahead, and a lot to accomplish. I'm not like you, already at the top."

Why the hell is he comparing us? "I'm a writer. You're an actor. We don't have to be the same."

Jude sighs, like I just don't understand. "You've had hit after hit. It's not like that for me. I don't expect you to get it."

Whoa. "But I do get it," I insist, trying to impress that on him because I don't want to go through the same thing again, not with Jude. "I understand what you're saying. I just think you need to give yourself a chance. You'll get there. You're already on the way." How does he not see this? "Your business is hard."

"I *know* it's hard, TJ," he says, his tone laced with frustration as he sets down his fork. After he drags his hand through his hair, he jerks his gaze away from me, stares down the street, his jaw ticking.

I'm quiet, giving him the time he needs, even though worry spikes in me. Are we arguing over a race he shouldn't be running between us? It's like saying *who has the bigger dick*? Really, who cares?

Except, I care deeply about how he feels. And I care intensely about what we could be. But I don't want Jude to judge me, or worse, judge himself by the metric of me. That's a recipe for romance disaster. I can see it playing out in a book. The scenes are writing themselves, marching toward a dangerous moment I've got to try to stop. "Jude," I say softly, puzzling over what to say next.

When he turns back to me, frustration is still etched in his eyes. "Look, it's a sore spot," he says, then lets out a long exhale, his expression softening slightly. "It's not your fault, though. I appreciate everything you're saying. But I'm still chasing my big break."

Even though I don't like how he's talking, I also know you need to read the room. I got lucky with *Top-Notch Boyfriend*. Yes, it's a good book. Yes, it's probably my best book. But it also came out at the right time, when gay romance started having a big moment in the publishing sun. Add in the Flynn debacle, and it shot up the list, then sent my other books back up the charts, coattails and all. But telling that to Jude won't change his desire to hit the next level. I try another tactic, since he's not Flynn. Not at all. He's the guy I want another chance with.

I reach for his hand. "Hey," I say gently. "I'm on your side. I'm rooting for you. We don't have to compete."

"You're right," he says slowly after a beat, linking our fingers. "Sorry. I was an arse."

I point at him with my free hand. "You said arse."

He laughs. Finally, he laughs. "I did it for you. I'm not annoyed with you, TJ. I get annoyed with myself sometimes. Over . . . *things* I've done," he says, but he doesn't elaborate on those things. "I didn't mean to take it out on you."

I squeeze his hand harder. "It's all good. But please know this—I do understand you. I like to think I always have."

Jude squeezes back. "You have. I was a dick to get annoyed."

I wag a finger at him. "Dick is a good four-letter word. It's not like carb." The waitress swings by with the pot of coffee, offering a refill.

I say yes, and when she leaves, Jude points to the cup. "Seconds at a café? I figured you'd turn up your nose. Have you given up your coffee snobbery?"

"Fuck no." I shake my head. "The coffee's horrid, but I like to punish myself with bad coffee."

He holds up his hands in surrender. "Nothing, nothing in the whole world, could be more you than that."

"You get me," I say.

"I do."

We both laugh, and this direction feels so much better. Still, I have one more thing to say on the prior topic. "Just know you don't have to compare yourself to me or anyone else. You're you. And comparison is the thief of joy."

"Is that from one of your books?"

"Please," I scoff. "It's from a mug or a pillow or a fucking Instagram post. But originally, it's from Teddy Roosevelt. Point is, you're going to keep chasing your dreams. You're going to land job after job. You said you have meetings while you're here, right?"

His blue eyes twinkle. "I do. Holly set up a number of them. One with a network about a show. Another with a studio. Then there's one on Friday about a possible streaming opportunity."

"Yeah?" I ask, already excited for him.

He crosses his fingers. "I don't want to get my hopes

up, but they've been talking about maybe developing a show around me, and the best part is that it's got some of *me* in it. It's a queer romance. Supposedly, they're talking to Christian Laird too. Not for the same part, though, since he's American of course. But I'd love to work with him."

I keep my mouth shut about my publisher going after the same guy. This is Jude's moment, not mine to humble brag about a slim-to-nil chance of him recording my books. "That's perfect. I'm telling you, queer romance is *the* thing."

"That's what *The Hollywood Scoop* said in an article the other week, and I say it's about time. What took Hollywood so long to figure out there's nothing better?"

I shrug, *what gives* style. "No idea, but I'm glad they did, because I love it. And it gets me hot."

Jude leans a little closer, whispers in his most seductive voice. "Tell me more about why it's so damn sexy."

"How about I show you later?" I tease, then slide a hand under the table and squeeze his thigh.

"You better show me tonight after the show."

I'm tempted to bring up something I want to do in the bedroom. But now isn't the time after that minor disagreement. I'll wait till the mood seems right. I'm patient like that. "I will, Jude Fox."

"Speaking of names, TJ Hardman, where did you come up with that perfect pen name?"

He truly doesn't know? Oh, this will be fun. This may jolt him further out of his funk. "At first, I considered TJ Cummings, but then you have to get into the whole is it c-u-m or c-o-m-e debate."

"Is this like the whole ass/arse debate we had before?"

"Oh, it's bigger, Jude. So much bigger."

"Gee, I wonder if I can figure out which one's right in your world," he deadpans, then stares. "I know the answer. I've read your books."

I snap my fingers, playing along. "Dammit."

He taps his chin. "But what I want to know is, which one is correct in *your* favorite book? That is, the dick-tionary?"

That's my Jude, giving it good in the word-play department. "If you must know, the Merriam-Webster dictionary says both spellings are correct," I say, enjoying the hell out of this answer. "And frankly, I like the way c-o-m-e looks written down better. But, let's be honest, they both feel the same on the tongue."

He murmurs his approval. "Mmm. They do. Though I might want to verify that before I leave for the theater."

"You want me to give you a good luck BJ before curtain? I'll allow it."

"Or maybe I want to give you one. Seeing as another name you could have considered is . . . Sweetcox."

Fuck, he's good. But so am I. "And if I ever need to launch a new name I could be *Phil . . . Accio*."

Jude slow claps. "You win."

From my seat at the table, I take a small bow.

The sound of wheels racing by on the sidewalk snags my attention. "Dude! Team TJ! Rock on!"

Jude jerks his gaze to the surfer guy already down the block on his skateboard. Then he levels me with an amused stare. "Does that happen a lot?"

I roll my eyes. "Less than before. But zero times would be my preference."

"Well, I've *always* been on Team TJ," he says.

"Thanks," I say, and that's as good an entrée as any to a secret I want to share. Something I wasn't sure I'd tell him but he was honest with me today, even though he was pissed. Still, he told me something that was clearly tough, something that revealed some insecurities. It's hard to make yourself vulnerable, so he deserves this intel.

"Do you remember the first night we went out?" I ask.

"The night you fell asleep at the table, you mean?"

"I did not fall asleep," I huff.

"You yawned your face off. And it slowed down our time to shag. We were going to fuck that night, and instead, I had to wait fifteen long and hard days."

"And was it worth it, Jude? All those long and hard days?"

He grumbles out a yes.

I cup my ear. "I can't hear you."

"Yes, fine, it was good. Fine, it was great. Okay, it was fucking amazing. So, what should I remember about the night we met?"

"At the bar, I wrote a note in my phone."

His eyes light up from the memory. "That's right! You did. I asked if you were taking notes on our conversation."

"Because you gave me an idea."

His eyes brighten. The memory must snap into place for him. "I said *I enjoy a hard man*. Are you fucking kidding me? That's where your pen name came from? That was the note you wrote down?"

"Yes," I say, and wow, did I just tell him something this big? I did, and it's a little scary being this open, but a little awesome too.

"I love that," he says, then sighs happily. "Did you happen to notice my handle on Instagram?"

I sure as shit did. "It's JustJude," I say.

He says nothing more. There's no need to since we both just said enough. That we matter to each other. That we've mattered for a long time.

Even though we might have had a minor argument, we can make it through.

* * *

After our late breakfast, we walk along the beach, pop into shops, and track down consignment stores where we both buy some new clothes.

It's London in Los Angeles all right, and it's a perfect day.

As the afternoon ends, we head back toward the promenade when a bus rumbles along, a poster for *Our Secret Courtship* with the new Victor on it.

I flip him the bird.

Jude laughs. "Thank you for the support. That bloke is a total twat. He took my role."

"It's a tough business," I say, hoping Jude doesn't get annoyed again.

"It is," he says, his mouth a straight line. "You just never know who has your best interests at heart."

I drape an arm around his shoulder, wanting to reassure him, even though I don't entirely know what he's dealing with. "I think I get it. I want to get it."

Jude gives me a soft smile. "I knew you'd understand," he says, and I'm thankful for that.

Very, very thankful.

When I spot a bookstore at the end of the block, that sparks an idea. Something I never did for him in London. Something I can do now.

35

DÉJÀ VU ALL OVER AGAIN

TJ

I'm not jealous of the way Jude stares at the abs on the cover. What I am is eager to get the hell out of this section of Read Between the Lines.

"I have one question for you," he says, holding up a copy of *The Size Principle*.

"Yes?"

"Did you pick the model for this cover?"

I roll my eyes. "No. The publisher did. And they're redoing it."

"Why? Do they hate abs? Men like abs. Women like abs. I'm giving up carbs for abs. How can anyone hate them?"

I shrug. "Illustrated is the thing now."

"I'm going to be blunt here. Illustrated abs aren't as sexy as real ones," he says, then sets down the book.

I seize my chance. "Can we please go to the memoirs?"

"Are you afraid someone is going to see you and ask you to sign a copy?"

That's not the issue whatsoever. I brought him here for him, not to ogle my covers nor to talk about me. "Yes, Jude. I'm afraid of random bookstore sightings," I deadpan, then I loop an arm around his waist and tug him away from the romance section toward the back of the store.

"Why don't you want to see your books? Don't tell me you're *so over it*."

I turn the question around on him. "Why do you *want* to see my books?"

He counters in a flash. "Are you excited to come to my play tonight?"

"Yes. An insane amount," I say as we reach the tell-alls.

"That's why I like looking at your books," he says, and I might float.

That's the problem. When he says those things, my heart goes crazy. I need to get it under control.

I move behind him, drop my chin on his shoulder, and nod toward the hardbacks. "I got a list of the most salacious celebrity memoirs from my friend Hazel. She said the juiciest is the Keith Richards. Have you listened to it yet?"

"Why did you get a list?"

"Answer the question, Jude."

"No, I haven't heard it."

"Good," I say, then dart out a hand and grab a copy. "I'm getting one for me."

"Selfish fucker," he says.

I laugh. "Just come with me."

"Isn't that what I did this morning?"

"And it's what you'll do tonight after the show."

"I better."

"I better too. You better. We better," I add.

"Wow. You sure can conjugate."

I crack up. Nothing, nothing at all, has ever felt like this—talking with Jude, teasing with Jude, being with Jude.

I bring him close, bite his earlobe. "You know I can, baby. We already conjugated this morning."

He leans back against me. "Speaking of dirty words, I've got something I've been meaning to show you for, oh, say, about five years."

I arch a brow in curiosity.

Jude just flicks his hand toward the register. "Buy your book, selfish fucker, then it's show and tell time."

I buy the Richards memoir for me, then when we leave the store, I grab my phone, click on an app, and send Jude a gift.

A minute later, his phone beeps.

Jude looks at the screen, then at me. "You just bought me an audiobook?"

"Well, I know you like to listen to celebrity memoirs rather than read them," I say, and my cheeks heat, like I'm revealing something personal.

Even though it's about him.

But this is personal, and he knows it. He knows, now. I asked Hazel for gift ideas for him. He knows, too, I've never bought him a gift before. This is a first.

Jude steps closer, brushes his lips to mine, and says softly, "You didn't have to get me something."

I feel woozy. "I know. I wanted to."

"Thank you," he says, then he takes my hand, and we walk along the promenade till we reach a coffee shop I can't stop staring at. Or sniffing. I lift my nose and inhale.

Jude takes the Richards book from me, then gestures to the shop. "Go. Get a coffee. And give the barista the third degree like you did with William when you met him."

I arch a brow. "Did he tell you that?"

"*Friends*. We're friends. Like you two."

Still, a tiny snake of jealousy slithers through me as I head into the shop. Not sure why. Maybe it's because William had access to Jude when I didn't. Does William even know how lucky he is? But that's a dumb thing to be jealous about. Still, as I order the drinks, I noodle on these strange feelings of envy. Except, is it envy? Maybe it's worry—the worry that the people I tell my secrets to aren't so safe after all. Maybe they'll eventually spill them to the people I keep them from.

Or maybe I'm a paranoid writer, always seeing ten thousand ways something can go wrong. Since that's what I do for my characters. Throw rocks at them, especially when things start to seem easy.

I shove the worries away.

With the cups in hand, I tip the guy at the counter, head outside, and sit with Jude, sliding the Earl Grey to him.

Jude thanks me, then grabs his phone. "And now, as I said, I have a little something for you."

My dumb heart flips before he even gives whatever it is to me. "Yeah?" I ask, probably sounding all dopey to him.

Jude moves closer. His shoulder touches mine as he shows me the screen. I freeze.

Are you kidding me?

I turn my gaze to him in slow motion, awe coasting down my spine. "You took a picture of *Yes Man* at An Open Book?"

The evidence is there on his phone, yet I can't quite believe it.

"I did," he says, sounding nervous, but happy too. "I figured you'd want to see it someday. I took it and held on to it."

I can barely catch my breath from what he's saying, and more so, what it's doing to the organ in my chest. "When did you take it?"

"When it released."

"You went in there. Took a picture of it on the shelves. And you've held on to this for five years?"

"I did. I held on to it for you," he says, his warm, rich voice reaching deep into my chest, touching me in a place only he ever has.

This can't be happening so fast. I can't let it. I don't even know what to do with *this*. My heart is out of fucking control. My emotions are spiraling. All I want is him.

I won't say that yet, so instead I tell him a story so he'll know what this gift means to me. "My brother bought a gift for me long ago. A travel journal. It meant a lot to me because he got it at that store on Cecil Court when we were thirteen. The one where—"

"Where we met again," he supplies, his eyes locked with mine.

"Yes. That one. Chance held on to it for ten years. He gave it to me when I went to London a second time," I say, and every word I share is like stripping off a layer of self-protection, letting Jude into my mind, into my most private thoughts. "It meant a lot to me because it said he knew me. I hadn't even told him I wanted to write a novel, but he knew I'd need to write down my thoughts." I take a breath, prepping to say the next thing. "I wrote in it when I was in London. About the city. About places," I say, swallowing around a knot of emotions as I start my true confession.

"You did?" Jude sounds like he's hanging on to the edge of the world.

"About people too," I add softly. "I even mentioned this guy I met."

"Did you?" he asks, like he's amazed that he inspired me.

Heat rushes over my skin. I'm caught in the haze of Jude once again. "I did."

"I hope you said nice things about him," he says, then runs his hand over my shoulder, along my neck, lighting me all the way up.

"Very nice things," I whisper.

If I say more I will tell him what I only ever admitted on paper. Deeply personal, deeply private words that I'd never want to share with anyone. "That journal meant a lot to me because Chance held on to it over the years. He waited for the right moment. He wanted it to matter. That's why I loved the gift. And now, this picture you took?"

"Yes?" That one-word question is full of the same hope I feel.

"It matters to me because you took it. You held on to it. That's why I love it. This is my new favorite thing."

And so are you, Jude Fox.

I'm so close to breathing those risky words out loud.

I do the only thing I can.

I cup his cheek, slide my hand into his soft hair, and cover up my feelings with a kiss on the sidewalk of Santa Monica.

Every kiss with Jude has been incredible. But this one might be the best yet. It's slow and lingering. It's hot and intimate. It makes me feel like the hero in my own love story.

It's also a kiss I'm sure I'll never recover from.

Because I know. I just know.

Less than twenty-four hours later, and I'm already falling in love with him all over again.

36

THE SPOTLIGHT'S ON ME

TJ

The fountains outside the Mark Taper Forum dance in the twilight. As I head to the doors, a canvas bag in hand with a gift in it, I stop to snap a photo of the theater and send it to Hazel. I'm so damn jazzed, and I need to share that with someone.

TJ: This is where I am right now.

Hazel: Are you telling me because you might die of excitement from seeing him and you wanted someone to know your whereabouts?

She's a witch. A fucking mind-reading witch.

TJ: Yes, Hazel. When I die, I'll be in a theater with seven hundred people and no one will be able to find me but you.

Hazel: I love being your person. Also, HOW THE HELL IS YOUR WEEKEND? Since this is the first I've heard from you, I assume it's been a non-stop sex fiesta of epic proportions.

I stop, park myself on a bench, and stare at her note with a stupid smile on my face. She's the only person who knows *why* I'm in Los Angeles. My other buddies just think I took off to the West Coast to see some friends.

Even though Hazel's question is the math test equivalent of two plus two, I take my time typing before I hit send on a one-word reply.

TJ: Amazing.

She writes back with an image of my reply, edited.

Hazel: I fixed your response. I added ten exclamation points!!!!!!!!!!

I laugh, writing back to her when a familiar voice booms. "Are you bloody kidding me?"

I swivel around. There's a blast from the past I didn't expect to see tonight.

The inked Brit strides across the concrete, looking every bit the rock star he's become. He's got a leather jacket slung over his shoulder, a white T-shirt stretched over his chest, motorcycle boots, and double the ink he had when he served me coffee in Piccadilly Circus.

"Well if it isn't TJ from Seattle by way of New York. Have I got a steam wand for you!"

I roll my eyes as William stops a foot away, then hauls me in for a hug. "I've missed your purges, William. How the hell are you?"

"Fantastic. I can't believe you're here."

"I can't believe *you're* here, man."

William gives me a look like I'm crazy. "I live in LA now. Course I'm here. I was touring, but I wouldn't miss this for the fucking world. I didn't know you'd be here tonight."

Well, why would you know?

Most of my closest friends in New York don't know what I'm up to. My brother doesn't know. But maybe William means Jude didn't tell him, and he'd have expected Jude to mention my whereabouts?

"I flew out last night," I say, and I'm dying to ask if Jude invited William to his play. But that feels like prying. "So here I am."

"Brilliant. The show's getting rave reviews. Our guy is doing so great, isn't he?"

Our guy? He's *our guy* now?

Settle down, jealous dragon. "He is," I say.

William drags a tattooed hand through his floppy hair—rocker hair now, then shakes his head in disbelief. "I can't believe I almost missed the chance to see him in this. I grabbed a ticket on StubHub last night when I knew I'd be back."

That answers one question I had. William bought his own ticket. I don't say Jude got me mine. But I sure as hell like that I'm the one with the star's house seat.

"So, do you have business in LA?" William continues.

My brow knits, but then I quickly rearrange my expression since I don't know if Jude wants it to be obvious that we're a thing.

Shit, are we a thing?

I'll deal with that later, but for now, I weigh possible answers to William's question, opting quickly for the easy way out. I'll omit. Besides, my agency has offices in Los Angeles. "Yeah. Agents and all, you know. So it made sense to see Jude's play too," I say.

William's green eyes twinkle. "Right. It *made sense*," he says, sketching air quotes. "You still have a massive crush on him, don't you?"

Jesus. Is it obvious? "Don't we all? He's Jude Fox, after all," I say, and *there*. Take that. I might not dance well on the dance floor, but I can tango my way around getting too personal.

"It's impossible not to have a crush on him. He's gorgeous," William says, and it sure as hell sounds like he's got a big crush. "Where are you sitting?"

"Front row."

"Bugger. You got better seats than I did, mate," he says, then glances at the canvas bag I'm holding. "Do you have flowers for him? Shit. I should get him flowers." William peers around the courtyard area, hunting for a florist, perhaps. His gaze seems to land on a black and red wooden cart, full of flowers but also chocolate. "Sweets. He loves sweets. I'll get him chocolate."

I *should* tell William Jude won't eat it. I should. But I don't.

"Cool. I'll see you later," I say, tipping my forehead to the doorway.

"Why don't we all get a drink afterward?" William suggests.

"If that's good for Jude," I say. I like William. At least, I did, and I think I still do. But I'm *not* making plans for the three of us unless Jude wants to.

We say goodbye, and William heads to the cart, while I go inside, relieved to get away from him. Which isn't how I should feel around a friend.

Once in the theater, I tighten my grip on the bag, and grab my seat in the front row.

When a cool modulated voice tells everyone to take their seats since the show's about to begin, I glance around the theater, soaking in the utter coolness of being here. As I survey the crowd, William snags his nearby chair and waves.

I nod, and a few rows behind him, a sharp-dressed man with a thick head of golden-blond hair swings his gaze around the auditorium from William to me.

The guy stops and stares at me for a few seconds. No idea what that's about. Then it hits me. He probably recognizes me from the viral video. Twice in one day. It was too good to be true that I'd remain anonymous in LA.

Three minutes later though, I don't care about

anyone else. My phone is off, my attention's on the red curtain, and the lights go down.

When they go up again, Jude walks on stage. *"Darling, have you seen my public persona? I seem to have misplaced it, and I need it to get through the Abernathys' dinner party."*

I laugh, and for the next hour, I hardly stop laughing. It's like a modern-day Noël Coward script, and every scene is a showcase of how fantastic Jude Fox is when it comes to deft, sharp stage humor.

The whole cast has me transfixed, but especially the lead. The guy I would fly across a country for again and again. The guy who makes my heart hammer. The guy I want to make mine, all mine.

When the first act ends, I stretch my legs and head to the lobby bar to grab a water. As I wait in line, someone taps my shoulder.

"Hey! Any chance you're TJ Hardman? Please say yes."

I groan privately, then fasten on a smile before I turn to face the good-looking blond dude behind me. "That's me."

He sighs in relief, even wiping his hand across his forehead. "I hoped so. I saw your video this morning. A colleague sent it to me."

Oh, joy.

"And I had to introduce myself. Couldn't miss the chance—I am one hundred percent Team TJ."

He reaches for his phone, and since I don't want to prolong this encounter, I cut to the chase. "Sure. We can take a selfie."

"I won't turn that down."

He slides in next to me, and we smile for the camera. When he slips the phone into his pocket, I'm ready to take off, but he puts a hand on my shoulder. "That's not the reason I'm interrupting your intermission," he says, his tone shifting to all business.

"Okay?"

"I started your book right after I saw the video. Holy balls. It's amazing. The romance, the humor, the angst as he falls for his best friend's brother. I'm halfway done and it's . . ." He presses his fingers to his lips in a chef's kiss.

"That's great," I say, my shoulders relaxing. At least the video's been good for one solid book sale.

"I work at Webflix. I could totally see your book being a film. A TV show. Anything," he says, then gives me his name.

Robert Walsh.

I flashback to the conversation Jude and I had in London.

Robbys are wankers.

This guy probably is. And besides, it's Hollywood. My agent's parting words on this topic were: *Hollywood will start calling, but don't believe a deal is done till the ink is dry. And even then, it'll likely be in disappearing ink.*

I do love being repped by a realist. I smile like Mason would want me to.

When Robert asks for my agent's name and says he'll be in touch, I figure nothing will come of it, even after I grab my water, then Google his name when I'm back in my seat, and learn he is indeed an executive at Webflix.

But who isn't these days? I don't even email Mason. Besides, I'm here for Jude.

I settle back in and watch the second act, where the entire cast transports me to London, the place where I was happiest. Except Los Angeles is making a damn good case to snag that top spot.

When the cast takes the curtain call together, I can't contain the biggest smile I've ever felt.

That's my guy, on stage, captivating a packed house.

After one more group bow, Jude scans the audience and quickly, very quickly, his eyes land on me. He flashes a smile that's both for the entire theater and for one guy only. And it says: *when everyone is gone, you're the one I'll leave with.*

It's the most intimately his spotlight has ever shone on me, and I don't want him to ever turn it off.

* * *

After a long line of autograph-hunters finally peters out, it's just William, Jude, and me outside his dressing room.

"So glad you could be here," Jude says to the fellow Brit. "I did not expect to see you."

"I like to surprise you," William says, then hands him a box of chocolates.

Jude grins. "You're the best. Thank you, mate."

Then William kisses Jude on the cheek. I burn a little. Okay, a lot. William steps back. "My band is playing at The Holy Cow this week. The club is ten times better than the hole-in-the-wall joint you saw me play at in London. You men should come see me. I'll get you VIP tix," he says to both of us.

I don't even have a chance to fashion a reply since

Jude's got this handled entirely. "Send me the details. You never know if it'll work out," he says and it's a perfect answer, since it's perfectly noncommittal.

William drops a kiss to my cheek and turns around. As his boots clomp on the floorboards, Jude surveys the backstage area, grabs my hand, and hauls me into his dressing room. "Love him, but I thought he'd never leave," he whispers, sounding relieved as he snicks the door shut.

"He wasn't even here that long," I say, completely forgetting whatever shards of jealousy stabbed me a minute ago. I have a selective memory with Jude. My brain clears everything away but the good stuff.

Like Jude's performance, like this chance I have to tell him what it means to me. "You were amazing. I laughed the whole time. I was completely transported. You're so real," I say, and it's everything I wanted to say when I watched *The Artificial Girlfriend, Our Secret Courtship,* and *Afternoon Delight*. "You make me believe."

"Really?"

While his question *is* a question, it's not full of doubt. It's imbued with hope.

I don't even try to lighten my answer with something cheeky like *And I'm not just saying it to get in your pants*. I keep it simple. "It's true."

"Thank you," he says, and I can feel, too, how much he wanted me to like his performance. "I have to tell you a secret now."

I tense, since secrets can destroy a good thing. "A good secret or a bad secret?"

"It's good." Jude runs a hand down my arm. "When I was on stage, I heard you laughing."

"You did?"

"You have a very distinct laugh."

"Huh. I didn't realize that."

He squeezes my biceps. "That's a good thing. I liked it. It gave tonight's performance a little something extra."

Before I get too caught up, I need to give him his gift. This isn't the moment to talk about anything but him. I hand him the canvas bag, hoping he likes what I got him and why. "I didn't get you flowers."

He laughs softly, glancing at a farmer's market worth of roses, sunflowers, and daisies in his dressing room. "Do you think I don't like flowers?"

"I actually don't know if you like flowers, but flowers felt like something anyone could get the star of the show."

"And you're not just anyone," he says, his tone warm and sensual.

I want to be his *only one*, but no way will I say anything resembling that. "So I got you a canvas bag. I figured you'd need it for the chocolates and flowers everyone else gets you," I say drily since I definitely need jokes right now.

He laughs, then peers into the bag, arching a brow. He takes a blueberry from the carton and pops it into his mouth. "You are the only person who's ever given me blueberries."

"I'm a practical guy," I say, but that's not why I stopped by Trader Joe's before the show. I wanted him to know I listen to him. I listen to *everything* he says.

Jude takes one more, then sets the bag down on the edge of the chair by the mirror. "But how does it taste on your lips, I wonder?" He returns to me, offers me the berry. When I part my lips, he brushes the tiny fruit seductively along my bottom lip.

I'm not into food play, but hell, I will be if it warrants that dark glimmer in his eyes. My tongue darts out, and I bite down on the berry, the juice hitting my tongue. I finish it quickly. "Find out," I whisper in invitation.

He dips his face, kisses me with the barest trace of his lips, then backs off. "Tastes like the start of my dirty fantasies."

I shudder, anticipation rushing through me from his heated stare . . . *at my duck shirt*. I'd been wondering when he'd finally notice what I wore. "You like this too?"

"Like it? I fucking love it." He darts out a hand, fingers the top button, plays with my chest hair right above it. He travels down the buttons, undoing the first one, then presses a hot, possessive kiss to my pecs.

"I thought you might," I whisper.

"As soon as I saw you at the end of the play, all I could think about was my dressing room fantasy. *This.*" Jude drops down to his knees, unzips my jeans, and frees my cock from the confines of my boxer briefs. "Do you have any idea how much I love sucking your cock?"

This man. I'm trembling already as I thread my fingers through his hair. "Show me."

He bends his face to my dick, presses a hot tease of a kiss to the crown. "Ever since I invited you to LA, I've been getting off to thoughts of *this* every night."

He draws the head of my dick between his lips, watching me watch him.

"Just . . . this?" I rasp out.

With a nod, he swirls his tongue around the head, then stops. "I get so fucking hard sucking you off. I love the way it drives you wild," he says, then licks a long, tantalizing stripe down the underside.

"*You* drive me wild, Jude," I say, my voice shaky as he plays with my dick.

"The way you taste. The way you smell," he says, letting go to run his nose along the space between my thigh and my pelvis, inhaling me. Then he returns to my dick, flicking his tongue over the head as he cups my balls. "Most of all," he says, slow and seductive even though he doesn't have to seduce me. I'm already seduced. "I love what it does to you."

My legs shake. My pulse surges to the sky. That's what he does to me. "The second you touch me, I want to explode," I confess.

"I know." He swirls his tongue over the head, then he drops his mouth down on my dick, taking me all the way.

"Fuck yes. Like that, just like that." My head thumps hard against the wall. My hands clamp around his skull.

All his teasing disappears as he sucks with ferocious purpose. I have to watch him. Have to record every filthy image. I stare down at the man on his knees, his gorgeous lips wrapped around my dick, his noises wet and obscene. His hands roam up and down my thighs, and the whole time, his blue eyes pin me with a daring look.

As I grip his head, I'm grunting, growling. Someone could walk by and hear us. Jude clearly doesn't care, since he unzips his pants, takes out his dick.

The sight of him hard sends hot spikes of lust straight to my balls. "Gimme your palm," I tell him.

He thrusts up his hand as he lavishes unholy attention on my shaft. I spit in his hand, then he grips his cock, stroking. I can't stand how good this feels. How turned on I am. How I want things I haven't wanted in ages.

Someday soon, really soon, I want to ask him to fuck me.

The second I picture him spreading me open, my orgasm taps on my shoulder then knocks on the door of my back. "Gonna come, baby," I warn, then I slam my fist against my mouth. I have to bite my knuckles so I don't shout in pleasure.

I come so hard my knees nearly buckle. As he lets go of me, I want to slump against the wall and savor the aftershocks.

But I've got a bigger mission.

In a heartbeat, I get down on the floor, push him onto his back, and kneel between his legs, taking over for his hand. I draw him deep, and that's all my guy needs. One, two, three sucks, and he's shuddering. "Yes, fucking yes. Take it all."

I happily, greedily swallow his orgasm, drinking every last drop, humming around his shaft till he laughs, then pushes me off. Then we slump next to each other on the dressing room floor.

I'm exhausted and elated. Especially when he whispers in my ear, "Are you really leaving tomorrow?"

I'm so high on him that all I can think is what a good question that is.

37

READING BETWEEN THE LINES

Jude

I've never been one to think I have a gift when it comes to acting. Mainly because it's a craft, and like all crafts, it takes work, time, and practice.

But there's one gift I might very well possess—reading between the lines of TJ Ashford-slash-Hardman. I've been able to do this since I met him seven years ago outside a discount shop in London.

I knew he was writing a book before he told me.

And I figured out the first night that he kept pieces of himself to, well, himself. I learned to be patient since eventually, he'd share some of those details with me.

Tonight, his damn shirt is so easy to read, and it gives me the balls to take the next step. Something I'm ready to do when a knock on the dressing room door stops me. "Hello, Mister Fox. We're going to lock up for the night," the stage manager calls out.

"Great. Thanks," I say as TJ and I spring to our feet, comically tugging up jeans, tucking in shirts, and smoothing our hair in seconds.

"Just checking to see if you need anything," she adds.

"Thanks, Maggie. All good. Cheers."

"Cheers to you," she says.

As TJ buttons his duck shirt—could there be a better sign, universe?—I mouth *this is all your fault.*

With a cocky smile, he just shrugs. "Sure is, Mister Fox."

"Shut it, Mister Hardman. Just shut it," I say with a laugh.

Five minutes later, he helps me carry vases of flowers from my agents, the show's producers, and my parents and friends.

Once we're outside the theater, his brow knits. "Do you want to take these to . . ."

"My Airbnb." I stayed near the theater for the first few weeks but switched to a cute little cottage on Venice Beach on Friday. "And I want to take you too. For more than tonight," I say, since why beat around the bush?

There's that twinkle in his eyes, that grin he tries to mask. Why does he hide his feelings? Or hide them badly, I should say. Doesn't he know I can eventually see through him?

As we walk, he clears his throat. "A few minutes ago, you asked *Do I really have to leave tomorrow?*"

"I did."

The twinkle multiplies as we walk past the fountains, glittering in the dark. "To answer your question, Jude . . . I bought a one-way ticket."

This is officially the best night ever. "Someone was hopeful," I say, as he's proved my point—eventually, he says what's in his heart.

"I was," he says, and it's the admission I wanted last night at the bar, but I suppose it's an admission I had to earn. Maybe one we *both* had to earn over the last twenty-four hours.

As we head toward the Lyft I ordered, he tells me he has to return to New York on Thursday for a book signing the day after.

"Good. Stay till then," I tell him. "I got this place on the beach since I figured I'd rather be there for these meetings and whatnot. I have a commercial shoot in Malibu on Wednesday, but it's only half the day."

"No problem. I'll write then. I can write anywhere, while you're in your meetings and whatnot," he says, always practical.

And I like that practical side. I want him to write while I handle business. I want our lives to mesh somehow. This week feels like the start, even though I know there are so many more hurdles—New York, London, the fucking ocean.

But one thing at a time.

An hour later, after we've stopped at his hotel to grab his things, we're in my one-bedroom Airbnb cottage on the beach. It's all white wood, with a wraparound deck and a view of the Pacific. In short—heaven. We set the flowers on the kitchen island, surf crashing softly in the distance. TJ leans against the counter, tipping his forehead to the daisies. "I guess you do like flowers."

"Yes, because I'm not a monster who hates flowers and musicals."

"Musicals suck, but I like flowers too, you dick." TJ grabs both my hands, yanks me flush against him, then rumbles something soft and sweet against my throat, a long, low *mmm*. He rubs his beard against my neck, whispering in my ear, "Are we doing this, finally?"

That fizzy sensation I had when I learned *Pillow Talk* was going to the US? It pales in comparison to what I feel now. "We are."

If I ever need to play a character who's falling in love, this moment is what I will draw from, and I will fucking nail it.

* * *

On Monday morning, I get out of bed and follow the smell of coffee. TJ's drinking a cup on the beach house deck, staring at the surf from the white wooden railing.

Or wait. Is he staring at a *Top Gun* scene?

I stride out onto the deck. "You fucking pervert. Are you watching those shirtless guys play beach volleyball?"

He shoots me the kind of deadpan stare only he can deliver. "Yes, Jude. I'm staring at other men when I'm with you." He nods to the phone in his hand and the notes app on the screen. "I was thinking about a scene on the beach for my next book. I was trying to figure out a volleyball meet-cute."

"Ah, so you came here to work," I tease. It's so fun to poke him.

"You figured me out. I flew to Los Angeles for work.

I finagled this invite so I could stand on the deck of a beach house and brood over a clever way to start the book I'm dangerously close to falling behind on."

That's surprising. TJ always seems to have his shit together. Moving behind him, I run a hand through his hair. "Just write about a fetching Englishman who charms the pants off a hot, broody, bearded volleyball player."

"You're so helpful. I even know who to suggest to star in it when it's made into a flick."

"Problem solved," I say.

I tell him I need tea before I solve any bigger dilemmas and go inside the house to put on the kettle. While I wait for it to boil, I grab my phone, touching base with Holly and Kenta about our meetings, then I click to my texts. Olivia tells me to get a job in New York before she dies from missing me, my brother teases that he liberated all my books from my flat, and William shares details of his show with both TJ and me.

Hmm. Do I want to go? William is a big fucking deal too, just like TJ, and I'm the guy who's trying to catch up to their level of success. But as TJ said, comparison is the thief of joy. So what if they're both a little further along in their careers than I am?

TJ always did like William's music, so I suspect he'll enjoy going. After I pour the tea, I head back to the deck, calling, "What's the verdict, stud—"

But he holds up a hand then points to his phone as he speaks into it. "Yes, of course. I love Amsterdam. If they want me there for the book show, I'll go." There's a long pause. "I'll believe *that* when it happens." Another beat. "Just like you taught me, Mason."

When he hangs up, the wildly curious center of my soul is dying to ask what that's all about. But it's not my business.

"That was my agent," he explains. "A lot's been happening."

No one in the whole world can downplay like TJ Hardman. "Sounds like it. Is your publisher sending you to Amsterdam?"

"Potentially. There's a book expo in a month. A big trade thing. My Dutch publisher is talking about me doing a meet and greet."

You should stop by London, I want to say. But more than that, I want it to be his idea. Or to ask me to join him for the weekend. I'd go. In a heartbeat. So, I wait for him to connect the dots. Let him be the impulsive one for once.

Instead, he glances at the phone screen. "You were asking me about this text, I think?"

I shift back to that topic. "Do you want to go? You always liked his music."

"I did. I still do." Then he scratches his jaw like he's about to say something, but maybe he thinks better of it. "But do you want to go? I know he's a good friend," he says carefully, maybe a little unsure of William's role in my life.

"We should. I think he'll appreciate it. He seems a little different than when I lived with him in London. Lately, I get the sense he's struggling with something."

TJ blinks. "You. Lived. With. Him?"

Oh, fuck me. "You didn't know that?"

"Um, you and I weren't in touch for seven years,

dude." His tone hints he's about to cross his arms and shut down.

I step closer. "But you talked to him, so I figured it came up at some point."

"We texted now and then. That was all."

"He lived with Olivia and me for a bit, but that was a couple of years ago," I explain quickly. "Does that bother you?"

He hesitates. "It shouldn't," he says, but it's clear it does and he sounds as frustrated as he did that rainy night at Wiseman.

"Why though? Why does it bother you?"

"He lived with you. He got to see you." TJ sighs heavily, then does it once more as if he's trying to get a handle on his emotions. "He got to see you over the last seven years. I didn't get to see you at all."

I set my mug on the railing then close the distance between us, grabbing a fistful of his shirt. "He's not you. Just know that."

TJ exhales in obvious relief as he jerks me up against him. "And I get to see you now."

"Yes, you do."

"We'll go, then. It's important. We'll show him our support."

It's settled.

More importantly, we've navigated that little speed bump. I take that as a good sign for us.

* * *

TJ tells me he wants to teach me pinball, so that night, he takes me to an arcade a mile away.

This will be thoroughly entertaining—because I am absolutely savage with the flippers.

His jaw hangs open after my tenth win in a row. "What the hell, babe? You didn't tell me you were the pinball wizard."

I smile for many reasons, but partly because I'm *babe* now. A nickname for when we're in the real world and one for when he's drunk on sex. I like having both.

We continue like that the next day. I head to meetings, and he disappears into his meet-cute world in coffee shops. On Tuesday night, we go to The Holy Cow to see Lettuce Pray. It's a packed house, and the crowd goes wild for the lead singer. When the show ends, William texts and asks us to meet him at a dive bar around the corner, someplace he won't be recognized. Once he's there, he slams back shots so fast he's unsteady on his feet after a mere twenty minutes.

That's what I was worried about.

"C'mon, buddy," TJ says gently. "Share a Lyft with us. Let's get you home."

"Awww, I thought you blokes would never ask," William says with a dopey grin.

When we're in the back seat, he's between us, wrapping an arm around me, then TJ. "You're both so fucking hot," he says. He kisses my cheek, then TJ's. "If you ever want to have a threesome . . ."

TJ shoots me a seriously deadly stare as he answers, "No, William. I'm not sharing Jude. With anyone. Ever," he says, firm and clear.

William laughs, shaking a finger at TJ. "I fucking knew you were here in LA for him, not business like you said."

"Of course I'm here for Jude," TJ says, his tone underlining my name and what I mean to him.

I get hot all over. I needed that—a little possession from my . . . obsession.

We deliver William safely into his home, where he flops onto his couch, humming a tune. TJ pours a glass of water and sets it on the coffee table, and I find some aspirin.

"My mates are the best," William says, and I tell him I'll check on him in the morning.

We return to our waiting car, and as the driver peels away from the curb and into the hazy night, TJ points back toward William's house. "I guess that's what he's struggling with."

"I think the fame is hard for him," I say.

"Good call on going to see him," TJ says, then he's clearly done talking about William since he pounces on me, pouring all that possessiveness into a kiss that doesn't stop when we get home. His ownership continues in bed for a good, long time.

The next morning, I take off early for Malibu, ruffling TJ's hair as he lies in bed. He mutters something about seeing me tonight—that he'll be in a coffee shop all day writing.

"Of course you will," I say, then I'm gone. Maybe tonight, I'll ask what happens after Los Angeles.

No, I won't *ask*.

I'll tell him I want him to see me in London when he goes to Amsterdam. Or ask if he wants company while he's there. I'll tell him I want an *After Los Angeles.*

38

SWIMMING WITH THE SHARKS

TJ

As I drain my morning joe at Doctor Insomnia's Tea and Coffee Emporium, an image of washboard abs lands in my email. There's no text in Hazel's email, just the subject line: *For my next cover—your rating, on a scale of one to ten?*

As I tap out, "Looks-like-he's-never-even-seen-a-carb-much-less-tasted-one," Mason's name flashes on the screen. I hit send quickly so I can answer my agent. "Hey, give me a sec," I say.

"Don't worry. I have all day," he barks.

"Dude. Cool your jets," I tease, grabbing my laptop quickly. I stuff it into my messenger bag and go outside. "Okay. What's up?"

"You. You're up. You're at bat, and Kristen wants you to get your fine ass on over to CTM in, oh, say, two hours."

Is he for real? He wants me to meet his LA counterpart for the first time, and he's giving me this little warning? "Two hours? From now?"

"Yes. As in noon. Was that not clear?" he deadpans.

"Back it up, man. You want me to go to the Beverly Hills offices?"

"Yes, sweetheart. They want to give you a foot rub and a hot-stone massage. Shall I send a car to Doctor Insomnia's for you? I can arrange to have the Olympic men's swim team waiting for you if that'll sweeten the deal."

I swing my gaze back and forth along this Venice street. "How do you know where I am?"

"I had your tracking device implanted last time you were here. Also, you're a creature of habit, so I took a good guess. Was I right, totally right, or of course I was fucking right?"

"Yeah, you're right. No, the swim team won't be necessary, but thanks for the offer. Also, if you're making your Christmas list, I like hand rubs, not foot rubs. And why the hell do your LA doppelgangers want to see me, stat?" He's hitting me with surprises left and right.

"Because everyone loves *Top-Notch Boyfriend*. Anyway, do you look decent? Wait. Who am I talking to? You always look good. Bet you're wearing one of your animal-print shirts and fashionable jeans that you've never washed in anything but Method detergent?"

I glance down at the armadillo print on my chest and the aforementioned denim. "That tracking device worked out really well for you. Anyway, why am I going to CTM at the last minute? Just to meet with Kristen and company?"

"Not just with the LA Masons. A producer is coming too, but you know my mantra."

"Don't believe anything till the check cashes," I fill in.

"And even then, who knows? But there's some stuff in the works, and we can sell your books better if we can also sell *you*. I figure I could have a little TJ showcase while you were in town for whatever secret tryst you're having."

Damn. Mason knows me too well. But hopefully, this secret tryst won't be secret for long. Jude and I have hardly been clandestine since we've been out in public. I'd like to make some plans with him beyond this trip, plans to see Amsterdam with him. I'd like, too, to make this thing more than a thing. I want him to be my boyfriend.

For now, though, I focus on Mason as he rattles off details about the meeting. When the town car he ordered arrives five minutes later, my head is reeling.

Still, I know better than to get excited about Hollywood.

Just like Mason taught me.

* * *

Only, it's not just a meeting. It's more like a full-court press in the sunlit, floor-to-ceiling glass conference room overlooking Beverly Hills.

CTM's catering brings in Costa Rican coffee, blueberries, and an assortment of kale-based snacks. Jude will get such a kick out of this when I tell him about the spread later.

Even though Mason prepped me, I'm still a little surprised to see Robert Walsh from the theater the other night. I was sure nothing would come of bumping into him. But after hellos, he takes a seat next to Kristen. Mason's zoomed in on Kristen's iPad.

The producer from Webflix leans forward in the orange chair, shaking his head in disbelief. "I literally can't stand how much I love this story."

"I'm happy to hear that." I'm still gobsmacked and sound like it.

Robert shoots me an intense stare. "Let me make it clear. I love it as much as my dog."

"And his dog has a private chef," Mason chimes in.

"Rocco, the Fiercest Chihuahua, has a personal trainer too," Kristen supplies with a smile. "Tell us what your vision is for the show, Robert."

"We'll stay as true to the book as possible," Robert says, then stretches his hands out like he's framing a marquee. "After the prologue when they meet, I see the camera pans to an establishing shot, Greenwich Village. Close-up on our hero. He's working on one of his cartoons when his best-friend-turned-business-manager saunters into their artsy office, tells him about the deal he just booked for our hero's illustrations. Then, we cut to the guys celebrating that night with ping-pong and beer at their favorite bar. In walks the other hero—duh duh *duuun*—the best friend's brother. Our hero has been crushing on him since that day in the prologue. AKA *for-evah*."

It's too good to be true. I know Mason's mantra, he's

repeated it ever since my book took off, so I do my best to stay super chill.

But man, it's really fucking hard when this guy tells me that Webflix loves my story and wants to make a deal.

Maybe I do finally understand musicals because it's also really hard not to burst into, well, an epic rock song right the hell now.

Especially when Robert shakes my hand at the end of the meeting. "I know this seems like luck because we ran into each other at the play. But it's not luck. Your book is gold, and we're going to mine it and give it a good home. I promise you that."

"I'm just glad you enjoyed the story," I say. That's about as much as I can process right now.

When he leaves, Kristen mimes her head exploding. "Some deals are the LA freeway system. Some are the autobahn. That deal is a Bugatti on the autobahn."

I don't even know what to say to her. It's all too much. Too Hollywood. Too unbelievable.

I thank her then slip my cell phone out of my pocket to snap a shot of the catering spread before I leave. I slide into the town car a minute later, my bones buzzing. When we're on the road, I call Mason back. "So, what did you think?"

"I think armadillos suit you, and so does LA. You look happy, so I'm guessing you needed sunshine. And . . . Robert just called to say he's sending a term sheet over tonight."

This feels so unreal. But as the car slogs through traffic, I'm struck by one more revelation. Even though I usually keep this shit to myself, I want to tell Jude.

I want to let him know about my crazy day. Find out what he thinks about it.

But I also don't want him to get weird like Flynn did. Or, really, like Jude kinda did on Sunday at the café.

Except, it should be okay if Jude has his own feelings about this maybe-kinda-sorta deal. He's an artist. I get that. But he's shown me his wounds; he's opened up about his sore spots. If I want to be a damn good boyfriend, I need to share things in a way that shows I give a shit about his sensitive heart too.

Share in a way that says, *Hey babe, what do you think?* and not, *look at me, look at me!*

If there's one thing I know about Jude, it's that he likes fun, sex, books, and food he can eat.

And, well, me. He likes me.

I send him a text.

TJ: Hey, want to go to the Silver Spinner Neon Bowling Lanes and see if you can beat me? Then, sushi? Just the fish for you, though, babe. I'll happily eat all your rice.

Then I follow with a second note.

TJ: If you're very good, I'll let you blow me after. Sixty-nine if you beat me like you did in pinball, you secret pinball wizard.

Jude: Fuck me. The shoot is running late. Can you

please be naked and covered in sushi when I return later? Like, on a table and all. I don't even require chopsticks.

TJ: Mark that down with things that will never happen. (Me covered in sushi, not me fucking you. The latter is of the name-the-time-and-place variety.)

Jude: Someday, you'll be my sushi feast. But for now, can I trouble you to order me some yellowtail rolls for takeout? Wait. Nope. Fuck me again. I mean yellowtail and edamame. Do not tempt me with rice. Seriously. Promise me you will never bring rice near me. I might want rice more than your cock at the end of a long day.

TJ: You said, "fuck me twice." What I hear is you want double-sex tonight. Got it.

Jude: At last! He gets my order right! Yellowtail and a long cock!

But when nine p.m. rolls around with no sign of Jude, it's clear neither sushi nor dick is on the menu for him tonight. His next note comes with a crying eggplant emoji.

Jude: I hate everyone. Hollywood time is a bigger lie than *It must have gone to my spam folder.*

TJ: Or *Your hair looks nice?*

Jude: Wait, are you saying you don't like my hair?

TJ: I like your hair all the time, especially when my fingers are tugging on it and your lips are on my dick.

Jude: It's sooooo late. I'm hallucinating about eating white rice off your dick. Send help soon.

TJ: Fine, fine. I'll be covered in yellowtail when you return.

Mason sends me a term sheet a little later, and it still seems too good to be true, so I go to bed.

It'll be there in the morning to sign, after all. Then, I can try again to share my news with Jude, maybe invite him to go to Amsterdam with me, and then finally ask him to be my top-notch boyfriend.

39

SHOW AND TELL

Jude

Lucky me. After a long day shooting a cologne commercial, I get to come home to fresh yellowtail in the fridge and an American hunk in my bed.

Fine, he's not covered in pancakes, or rice, or bread. But TJ still looks good enough to eat, even sound asleep.

I'm quiet as I brush my teeth, shed my clothes, and pad to the bed. If he happens to wake up, though, I won't complain. I'll reward him.

After I slide under the covers, I snuggle against this warm man.

"Hey," he murmurs.

"Hey, you," I whisper.

I wait to see if he'll wake up. He's quiet for several long seconds, then he slurs, "How was your day?"

"Good. Yours?"

More silence. "Good. Meeting. Stuff."

I laugh to myself. Press a kiss to his shoulder. "See you in the morning," I say, and I won't even be upset that it's our last morning before he returns to New York.

There will be more. I'm sure of it.

* * *

The sun blasts its get-the-fuck-out-of-bed rays at me. I rub my eyes and grab my phone. Ugh. It's only nine.

I'm tempted to hit snooze and catch some more winks before it's time to prep for my Webflix meeting.

But my notifications blink like mad red dots.

With a heavy sigh, I push up in bed and click on the text from TJ first. He's out for a run but wants to talk to me when he returns, especially since he needs to catch his flight.

That sounds ominous, but sometimes he comes across that way because he doesn't use emoticons and hates exclamation points. Weak writing, he'd say. Writing snob, I'd say.

I'm about to reply when I spot a text from Holly. ***Webflix meeting canceled. But don't stress. We'll sort it out. Call me!***

I groan, then slump back in bed.

But wait.

Just because it's canceled doesn't mean it won't be rescheduled. After all, meetings get changed all the time. Plus, Holly used exclamation points, so this must be just a blip.

After I turn on my ringer, the phone pings with a text from William: ***Does this mean I'll be seeing more of***

you and your man in Los Angeles? Sweet! You guys are the best! And seriously, I KNEW he was here for business.

What?

Alarm bells begin to blare. William did say something the other night about TJ being here for business. But what the hell does that mean?

The next text is from Olivia. ***There better be a British character for you, or I'm suing the world.***

My stomach curls with dread as I click on the link she sent.

It's from *The Hollywood Scoop*, the insider gossip blog for the industry that's pretty much never wrong.

With a knot in my throat, I read.

Word on the street is Webflix just acquired the film and TV rights to bestselling author TJ Hardman's most recent romance, Top-Notch Boyfriend. *You remember this one, right? The author was dumped on TV by a guy who runs a chicken café and was in a jealous lather over Hardman's skyrocketing popularity. (For the record, I'm Team TJ.) The viral video took off, and so did the book. But that's not why Webflix's recently elevated Head of Acquisitions, Robert Walsh, inked the deal late last night after meeting Hardman and his LA agents at CTM yesterday. "It was a whirlwind romance with this book and the author. I fell in love with the story from the first page, and we're thrilled to bring this fun, sexy, heartfelt queer romance to our millions of streaming viewers worldwide," he told me when I called him this morning for a comment.*

. . .

All my hackles rise. It turns out TJ wasn't writing at a coffee shop during my shoot after all. He was off wooing the head of the world's biggest streaming service. And he didn't think to mention that when he was texting me about sushi.

But no matter.

It's fine. TJ has his writing business to tend to, and he's always played business close to the vest.

Deep breath.

This is probably something that's been in the works for a while. Deals like this take time. Except, wouldn't that then mean he came to LA for a meeting, rather than . . . for me?

My stomach drops with an all too familiar feeling.

Then plummets when the top of a photo peeks out from the screen. I scroll down, and I burn as it fills the screen. It's Robert Walsh and TJ smiling for the camera on Sunday night at the Mark Taper Forum.

The caption reads: *Robert Walsh working his deal-making magic with author TJ Hardman at intermission Sunday night during* Pillow Talk.

I close my eyes, draw another deep, calming breath like I'm doing yoga. But fuck yoga. I get out of bed, frustration fueling me as I pull on boxers and workout shorts then call Holly.

My fingers slip as I hit her name. Dammit. I try again, and she answers after a quarter of a ring.

"Good morning, Jude."

"Hi, Holly. But is it really a good morning?" I ask, strained. "What in the bloody hell is going on with the Webflix meeting?"

She sighs sympathetically. "Ah, did you see *The*

Hollywood Scoop? Webflix acquired another property instead. They're going forward with that one. It's total bollocks if you ask me, and I hope it fails magnificently."

I want to laugh. I love her support.

But instead, I huff, drop my forehead into my hand, and look for a silver lining.

"And so when are we rescheduling? They said they wanted more queer romance. That's what we're going to do, right? Reschedule? There has to be room for more than one? Christian Laird was keen on signing up. That should help greenlight a project," I say, and I sound desperate because I *feel* desperate. I'm hanging on for dear life, clutching this opportunity.

She sighs. "It's not being rescheduled, Jude. I'm so sorry. They backburnered your project."

I can barely speak. All I manage is a strangled "Why?"

"They greenlit this book late last night, and it's replacing the project they wanted to develop with you. It's called *Top-Notch Boyfriend*. I hate it on principle. Like, with the fire of a thousand suns. Have you heard of it?"

Yes, the author fucked me. In every sense of the word.

No wonder he's out for a run. He's probably formulating a script of what to say to me. Because he clearly came to LA to work a deal. Then he learned of my projects, called his agent, and used my inside information to steal my opportunity from under me.

The guy likes Agatha Christie. He loves to weave tales of mystery. But I learned a thing or two from him about following clues.

That call I overheard Monday morning? When he said *But I'll believe that when it happens?*

He knew this Webflix thing was in the works then, even if he doubted it. And he chose not to say a word to me.

I shake my head, amazed that he almost pulled it off. But I've cracked the case of TJ Hardman. My visitor was working the deal on my deck. That's why he didn't invite me to Amsterdam. There's no Amsterdam. Amsterdam was probably a code name for this secret deal. And if so, he had time to tell me, but he didn't.

"Yes. I'm familiar with the author," I say to Holly.

"Seems they're making that project the Webflix marquee gay romance."

It's ten thousand slaps in the face.

I am such a sucker.

"Which is a total mistake if you ask me," Holly goes on. "Everyone loves Brits. There are literally studies out there about how much Americans love our accents."

I can't believe I'm about to say this. It's the end of any self-respect I have left. But I say it anyway because, apparently, I've lost all my dignity. "Any chance there's a role for me?"

"That's what's so mad about the whole thing. It's like they didn't get the memo about sexy accents," she says, clearly disgusted as an agent should be. "The leads are both American. And supposedly, Christian Laird is attached to this project now. Which is ridiculous."

The floor drops out from under me.

TJ took every single detail about my hopes and dreams and used them.

My heart hurts. Literally fucking aches. Why do I always fall for men who use me?

I draw a shaky breath. "So, that's it?"

"That's it for now, love. But chin up. Kenta and I will find something. That's our job, and we're not going to fail. We love you madly, so put this out of your head, go enjoy the sunshine that we never get back home, and we will carry on."

"Thanks, Hols."

"Let's have lunch tomorrow, okay? We'll strategize over kale and tofu and tea."

"Sure," I agree, and she hangs up.

I want to believe this is a misunderstanding. I want to believe it's a coincidence. But every detail adds up to *I got fooled again*.

William let slip on Tuesday night that TJ came to LA for business.

TJ bought a one-way ticket.

TJ arranged his schedule for a meeting while I was at a shoot.

The worst part? He wooed the guy the night he came to my show and gave me those fucking blueberries. And then I blew him.

I stare daggers at the photo of him during intermission at my show, romancing my work right out from under me. And he didn't say a word to me.

Just like Arlo didn't say a word when he was wooing my agent and then stealing my role. Talk about déjà vu.

This is Arlo all over again. My boyfriend used me to get to someone else.

And the irony of it all? TJ's not even my boyfriend.

The front door clicks open, and I seethe like a volcano.

"Hey, baby, I'm back," TJ calls from the foyer. "Want to get kale for breakfast, and I can tell you something? I have a funny picture to show you."

Ha. I have a damning picture to show him.

Slowly, I head out of the bedroom, my jaw tight. My eyes lock on him as he pushes the front door closed. His T-shirt clings to his chest, and I don't fucking care.

I hold up my phone, and the volcano erupts. "Why the fuck did you really come to LA? Because it sure as hell seems like it wasn't for me."

40

YOUR DREAM GUY

TJ

Jude holds the phone like a cross-examiner holds damning evidence. His eyes are steel—no, guns—and they're aimed right at me.

My neck prickles. I have no idea what he's getting at, but when he shoves the phone near my face, I groan.

The shot of Walsh and me is a neon Vegas billboard advertising all the misunderstandings in the world.

"I can explain," I say, and with those awful words, I sound like every cheating jackass in history.

With a twist of his lips that's not a smile, Jude gestures to the living room. "By all means. You have the floor. Don't leave out a tawdry detail."

Holy shit. I've never seen him like this. "I wanted to tell you last night about the deal." Wow. That sounds bad. Even though last night my plan seemed brilliant.

He arches a doubtful brow. "Did you now? Were you going to tell me, over, say, sushi and bowling? Was that your plan?"

"Yes, but it all came together quickly. I didn't even sign the term sheet until this morning."

He tilts his head. "Awww. Did you sign it while I was sleeping? So fitting, since you've hidden the whole bloody deal from me. You fucking knew on Monday morning when you were talking to your agent. You said *I'll believe that when it happens*."

I shake my head. "We were talking about the Amsterdam thing."

"Right."

My chest caves. "Jude, I'm sorry I didn't tell you. I just didn't think it would amount to anything, and once it came together, I wanted to tell you."

"That's awfully convenient. But oh, hey, did you know they fucking backburnered my project for yours?"

A black cloud of regret swirls over me. "Shit, babe. I'm sorry. I had no idea."

"Don't *babe* me. You brought them a project pretty much identical to the one they wanted to talk to me about. You brought them Christian Laird. You knew he was part of the project they were talking to me about developing. But you swooped in and gave them a queer rom-com. You probably already adapted the book for film and TV. Oh, except yours has two Americans and zero Brits. Thanks, TJ."

I grab at facts to try to explain this to him. "I didn't bring them Laird."

"Well, he's on it. Funny how that works."

This looks so bad. But it's not, and I have to prove it. "A few weeks ago, my agent told me my publisher was pursuing him to narrate my audiobooks, but he didn't think it would happen."

"Well, what do you know? It happened. You got Laird. I got nothing."

But this isn't a zero-sum game. "That's not how it works."

"Oh, really? I thought Hollywood wasn't your thing. On Sunday, you literally said, *Not everyone's goal is to work in Hollywood. It's not mine.*" Jude makes my words sound so damning. "Care to revise that now, stud?"

"It wasn't my goal. I swear. It all happened so quickly."

He rolls his gorgeous blue eyes. Today, though, they look mean. He's never looked mean before. "So you finagled this deal with a Hollywood A-lister at the center of it at the same time you were busy *reuniting* with me. Romancing me like one of your heroes, in fact. My God, it's all so obvious in retrospect. You were playing a part the whole time. How did I not know you were such a good actor?"

Jude doesn't pull punches. He hits hard, square in the jaw, and I'm reeling. "I told you why I did that, and you did the same thing."

"Hardly to the same degree. Plus, the next day, we made an agreement. No bullshit. And what did you do? You fucking bullshitted me. I told you about my meetings. I told you about this project. I told you about Laird, and you pretended you understood. You gave me that whole *comparison is the thief of joy* shit." He shakes his head in pained disbelief, more hurt than angry, and I hate that he feels this way.

"That was all true." The sun keeps rising, casting bright rays through the open deck. The warmth feels all wrong. A hurricane should hit the beach right now. "I didn't come here to do anything but see you."

He's unmoved. "Your *one-way ticket*? Right, sure. Oh, and didn't you tell William you were here for business?"

I groan, scrubbing a hand over my beard. "Jude, I didn't know if you wanted me to say anything about us to William."

"Us? What does *us* even mean to you—except when it's convenient." He snorts bitterly, not hearing a word I'm saying. "Everything you say is so fucking convenient you could have scripted it." Jude turns that spotlight on me only it's cold now, a search light rather than a warm stage light. "It all adds up to the fact that you used me."

I hate the look on his face. The hurt in his eyes. The anger in his voice.

I edge toward him like he's a wounded animal who'll bite if I touch him wrong. "I didn't use you. I would never use you. I wanted to tell you last night. I wanted to share this with you and get your opinion."

He brings a hand to his heart. "That's so sweet. But hey, why not get my opinion on, oh, say, Sunday night, when you courted Webflix at my play?"

Does he not get it? "Oh, that would have been classy. *Hey, Jude, congrats on your amazing performance, and oh, by the way, I met a Webflix exec during intermission, and isn't that cool?*" I stop to take a breath. "I didn't want to steal the limelight from you."

"Well, guess what? You did anyway, TJ." His shoulders relax, and his expression softens and I feel a glimmer of hope that we can fix this horrible misunderstanding. "But if you'd been honest with me from the start, this wouldn't matter. You could have told me."

"I wanted to celebrate you. You deserved it; you worked hard for your show," I say, imploring him to see that.

His softer voice prevails again. "You had Sunday night to tell me. Monday. Tuesday. This wasn't about last night. This is about you keeping secrets." But then his anger builds a new head of steam. "You always keep all your stuff to yourself. You hold everything inside . . . *until it suits you.*"

"I was protecting you," I explode. Because what the fuck?

"From what?" Jude matches my intensity. "Protecting my poor little ego because I can't handle you being more successful than I am?"

If the shoe fits—

But I bite my tongue.

"Is that it?" he pushes.

I point at him. "Yes, this is ridiculous."

"You want to know what's ridiculous?" he demands. "Me opening up to you. Me trusting you. And you taking every bit of information and using it for yourself." He jerks his gaze away, swallowing whatever emotions have a hold on him. "I'm such an idiot. Arlo did this to me. He got my agent, fucked him, and then . . ."

He breaks off and waves the phone at me, and he's one step shy of an accusation I will never forgive him for.

My jaw ticks. I hold up a hand. "Think *real* hard before you say the next thing."

Jude purses his lips like he's holding something in. Good. He fucking better.

"And then after that, my career just—" He can't seem to finish, and I know he's talking about those years when he didn't work. For the second time, I hope so hard that he simmers down, that he sees I would never do this to him. Maybe, just maybe I'm getting through. But then, he breathes out hard, his eyes darkening. "I'm going to ask one more time. Did you use me?"

I've had enough.

I'm not the bad guy and I won't let him treat me like one. "I already told you what happened. You know I wouldn't betray you."

He scoffs. "Do I? I'm wondering if I ever knew you at all. And do you even know me? Maybe I'm not your dream guy. Maybe I'm not the swooniest man you've ever known. Maybe you're not as far gone as you think."

My brain goes eerily quiet. I freeze for terrible, stretched-out seconds as the world turns deathly silent too. I stare at Jude like he's a math problem.

But I've already solved it. I just can't quite believe the answer.

"Did you—?" I hiss, but I don't have to finish. I know what he did. He knows what he did.

Jude blinks, eyes wide. Busted. "It was open. On your computer," he says, scrambling. "When you showed me your book in London. I didn't mean to."

That sounds exactly like *I can explain.*

I back away from him, holding up a hand. "You read my journal seven years ago, but I'm the one hiding things?" I glance around at the living room couch where we crashed into each other the first night, then the deck where we made out under the stars, then the bedroom where we came together. Everything looks wrong, like this house is contaminated. "I'm leaving."

I spin around, stalk into the bedroom, and throw my stuff together, slamming clothes and toiletries into my suitcase, yanking my charger from the wall, stuffing my laptop into my messenger bag.

A minute later, Jude crosses the creaky floor. "I'm really sorry. I can explain about the journal," he whispers from behind me, sounding so contrite I nearly want to cave.

I stand my ground, though, and wheel around, fueled by his long con. "We're kind of past explanations now. You shouldn't have *done* that, and you know it. But you did it seven years ago and didn't say a word—"

"But there's a reason."

"You're past the grace period," I bite out. "And yet you're mad at me for something that snowballed over the past four days that I was going to tell you last night?"

I couldn't write the shitstorm unfolding in front of me. There's no coming back from it. And I peddle happy endings.

"I know. I'm an ass. I'm sorry," Jude shovels his hand through his hair and tightens it into a fist as if reining in runaway emotions. He closes his eyes in pained regret. Like he wants the world to rewind. Yeah, same here, but life doesn't work that way. When he opens them, they're full of fear and sorrow and what I think is genuine remorse. "I just wanted this so badly, TJ, and it didn't happen. I feel so stupid for this whole thing – wanting it so badly I blew up at you."

But I feel foolish too.

Foolish for falling in love with him again.

Foolish for thinking he was the one.

Foolish for putting on rose-colored glasses with him. The one guy I thought would never hurt me has punched below the belt. The Jude Graham I knew would never have done this. But he's now so clearly Jude Fox.

Even if he's sorry, and even if I'm sorry, this fight is a sign.

Jude will always devastate me.

He's doing it now and he'll do it again in a week, a month, a year.

I can handle the hurt in this moment. But if he breaks my heart down the road, when I'm even deeper in love with him, it will wreck me forever.

I strip the anger from my voice. "I'm sorry too. Sorry I didn't tell you sooner. Sorry I handled this badly," I say, then draw a deep, soldiering breath. "And I'm sorry that I can't be in this with you."

His lips part. He shakes his head adamantly, refusing to accept that. "What do you mean?"

His words are a plea, and it's hard to resist. I want to drop everything, take him in my arms, and say, *Let's forget this happened.*

But I've got to look out for future me, so I gird myself and do the hard thing. "This isn't what I wanted when I came to LA. Goodbye, Jude."

I grab my bag, leave for the airport, and I don't look back.

Not even when he calls me a few days later and leaves a message asking to please talk. Not even when he texts begging for the same.

I don't answer. I don't reply.

We. Are. Over.

EPILOGUE

IF FOUND, PLEASE RETURN

Ten Months Later

Jude

A taxi trudges by on Fifth Avenue, and Holly shakes her blonde head then tuts.

"Jude, darling . . ." A sigh comes next, a blown-out breath that says *I can't believe this picture of you is in the paper,* and *I certainly can't believe you'd let this kind of salacious mess happen after everything we've accomplished in the last ten months.*

But this picture—this fucking picture of me in a supposed salacious mess—isn't what everyone thinks it is. "I can explain," I say, and déjà vu sweeps over me.

Someone I was once in love with breathed those words to me in a beach house in Venice. And here I am at a sidewalk café in New York City, my new home, saying them to my agent.

"Of course *you* can explain it," she says in the friendly tone that always tricks me into thinking she's the lovable aunt type. But she's actually a lion, with sharp teeth she hides behind a Hollywood smile. "But I can too."

She swivels an iPad around and stabs a finger against the offending photo on the screen. I cringe again. That really does look bad with a capital B. "This, in the business, is what we call a PR crisis," she says.

"It is. It definitely is," I say, hoping the agency isn't going to explain it away by dropping me. When Holly took a new job at CTM a few months ago, she brought most of her clients with her, me included. But CTM is not only the biggest and most successful talent agency in the world, it's also more buttoned-up than Astor. CTM has its own reputation to maintain as entertainment royalty and is notorious for tossing out bad sheep clients. With nerves rushing through me, I ask the uncomfortable question.

"Does this mean we're . . . through?"

She laughs. "Don't be silly, love. We're certainly not going to drop you when you're the talk of the town thanks to *If Found, Please Return* being all the rage in film right now." That's sort of reassuring and sort of not. "And PR crises have PR solutions."

I square my shoulders, smile, letting her know I'm game for literally anything. "Whatever it is, I'll do it."

Holly pats my hand then lifts her teacup, looking ever so proper. "Good. Because here at CTM, we pride ourselves on looking out for our clients' best interests."

"And I'm so, so grateful for that," I say.

She drains the rest of her tea then sets the pink and white cup down with a clink. "Then you'll be grateful to know we've arranged to fix this by giving you a very appropriate fake boyfriend. We have quite a vast client list, after all."

That's it? That's the PR solution? Well, that's as easy as saying yes to a night out with friends. "Brilliant. I can do that, no problem." I rub my hands, ready to tackle this simple challenge to fix my tarnished rep. "Who's the lucky guy?"

Holly sighs, the kind that says *I wish there were another way, but there isn't, so don't fuck this up*. "Someone who desperately needs a fake boyfriend too."

"Even better. What did the bloke do to mess up his life?"

"I'll let him explain when you meet him. Though *meet* isn't exactly the right word." She gives a laugh—the conspiratorial kind. "You already know him."

I make a beckoning motion. "Tell me who he is. I can't wait to charm him for the cameras."

"And you will be so bloody charming," she says. It's unquestionably an order.

I straighten my spine. "Absolutely."

"Perfect. Then it's settled. We have another client who needs a little help too. TJ Hardman will be your fake boyfriend for the awards season. Won't that be fabulous?"

I freeze.

This has to be a lark. But there's no laughter coming my way. "You're serious?"

"Dead serious."

The only way I can save my career is by acting as if I'm in love with the man who destroyed my heart.

I guess we'll see just how good an actor I am.

Whoa. How the hell will these guys find their way back to each other after that epic, painful ending? Find out what happens next when TJ and Jude, now enemies, are forced to pretend to be boyfriends in HERE COMES MY MAN!

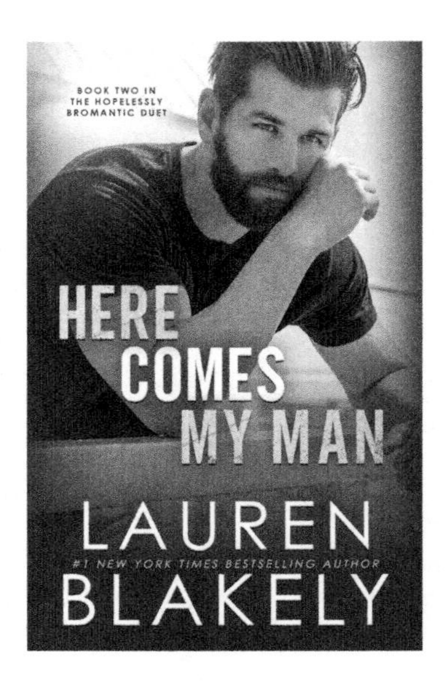

Want to be the first to hear about new MM releases? Sign up for my exclusive MM mailing list!

And be sure to try all my USA Today Bestselling MM romances!

Men of Summer Series

One Time Only

A Guy Walks Into My Bar

The Bromance Zone

Author's note: Some of the bands, authors and celebrities referenced in Hopelessly Bromantic are real as you likely noticed, and many are made up too. Among the fictional ones created for your amusement are: the bands Too Big For Their Britches, Lettuce Pray, Astronaut Food, and No Name; the authors Caroline Vienna, and Alistair Edwin and his international spy character Rhys Locke; Jude's play Pillow Talk and his show Our Secret Courtship, and many others...

ALSO BY LAUREN BLAKELY

FULL PACKAGE, the #1 New York Times Bestselling romantic comedy!

BIG ROCK, the hit New York Times Bestselling standalone romantic comedy!

THE SEXY ONE, a New York Times Bestselling standalone romance!

THE KNOCKED UP PLAN, a multi-week USA Today and Amazon Charts Bestselling standalone romance!

MOST VALUABLE PLAYBOY, a sexy multi-week USA Today Bestselling sports romance! And its companion sports romance, MOST LIKELY TO SCORE!

WANDERLUST, a USA Today Bestselling contemporary romance!

COME AS YOU ARE, a Wall Street Journal and multi-week USA Today Bestselling contemporary romance!

PART-TIME LOVER, a multi-week USA Today Bestselling contemporary romance!

UNBREAK MY HEART, an emotional second chance USA Today Bestselling contemporary romance!

BEST LAID PLANS, a sexy friends-to-lovers USA Today

Bestselling romance!

The Heartbreakers! The USA Today and WSJ Bestselling rock star series of standalone!

P.S. IT'S ALWAYS BEEN YOU, a sweeping, second chance romance!

MY ONE WEEK HUSBAND, a sexy standalone romance!

CONTACT

You can find Lauren on Twitter at LaurenBlakely3, Instagram at LaurenBlakelyBooks, Facebook at Lauren-BlakelyBooks, or online at LaurenBlakely.com. You can also email her at laurenblakelybooks@gmail.com

Printed in Great Britain
by Amazon

82818532R00200